DEADLY FORTUNE

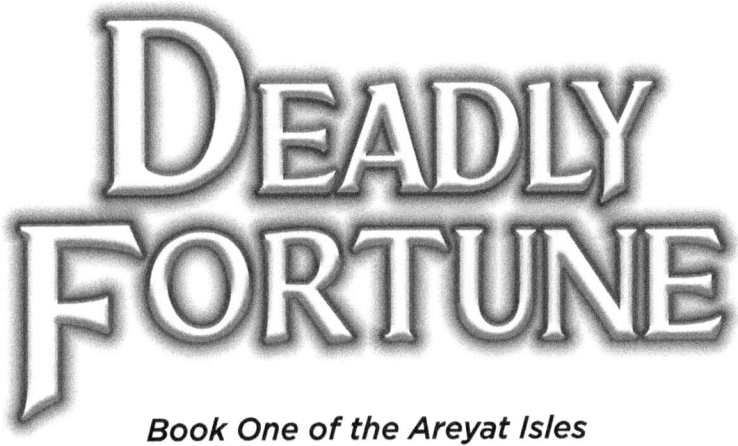

DEADLY FORTUNE

Book One of the Areyat Isles

AARON ROSENBERG

CRAZY 8 PRESS

Crazy 8 Press is an imprint of Clockworks

DEDICATION

*To Jenifer, Adara, and Arthur,
the greatest Gifts anyone could ask for.*

WHAT IS ELDROS LEGACY?

The Eldros Legacy is a multi-author, shared-world, mega-epic fantasy project managed by four Founders who share the vision of a new, expansive, epic fantasy world. In the coming years the Founders committed themselves to creating multiple storylines where they and many others will explore and write about a world once ruled by tyrannical giants.

The Founders are working on four different primary storylines on four different continents. Over the coming years, those four storylines will merge into a single meta story where fates of all races on Eldros will be decided.

In addition, a growing list of guest authors, short story writers, and other contributors will delve into virtually every corner of each continent. It's a grand design, and the Founders have high hopes that readers will delight in exploring every nook and cranny of the Eldros Legacy.

So, please join us and explore the world of Eldros and the epic tales that will be told by great story tellers, for Here There Be Giants!

We encourage you to follow us at www.eldroslegacy.com to keep up with everything going on. If you sign up there, you'll get our newsletter and announcements of new book releases. You can also follow up on FaceBook at:

facebook.com/groups/eldroslegacy

Sincerely,

Todd, Marie, Mark, and Quincy
(The Founders)

ACKNOWLEDGEMENTS

First off, huge thanks to Chris Kennedy for bringing me into the fold and introducing me to everybody at New Mythology Press. Special thanks to the Eldros Legacy crew, and Rob Howell in particular, for inviting me to play not only in this world but on his continent (and for being a good sport when I pointed at a barely sketched out part of the map and said, "Ooh, I want to set stories there!"). I also want to thank Courtney Farrell and Jonathan Miller for helping me make this book that much better, and Caio Cacau for doing his usual fantastic job on the cover.

As always, writing is something I do alone but never in a vacuum, and without my friends and family I'd be nowhere and no one. So thank you all for being there for me. I love you all.

Finally, to my readers, new and old. If you've read my work before, thank you for coming along on this strange new adventure with me. If this is the first of my books you've picked up, thank you for taking a chance on it.

I think we're going to have a lot of fun together.

Maps

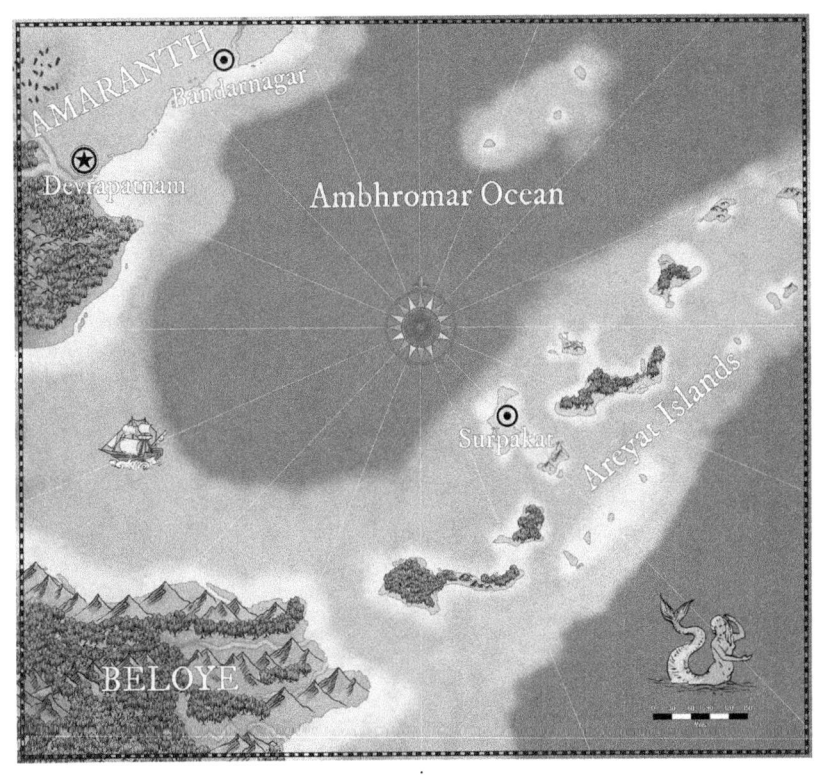

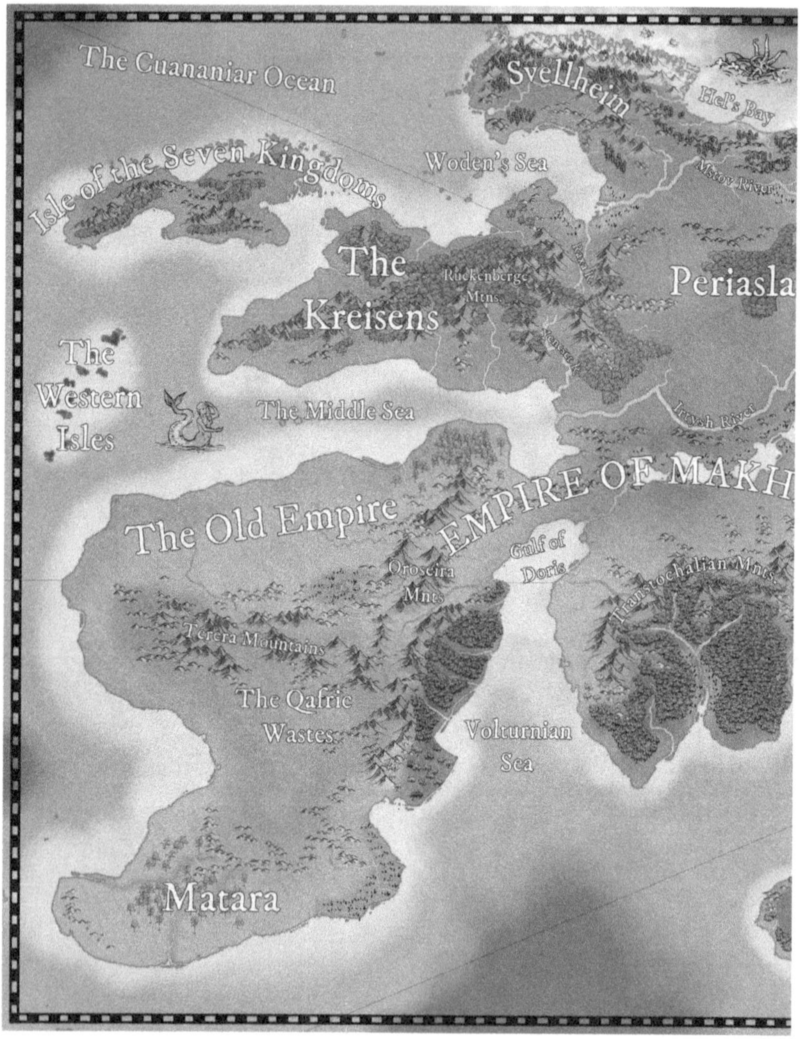

The Cuananiar Ocean
Svellheim
Hel's Bay
Isle of the Seven Kingdoms
Woden's Sea
Mstov River
The Kreisens
Ruckenberge Mtns.
Periasla
The Western Isles
The Middle Sea
Irtysh River
EMPIRE OF MAKH
The Old Empire
Gulf of Doris
Oroseira Mnts
Transtochalian Mnts.
Terera Mountains
The Qafric Wastes
Volturnian Sea
Matara

The Continent of
LATHRANON

By Sean Stallings

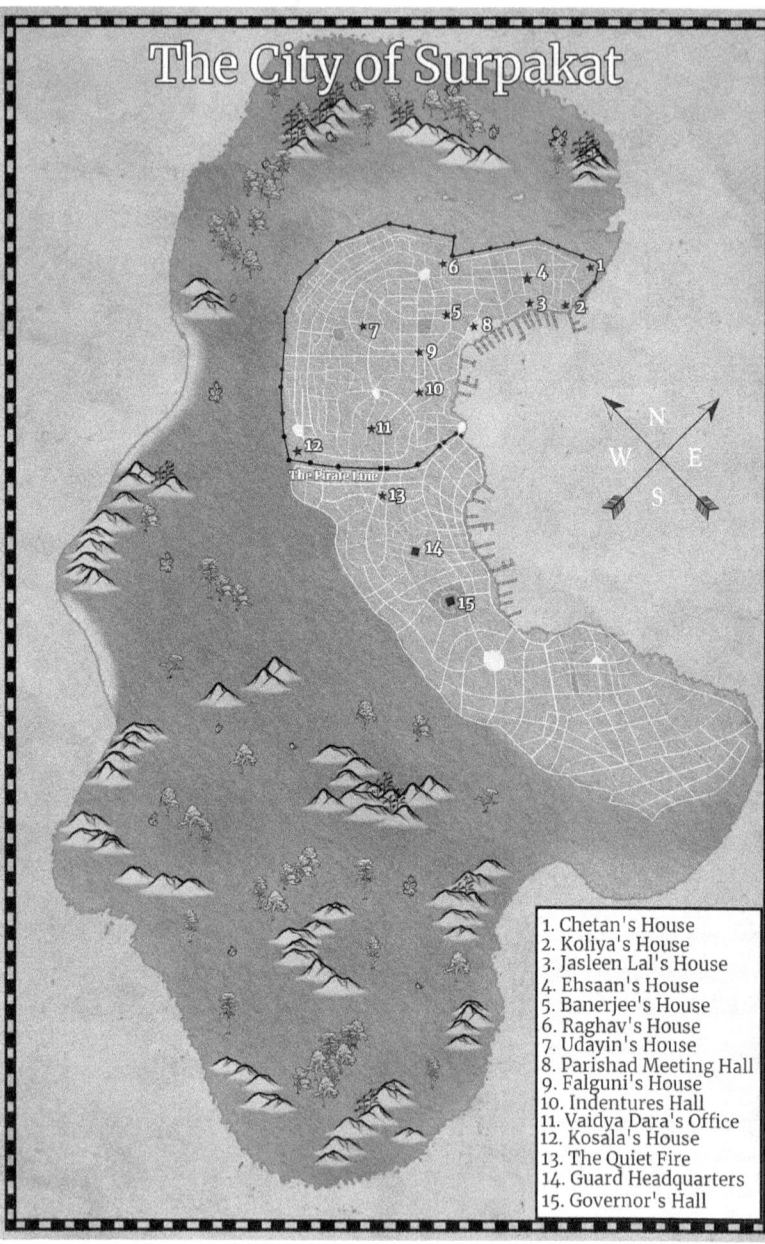

The City of Surpakat

The Pirate Line

N
W   E
S

1. Chetan's House
2. Koliya's House
3. Jasleen Lal's House
4. Ehsaan's House
5. Banerjee's House
6. Raghav's House
7. Udayin's House
8. Parishad Meeting Hall
9. Falguni's House
10. Indentures Hall
11. Vaidya Dara's Office
12. Kosala's House
13. The Quiet Fire
14. Guard Headquarters
15. Governor's Hall

CHAPTER ONE

SUNDRA

Sundra Aruvar knew he was in trouble the instant he felt the blade of his talwar slide home. Desperately he tried to twist aside, but it was too little, too late—the sword sank deep and true with an ominous *thunk*, and already its length grew slick from the blood that gushed forth around it.

Why, oh why, had the noble Sirdar Jivaka Pawari chosen to flinch at that precise moment? Sundra's slash had been carefully planned to give the elder noble a telling but purely superficial cut across his bare chest, letting his opponent acknowledge defeat without taking any lasting damage, except perhaps to his already overinflated ego. All the other man had needed to do was to stand his ground. Surely that wasn't too much to ask, especially from a noble of his stature?

Instead the fool had shuddered and turned away in exactly the wrong direction—and what should've been a light, sweeping slice had stabbed deep into the sturdy sirdar's chest.

Jivaka fell to the ground, gasping, dropping his sword as both hands flew to the wound in a vain attempt to stanch the blood now pouring forth.

Sundra stared at the older man, not sure what he could do in this situation. There was no one else around—often such a duel would've called for seconds, but Sirdar Pawari had insisted this was a private matter and so must be handled by just the two of them. Sundra had happily agreed to that suggestion, figuring that this way the older man could yield without losing face.

Now, however, he desperately wished there was someone else around—anyone to tell him what to do. He was no doctor or surgeon, he had no skill at healing, no poultices to apply or bandages to wrap. Perhaps he could use his mekhela? But even as Sundra struggled to unknot the heavily beaded and jeweled belt from around his waist, Jivaka shuddered and then froze for an instant before slumping completely.

Oh, blessed Eldroi, no!

Dropping to his knees beside the limp figure, Sundra checked the older man's wrist. There was no pulse. Next he studied the man's eyes, which were still open but clearly unseeing. Lovely.

"Did you really have to go and die on me?" Sundra demanded, tempted to give the sirdar a strong shake. "This is all your fault!"

Which was at least partially true. Oh, certainly Sundra had been flirting with the man's daughter at the festival two days ago. And with his wife later that night. And also with his sister. And *her* sister, for that matter. But what of it? It'd been a party, and they'd all partaken a bit too much of the mango wine. Sundra had been more than happy to demonstrate his many gifts and talents. Why had Jivaka needed to get so upset about it all? So the women had been lavishing all sorts of attention on Sundra, oohing and aahing over him—and perhaps a bit more than that in the back rooms when they thought no one was looking. Was that a crime? And could anyone blame them? Not Jivaka, who was twice his age and had perhaps half his looks at best?

Yet the sirdar had indeed taken offense. So much so that, at the end of the evening, he'd sought Sundra out and delivered him a sharp slap to one cheek then the other. "You've besmirched my honor," Jivaka had declared, jabbing Sundra in the chest. "I demand satisfaction. Swords at dawn, two days hence, in the marshaling yard behind my estate."

Sundra had not dared refuse. He knew Jivaka would spread the word of it if he didn't show, branding him a coward, and that his father would be furious with him for damaging their family's reputation.

Well, father, Sundra thought, reaching out and closing the dead man's eyes with the palm of one hand then shuddering and wiping his hand on his pants. *What do you think* this *will do for our reputation?*

Which was in fact a serious question, and the answer was nothing good. Rising to his feet, Sundra grabbed up a handful of grass and used it to wipe the blood from his blade. Sheathing the slim, curved sword, he backed away, putting on his long cotton kameez and heavily embroidered achkan over that before finally turning and running, putting the dead man as far behind him as soon as possible.

Their two estates weren't far apart, and in less than an hour, Sundra slowed to a jog as he approached the hedges that marked the boundaries of the Aruvars' land. Here he was forced to slow, picking his way carefully between the vatsanabha that grew all along their estate's border, arms held high to keep his brocaded sleeves from brushing the petals. The upright clusters of vivid purple flowers were pretty enough, but he'd had more than enough close encounters with the toxic plant over the years to give it a wide berth.

That was made more difficult by its deliberate use as a barrier, mainly against animals but also effectively against men. Fortunately Sundra knew exactly where the plant growth was thinnest and where, in one particular spot, one of the deadly plants had withered away, leaving a small gap if you knew where to look.

He slipped across the broad rear patio, through the back doors, and into the house proper. It was still cool and quiet, the sun only just starting to rise in earnest and the flames from the nilavilakku still burning low, but Sundra knew that, before too long, the whole household would be stirring, the servants and other workers rising to do their chores, his mother and father and little brother readying themselves to start the new day.

A day that was, unfortunately, going downhill.

Sundra moved quickly, removing his boots so his bare feet would make little noise upon the tiled floor as he hurried past Sumana's quarters. At least the little brat wasn't up yet, or else he'd already be out here begging to know what Sundra was doing. Once inside his own room, Sundra grabbed a sturdy leather satchel and began stuffing clothes into it, along with what money he had on hand, his jewels, and a few other accessories. He was sitting on his bed to tug his boots back on when there came a soft but firm knock upon his door.

"Sundra? Are you awake yet?" It was his mother, Devi, and before he could formulate an answer, his door had opened enough for her to peek in. "Ah, good." She pushed it open wider and stepped inside, but her words died as she took in his attire and the bag at his side. "What are you doing?" she demanded, shutting the door firmly behind her. "Have you been out this morning? What's going on, Sundra?"

"I need to leave, Mother," he told her, rising to his feet and crossing the room to take her hands in his own. "Right away. I don't have a great deal of money though."

"Money? What have you done?" she asked, her eyes going wider. "What kind of trouble are you in this time?"

"It wasn't my fault!" he protested, remembering at the last second to keep his voice down. "He shouldn't have moved!"

His mother's eyes bored into him. "He who?"

"Jivaka Pawari," he admitted, shuffling his feet and unable to meet her eyes. "After the festival last night, he challenged me to a duel. What could I do?"

"How bad?" the question was little more than a whisper, but in the still room, Sundra heard it. He didn't want to answer but knew she'd find out soon enough.

"He's dead," he admitted quietly. "I'm sorry, Mama. I didn't mean for that to happen."

"Dead!" Her face was pale and she wrung her hands together. "Oh, Heavens above! A sirdar, dead! And at your hand! When they learn of this…"

"I know," he told her. "That's why I need to go. Better I run, and all the ugliness is cast after me, than I stay and damage our whole family." *And embarrass my father,* he meant but did not say. There was no need.

"Yes," she agreed after a moment's daze. "Yes, you will need to run, my son. As far and as fast as you can." She seemed to regain her senses. "Meet me out back." And, without another word, she pulled away and retreated out into the hall.

Sundra wasn't sure what she was up to, but he trusted her completely so he grabbed up his bag and his sword and made for the door. A few servants were hurrying past, but he ignored them, slipping out into the hall and toward the back stairs.

He made it out onto the patio without more than a few questioning glances, but there he faltered, unsure what to do next. He dithered, pacing back and forth across the mosaic floor, and froze when he heard the glass doors whisper open.

It was only his mother.

Devi crossed the space quickly and moved to join him. "Here." She thrust a heavy pouch into Sundra's hands. He could tell by the weight of it and the way it shifted under his fingers that it held a great many coins. Moreover, the instant his skin came in contact with the leather, Sundra's Gift kicked in.

It wasn't real magic, not like the kind the kurioi of the Jadugara Council. No, it was just a bit of Lore Magic that helped him see where things had been, and it showed him an image of the pouch, but it wasn't here in back of the house. He saw it as it had been that morning, in a heavily carved wooden chest he knew resided in his father's study in the cabinet behind his father's desk. This was the money Sangram Aruvar used to pay their workers and cover other household expenses—and which

Sundra had dipped into a time or two on the sly to cover a night of drinking with friends.

"Mother, no," Sundra protested, trying to push the bag back at her. "I can't. If Father knew…"

"He'll know soon enough," she replied, "and I'll tell him the truth, that I took it." She lifted her chin defiantly, her eyes sparking as they did when she was up to something. "What will he do, send me to my room?"

Despite his situation, Sundra had to smother a laugh. If their neighbors and friends and other acquaintances only knew! Everyone always commented on how kind and polite and gentle Devi was. So few of them ever saw past that. But it was the real her, with all her charm and grace but also stubbornness and wit, that he was going to miss.

"Head to the docks," she instructed, cutting through his daze, her voice low and quick and her gaze intent. "Find a ship, one going well away from here and leaving as soon as possible. Book passage. This should be enough to get you settled somewhere, at least for a little while." She had a small bag slung over her shoulder. She lifted the strap over her head and offered it to him while he tucked the money into the pouch at his waist, which previously had held only a few silver dirham and some copper falus for buying trinkets and trifles and sweets. "Some food and drink for the trip."

Sundra reflexively took the proffered victuals, his inner eye showing that this bag had been hanging upon a hook by the back door to the kitchen even as his own thoughts ground to a halt. "But—" he started. "What—" He couldn't complete either sentence, his mind too fogged to speak and his eyes beginning to tear up from the same haze.

"I know." He could see water in her eyes as well, and then she hugged him tightly. "I love you, my son," she whispered in his ear. "And I hope you find a good life for yourself somewhere."

She pushed him away. "But you can't stay here. Not now. You must go, and quickly, before word reaches your father and he is forced to detain you himself."

Sundra knew she was right. As a sirdar, his father was honor-bound to uphold the laws of the land and to mete out punishment for any crimes committed in the region. Even if the crime in question had been accidental and the criminal was his own son. Sangram Aruvar would not hesitate, however much it hurt him. Better for all of them if he wasn't forced to face such a heavy task.

"I am sorry, mother," Sundra told her simply. "I love you and Father and Sumana." Ah, his little brother would be crushed! He followed Sundra around like a puppy dog, always wanting to imitate him. But hopefully this was one way in which he would not be the same.

"And we you," she replied, tugging his head down so that she could bestow a kiss upon his forehead. "Now go. Quickly."

CHAPTER TWO

RUHI

With a bitten-back groan, Ruhi Naidu turned at the sound of her name being shouted across the warehouse floor. *When would her aunt ever learn?*

But Auntie Rudra showed no signs of changing her habits any time soon. "There you are!" she called out, bustling across the dusty floor, the swish of her skirts raising puffs of dust and meal in her wake. "What are you doing out here? There's dinner to be prepared! Come along!" She turned to go, her tone and bearing making it clear she expected to be obeyed without question.

But Ruhi was no longer the frightened little girl she'd been when her mother had died and this stern aunt had come to live with them. "That's as may be, Auntie," she replied, keeping her own voice as sweet as possible. "But dinner can wait. This inventory can't."

She swept out a hand to indicate the row upon row of bale and barrel and box, each a different item to be sold or bought or traded. That was what her father did, after all. He was one of the finest merchants in the region, known as much for his careful organization as for his high quality and reasonable prices. But there was so much here, no one person could hope to keep track of it all.

Yet Ruhi did. She knew where everything was, right down to the last tomato or mango.

Knowing the quantities of everything here did nothing, however, to protect her from her aunt's sharp gaze or acid tongue.

"How many times have I told you? All of this—that's man's work. Leave it to your father. You come with me." Her aunt reached out and grabbed her by the wrist. "And none of your tricks," she warned. "Don't even think of using that thing on me."

"Yes, Auntie," Ruhi agreed with a sigh, forcing her Gift down as it tried to rise up within her. She did her best to be dutiful as she followed her aunt back through the warehouse, into the counting room, and then up to the family quarters.

Rudra dragged Ruhi straight to the kitchen, relenting only enough to let her rinse the dust from her hands before pointing her toward one side of the kitchen counter where a small cask of wheat flour sat beside a pitcher of water, a smaller one of oil, and a little tin of salt.

"Get to work," her aunt insisted, and Ruhi decided not to even bother arguing again. Not right now. Instead she began mixing the ingredients together, then kneading the resulting dough. She divided the dough into balls and flattened each into a thin disc. Those she tossed one by one into her skillet, cooking each one for a minute before adding the now piping hot roti to the plate there beside the stove, all under her aunt's watchful eye.

"There, you see?" her aunt told her when the plate was piled high. "That wasn't so hard, was it?" She frowned as she eyed her niece up and down with a dismissive gaze. "You'll need to know how to cook if you're ever to get a husband. Heavens know it won't be by your looks!"

As she had so many times over the years, Ruhi swallowed a retort. Her life would've been so much easier if she'd taken after Rudra, who was short and stout with a pronounced flare at bust and hips. Instead, she more closely resembled her dear, departed mother, being tall and slim. Sadly, she lacked her mother's beauty, her face too long to be heart-shaped and her eyes too small to be considered luminous, but she'd long since learned to accept such things—or would have, if her aunt would ever stop harping on them!

They worked in silence to prepare the rest of the meal, savory goat stew and curried rice and peppered lentils. Ruhi had been assisting in the kitchen since she could walk, and in truth she didn't mind the work—she was good with her hands, and she liked creating something with such a clear and immediate use. Plus it filled the whole upstairs with the rich smells of cardamom and pepper and chilis. It was also the only time Rudra even came close to being nice to her.

As was often the case, her father emerged from the stairs just as she was setting the last of the dishes out upon the table. "Smells divine," he told her, and Ruhi smiled, leaning into him as he came around the table to hug her and kiss her cheek. "How did the shipments look?"

"Good," she replied reflexively. "Except that the mangos were packed poorly, and many of them are bruised. You need to speak to Ganath about that." Ganath was their foreman, and at times he was too willing to let little matters slide. Matters like correctly packing the delicate fruits into their crates.

"I will," her father promised, crossing to the table against the far wall and pouring water into the shallow basin so he could rinse his hands. He settled at the head of the table as Rudra and Ruhi fixed a plate and set it before him. "Thank you both," he told them sincerely, "and thanks also to the spirits of the world and to the elements that watch over us."

"Spirits and elements," Ruhi repeated, her aunt only mouthing the words. Then they sat and took food as well.

After his first few bites, Ruhi's father began questioning her about his inventory again, and Rudra's eyes grew narrower and her grimace tighter as they discussed details of trade.

"Enough!" she announced at last, slamming one hand down

upon the table. "Look what you do to her, Ratan! She speaks like you, like an old man! How is any man to be interested in a girl who wants to talk about the price of grain and the weight of mangos and the shipping requirements of cloves and ginger?"

"Many men would be happy to have a wife who could converse with them on such useful things," Ruhi's father replied, a twinkle in his eye, and Ruhi grinned back at him. *Good thing we never told Rudra everything we've done, like about Manpreet teaching me to pick locks.*

Both of them winced, however, when Rudra slapped the table once more.

"You think it's funny now," she warned. "But you won't find it so when you're on your deathbed and she's an old maid, unmarried and unwanted."

So, like you, then? Ruhi thought, but her father's headshake stopped the words before they could spill free. And thank goodness. Her aunt's pique was nothing compared to her temper!

"I don't need a husband," Ruhi stated, holding her head up high. "If I find one, so be it, but I won't sit about pining away for one."

The gaze her aunt turned upon her was stony and as cold as shaved ice. "You can say that now, while you're safe within these walls, but when you're out there in the world, you'll feel differently. By then it'll be far too late. Your bad habits will have been etched upon you forever for all to see."

Ruhi's father frowned. "I don't think—" he started before his sister cut him off.

"No, you don't," she agreed sharply. Then her tone softened. "Who was it who helped you, brother, after Fia died? Who has been here for you, all this time? Trust me on this, Ratan. I know of what I speak. And I'd not see either of you unhappy or alone."

Which Ruhi supposed to be true. Whatever else her aunt was, Rudra wasn't so cruel as to wish them sorrow. Only her way would do, or indeed made any sense to her at all.

Ratan was far less opinionated. Sadly, he was also easily swayed by those who were, at least in personal matters. Thus he had always been, particularly by the women who'd ruled his life: first his own mother, then his wife, and now his sister. "Yes, perhaps you're right," he began, and Rudra pounced upon that statement before it was fully out of his mouth.

"Good!" she declared. "Then at last the time has come to take steps. Ruhi, beginning tomorrow you will no longer help in the warehouse. Instead you will sit with me and sew and weave and cook. You will set aside that ridiculous garb—" she eyed Ruhi's loose cotton shalwar and equally plain kurta, her only concessions to fashion or color being the lightly embroidered red vest atop the trousers and shirt "—for more appropriate attire." Here she patted her own handsomely detailed blue sari, which did indeed go nicely with her fitted choli and the pleated ghagra below that. "We shall make a lady out of you yet."

"But I like working in the warehouse!" Ruhi burst out. "Father, please!" she begged, appealing to him for help, but though his eyes were sympathetic, he shook his head, cowed by his sister as usual.

"Perhaps it is for the best, dear," he murmured. "I do wish to see you happily wed."

Ruhi wanted to snap back that those two statements— "happy" and "wed" —were incompatible in her eyes, at least right now, but she knew it would do no good and would only further anger her aunt and upset her father. So she bit her tongue and returned to her food, eating with forced gusto even though the meal now tasted like sawdust in her mouth.

It was clear what she'd have to do. The time had come at last.

❦ ❦ ❦

That night, after clearing away and cleaning the dishes, Ruhi bade her aunt and her father good night and retreated to her room. She took care to give her father an extra hug and kiss and tell him that she would always love him before she exited.

She hadn't wanted to risk leaving with that unsaid.

With her door securely shut and latched, Ruhi went to her closet and chest and began to haul things out she'd hidden behind and beneath other items. First came a sturdy shoulder bag Ganath had tossed aside because the shoulder strap had torn—she'd secretly repaired it late at night and then tucked the bag away in case she ever needed it.

Next were trousers and shirts like those she already wore but also a sadri and even an achkan. Most of those had been items of her father's that he'd worn out or simply chosen to replace, and Ruhi had carefully patched and adjusted them to suit her slimmer frame.

There were toiletries, already wrapped together in a long strip of muslin, and a pouch of coins she'd carefully scraped together, some by bargaining better than even her father realized and some by winning at dice and cards against Ganath and the others.

A few pieces of jewelry joined the pile—not the ones her mother had left her, sadly, but plainer, simpler earrings, chains, and rings that would not look amiss in her new guise. There was a plain cotton cloth, several inches wide and stained a light reddish-brown, and then what looked like a clump of dark hair.

Ruhi regarded all of this with a sigh. Was she really prepared to go through with all this? But what other choice did she have? To sit and wither away while Rudra tried to make her over into something she was not and never would be? No, that way lay madness. At least this way she would still be herself.

Even if, in order to do so, she must first become someone else.

Deciding there was no point in putting it off any longer, Ruhi rose to her feet and stripped off her clothes. Fortunately, her monthlies had been last week, so she had some time before she needed to worry about that complicating matters. The band she wove thrice around her chest, glad for once that she was so slight there. The color matched her skin close enough that it would not be noticeable even if someone should glimpse it through her shirt, yet it altered her profile sufficiently. A wad of cotton was stuffed into the front of her undergarments, creating at least a rough copy there of the bulge she so often saw among the men. The rest of her clothes were then restored, but they fit somewhat differently now.

Next came the hard part. Ruhi undid her hair from its customary bun and shook it out, using her fingers to unkink the thick, dark strands. Then she took up her scissors and began cutting. She trimmed back over a foot of length, cropping it in slightly in the process, so that in the end her hair still fell to her shoulders but in a more restrained fashion. Just so.

The jewelry went on next, nothing ostentatious but enough to show that she had some means, at least. Except for one piece, which she had purchased in secret from an old woman wise in the ways of those forces that made up the world and bound it together. Though unprepossessing enough, the crescent-shaped silver medallion with its insets of garnet and aquamarine contained a power Ruhi barely understood—but was determined to use.

Finally, she took up the strange clump she'd set out last. It was more of her hair, secretly trimmed away, woven together at the base, and then waxed and braided into a sort of mask, one that only rose to just beneath her nose in front but far higher on both sides. She slipped the tops of those sides over her ears, hiding them beneath the curls there, and used resin from a small pot to glue it into place along her jaw.

Shrugging on the knee-length coat before studying herself in the mirror, Ruhi had to smile. Between the beard and the shorter hair and the clothes, she looked like a proper gentleman. At least, that was how she saw herself and how others would as well, thanks to the amulet—it encouraged that interpretation, even as her own Gift encouraged people to let down their guard. On its own, the beard would never convince anyone, but between it and the necklace, her disguise should be impenetrable.

She gathered up the cut hair, wrapping it in a cloth scrap to be disposed of later. That way they would not know what she'd done or how to look for her in her new guise.

Then there was nothing left but to leave a note upon the small table by the front door:

> *"Dearest Father,*
> *I love you but can't remain here and be made into that which I am not. Instead I go to seek my fortune. Think kindly of me and know that I'll always adore you.*
> *— Your Ruhi"*

She snuck out, bag slung over her shoulder. She didn't dare breathe or straighten until she was out of the building entirely, standing alone in the cool air, the sky lightened with the dawn. Once she was, however, Ruhi felt as if a great weight had been lifted from her, even as a pit opened in her stomach. She was now free to go wherever she chose, to be whomever she wished.

The only question was, who and where would that be?

Chapter Three

SUNDRA

Despite the circumstances behind it, Sundra found himself growing less apprehensive and more excited once he'd reached the port.

The smell of planed fir, underlain with that acrid hint of quicklime, mixed with the salt from the sea to create a particular scent that could only be found down by the docks or onboard a ship. Sundra had sailed many a time, of course, though typically either on his family's barijah or that of other nobles, and he was well acquainted with sail and rudder.

He'd briefly considered taking their boat, the *Noonday*, but had decided that would ultimately compound his transgressions. Besides which, he would have difficulty sailing her alone and wasn't sure he could convince any crew to join him in the absence of his father's authority. No, better to book passage instead.

There was an abundance of other vessels here, even though it was now past dawn—the fishermen were long gone, but the traders didn't require such an early start and would typically wait until the warehouses had opened for the day in order to take on any last-minute cargo.

Sundra strode along the docks, dodging men hefting bales and barrels and sacks, studying each ship as he passed it. Many were too small to be intended for a great distance, so he discounted those. Others were too run down, their decks covered in muck and mire, their hulls peeling, and those he dismissed as well, though not from mere fastidiousness, for he knew that a poorly maintained ship was more likely to leak and founder. At last he arrived at one he felt would be suitable.

"The *Aden Star*," he read off the handsome plaque carved into its prow just below the sculpted parrot put there to guide its way. It was a baglah, he judged, one of the largest of the dhow and handsomely maintained, its hulls freshly treated, its sails and riggings neat. The captain clearly took pride in his ship, and that was always a good sign. Plus baglah were deep-sea vessels, which meant this one would be going a long ways indeed. Yes, this was the ship for him.

Hopping up onto the loading plank, Sundra made his way up to the foredeck, not needing the knotted rope railings on either side. The sailors paused in their work to regard him as he stepped out onto the fir planks, then resumed their regular activities. All save one, a stocky man who stomped toward him. He was dressed only in trousers and an open vest, his hair tied back beneath a kerchief. His skin was deeply weathered from extended time upon the water.

"Yes, good sir?" the man asked, his tone polite enough even if his speech was gruff.

"Apologies, I seek your captain," Sundra replied, executing a shallow bow. "I wish to inquire about booking passage."

The man nodded, indicating that, as Sundra had hoped, this wasn't a completely unfamiliar request. Ships of this size could carry a great deal of cargo but often had a few cabins belowdecks and would rent those out to travelers upon occasion.

"This way," the man said and turned, leading the way toward the rear and up the short flight of built-in steps to the raised deck there. Two men stood by the wheel, one of them dressed much like Sundra's guide. The other wore a sun-bleached turban and a sturdy canvas coat cut like a sherwani sporting some embroidery at cuff, collar, and hem. The turbaned man glanced up at them as they approached.

"Got someone seeking to book passage," the man with Sundra explained, and the turbaned man nodded and stepped forward slightly.

"Kaptana," Sundra began, bowing more deeply. "Apologies for disrupting your preparations."

"S'all right," the captain replied, offering a callused hand. "Nizami Mitra, captain of the *Aden Star*."

"Sundra... Devi," Sundra responded, clasping his hand—his mind had blanked in panic for an instant, knowing he couldn't give his true surname here, and so he'd thrown out the only name he could think of in its place, that of his mother. He hoped the pause hadn't been noticeable, but if it was, the man hadn't reacted. "It's a handsome ship, captain. Whither are you bound?"

"We travel up to Euskalerria," Captain Mitra answered, resting both hands on his hips. "We'll put in at the ports there, where they're always eager to get mango, bananas, rice, and other goods from here." He eyed Sundra's fine clothes. "We do have cabins free," he admitted after a moment. "So if you're looking to travel up that way, we can accommodate you. It's two dinar to sail with us."

Sundra had no idea if that was reasonable or utter robbery, and the other two sailors were carefully blank-faced to avoid giving any hint, but it didn't matter. He needed to be away from here, and quickly, and this ship looked solid and well-maintained. Once in Euskalerria, he would be free from any possible retribution and could then determine what to do next.

"Fine," he agreed, holding out his hand again, and he and Mitra shook on the deal. Then he reached into his pouch, extracting one of the heavy gold coins by feel. "Half now, half upon arrival," he declared, feeling more worldly for having insisted upon such an arrangement, and proffered the dinar.

"Agreed." Mitra took the coin, tucking it into the pocket of his coat. "Munda will see you settled." He turned back to the steersman, their business concluded, and the man at Sundra's side tapped his arm. This, then, must be Munda.

They returned to the foredeck only long enough to duck down the narrow stairs that ran beneath the raised aftdeck and led to an equally cramped corridor that ended in a cross-hall with five doors facing them. "This'll be yours," the mate explained, pushing open the first door on the left. "Meals're dawn, noon, and dusk. Freshwater's in the barrels stationed topside, free to use as needed. You'll have the run of the deck once we're out to sea."

"Thank you."

The sailor grunted and departed, leaving Sundra to survey his new quarters. The cabin was small and dark, the wood heavily shellacked, but the bunk built into the side looked comfortable enough, and there were drawers beneath to stow his belongings. A fair-sized window at the rear allowed light and could be opened for fresh air, and an oil lamp hung by ropes from the ceiling, the distance carefully measured so it could swing freely without risk of shattering against the walls. Far different from his own rooms, so light and airy, but at least it was clean and cozy. Yes, this would do.

Tucking his bags away in the drawers, Sundra sat on the bunk and forced himself to relax as much as possible. Soon they would weigh anchor and be off, casting his old life behind him like so much trash, the bits and pieces floating behind him on the water.

CHAPTER FOUR

RUHI

R uhi strolled through the docks, trying not to look as confused as she felt but suspecting she was failing at it badly. She'd worked in her father's warehouse since she was small, first in the counting office and then out in the bays themselves, and so the various cargoes were at least familiar to her. But she'd only ever seen boats from a distance. Who knew they were so huge? Or that they smelled almost woodsy somehow?

There were all different sizes displayed here, all securely tied to heavy pylons and all bobbing in the water. Is that what boats did? The very sight of that constant, rhythmic motion was making her queasy. And how was she to choose between them? Some were, she suspected, too small for her to consider—if they even took passengers, those people would be bunked in with the crew, and she couldn't risk such exposure. No, she required a boat big enough to have separate cabins for its guests.

She spotted a few that might suit in that regard, but the first one she saw was so grimy and smelled so foul of rotted fish and moldy produce that she couldn't even bear to approach it. The second was better, but there was something about its exterior, which seemed oddly lumpy like dripped wax, that made her hesitate. The third, however, appeared clean and neat, and so, with an attempt at confidence, Ruhi stepped onto the plank serving as its ramp and, clinging tightly to the rope guides, hurried up onto the deck.

It was so high off the ground! And that swaying she'd seen was now beneath her feet causing her to stumble and stagger and her stomach to roil in sympathy. *Oh, Eldroi, could she truly go through with this?*

"Help you, sir?" a man had approached her unawares. She straightened, struggling to quiet nerves and stomach both. He was shorter than her but nearly twice her breadth, and beneath an open vest, his bare chest gleamed with sweat. The gaze he bestowed upon her in return was frank, but at least there was no hint of a leer, nor even that speculation she so often saw on the face of the warehouse staff. It appeared that, for the moment at least, her disguise was holding.

"Yes, good day," she replied, careful to deepen and roughen her voice in an imitation of Ganath, who she'd spoken to most, after her father. "Are you taking passengers?" She didn't even know where the ship was bound, but it scarcely mattered.

He nodded and turned, glancing back to indicate she should follow him. His steps were sure, and his gait somehow rolled like the ship's as they headed back to where another level stood across the ship's rear. Stairs led up along its side, and they took those, Ruhi clutching the brass rail to steady herself. At the center of this smaller section was the ship's wheel, and beside it stood two men who broke off their conversation as she approached.

"'Nother passenger, Captain," her guide stated, jabbing a finger back in her direction. His statement had clearly been aimed at the second man, whose jacket proclaimed his rank, and it was to him that Ruhi turned as well.

"Good day, sir," she declared, bowing and secretly relieved that her beard didn't slip from the motion. "Rawal Chera, at your service. I was hoping you might allow me to book passage."

"Nizami Mitra," he replied, offering his hand. "Captain of the

Aden Star." They shook, and Ruhi let her Gift rise to the fore, watching as the captain's harsh, even suspicious glare softened. "Aye, we're taking on passengers," he agreed, and his tone was far less gruff than a moment ago. "We're heading up to Valkaria, if 'n you're going that way."

That was fine—Ruhi knew little about that land, other than some of the goods they exported, but it was civilized and therefore would have opportunities. And if she found it not to her liking, she would move on. Perhaps return to Amaranth, just to a different city than Sratapanara, one where no one knew her. Perhaps after a sojourn in Valkaria to save up some money. That was for the future, however. She needed to focus on the present.

"What sort of accommodations do you provide?" she asked next, waiting with bated breath.

"Your own cabin," was the answer, exactly as she'd dared hope. "Meals and freshwater provided. Safety guaranteed, end to end."

"Very good. And the price?" She had money, but not a great deal. Fortunately, she was well accustomed to haggling. And with her Gift in full force, she knew the captain would be more amenable than he might otherwise.

"A dinar," he told her, and she frowned beneath her beard, though inwardly she had far less concern. That was within her means, but she also knew it to be merely his opening bid. And, judging by the quickly concealed scowl of the man at her side, far lower than usual.

"I can pay you six dirham," she responded. "Up front."

"Two daniq, six dirham," he countered, trying for a scowl but the twitching at the corner of his lips gave him away. He was enjoying this back-and-forth, as was Ruhi. Here was something she was used to.

"One daniq, six dirham."

"Two daniq, four dirham."

She tilted her head slightly. "Two daniq, two dirham. Half up front."

After a second, he nodded, as she knew he would. "Done." The captain offered his hand again, and they shook on it. Ruhi carefully withdrew one of the small gold coins and one of the large silver ones from her pouch and passed them over. "Munda, show our guest to his quarters," the captain added once the transaction was complete. "We leave within the hour."

Munda muttered a bit, seemingly put out by how easily his captain had been out-bargained, but led the way downstairs and opened the second on the left. "This is yours."

"Thank you," Ruhi told him, though he hadn't waited, just grunted and fled back to the open air. Not that she could blame him; it was dark and cramped down here. The room, at least, was marginally better, with an oil lantern swaying above and a window at the back for light. There was a narrow bed, cleverly built into the wall, and drawers beneath it. The only other item in evidence was a brass chamber pot. Charming, but at least it was far better than trying to relieve herself in the presence of others!

Sitting there in that strange place, Ruhi couldn't decide if she was more excited or scared. Was it the start of something grand, or the worst mistake ever? Time would tell.

CHAPTER FIVE

SUNDRA

Sundra waited only until the *Aden Star* had set sail before quitting his cabin and venturing up onto the main deck. The crew were busy about their business, and he was careful to stay out of their way, veering off before the main mast and going straight to the starboard rail.

Ah, to be at sea! He closed his eyes and smiled, letting the wind whip at his face and hair, inhaling the saltiness of the air. All three sails were full, belling in the stiff breeze, and the big ship was all but skipping over the shallow waves, sailing along at an excellent pace. Clearly Captain Mitra and his men knew their craft. It was a pleasure just to lean upon the rail and listen to them work, hearing the rhythmic calls of helmsman and first mate and the answering cries of the lookouts and those adjusting the sails.

After a moment, however, another sound intruded. It was a far harsher noise, ragged and heartfelt. At first Sundra thought it might be someone weeping, but then he recognized it fully and straightened, frowning both in surprise and in some sympathy. For who, on a ship like this, could be retching?

Glancing about, he soon located the source. A man was curled over the rail some yards to his left, clearly hurling his guts out into the waters far below. Sundra started to approach, then stopped himself. Mere sympathy would be little help, and an audience even worse. But there was something he could proffer that would be far better, provided he could convince the ship's cook to provide it.

Venturing back downstairs, he stopped at the ship's galley. A big, burly man was already ensconced there, stirring a large pot. The smells that rose from it were that of fish and lentils and spices, and Sundra was pleased to note that meals aboard this vessel would not be so dire as he'd feared. That, however, wasn't his current focus.

"Hello," he greeted the cook. "Have you any roti or chapati? A fellow passenger is in distress."

The other man barked out a laugh. "Aye, I saw him run past, that one. Some just can't abide the sway of the sea." He was already reaching behind him and drawing out a small, cylindrical basket with a tight-fitting lid. "Here," he said, handing it to Sundra. "From this morning, but still good."

Tugging off the lid, Sundra found roti packed inside. "Perfect," he said, extracting two of the bread discs and returning the container. "Thank you. I'm Sundra, by the way." Always make friends with the cook.

"Druv," the big man replied, nodding and tucking the basket back away.

Sundra returned abovedecks. He stopped at the nearest rain barrel to extract a dipper of water, then carried both that and the roti over to where the other man still stood miserably. "Eat this," he said, holding out the food. "And drink this. But slowly on both."

The man glanced up at him, his narrow face creased in agony, sweat beading across his forehead. "Eat?" he rasped, his voice higher than Sundra had expected. "How can I? I just emptied what I had in me, and you want me to add more?"

"It will settle your stomach," Sundra insisted. "Try it."

The stranger frowned, but after a moment, he straightened some and accepted the roti, nibbling at it first and then taking proper bites. Next were a few sips of water, then the second piece of bread, after which he finished the water.

"Thank you." His voice was far less shaky and a trifle deeper as he stood up straight and then bowed. "I do feel a bit better." His hand, however, was still clinging to the railing.

"First time at sea?" Sundra asked with a smile. "Not to worry. You'll grow used to it soon. Until then, stick to plainer foods and to water. Nothing to upset your stomach further." Then he held out his hand. "Sundra Devi."

"Rawal Chera." They clasped hands. "I'd heard I wasn't alone as a passenger."

"No, though it does seem to be just the two of us," Sundra replied. He leaned on the rail, gazing out at the water rushing past. "I'm not used to that. Usually I have others with me, friends if not my father."

"Oh? Do you travel much then?"

He laughed. "Hardly at all and only under my father's supervision. But I do like to sail, and we have a barijah, so I take it out whenever possible. That and riding my horse are two of my favorite pastimes." Much to his father's chagrin, since both took Sundra away from home for hours on end and meant time he wasn't spending learning or accompanying his father to boring meetings.

Rawal nodded, though there was the hint of a frown beneath his mustache. "Your family must be quite comfortable to afford a boat of your own."

"Oh yes, we are," Sundra agreed easily. "Can't have a poor sirdar, can you?" Realizing what he'd said, he gasped. "Please don't tell anyone," he begged. "I've no wish to trade upon my family's reputation, and I don't want anyone to know I'm here."

"I won't say a word," his new acquaintance promised, and Sundra felt a flush of warmth toward the man.

"Come," he said, pushing off from the rail. "Let me show you the ship. A little walking about will help you get your sea legs, and once you have those, you won't feel nearly so sick."

Rawal hesitated, and Sundra stepped toward him and laid a friendly hand on the other man's shoulder. "Come on," he urged. "It will—"

The rest of his entreaty fell away, however, as Sundra's Gift kicked in. He saw the jacket he was now touching, which was of decent cut and acceptable embroidery, if somewhat worn and not of the finest materials. It lay upon a bed in a small but clean bedroom, beside several other articles of clothing. A hand reached for it, and as the person tugged it on, Sundra saw that it was Rawal—only it wasn't. For, in his vision, he could clearly see where his companion's beard was settled over his ears—and also make out her chest binding beneath the kurta as the coat was shrugged into place.

"You're a woman!" he blurted out, staring at this stranger he had just helped but who was now even stranger than he'd thought. "What—?"

"Shhh!" Rawal—clearly not his name, Sundra realized—clapped her hand over his mouth. "Not so loud! How did you—?" She shook her head. "Never mind, it doesn't matter." She sighed.

Now that he was looking for it, Sundra noticed the shape of her eyes and lips were too feminine, and her jacket hung oddly over slighter shoulders and a fuller chest than might be expected.

"Yes," she admitted. "My real name is Ruhi, all right? I wasn't sure how a woman alone might be treated, so I felt it was safer to go as a man."

She finally removed her hand, stepping back to watch his face, and Sundra nodded.

"Yes," he agreed slowly. "I can see where that would make sense. I'm sorry. I didn't mean to shout it. I was just surprised."

"How'd you know?" she asked. "Did I make a mistake some-where?"

"No, no," he told her quickly. "You were—are—very convincing as Rawal! I... it was my Gift. I can see where things have been. I saw your achkan as you put it on." Even beneath the beard—which was fake, obviously, but well-designed—he could see her blush. "I won't tell anyone," he assured her.

"Thank you." He could see the relief in her eyes. "And I won't tell anyone your true identity either." He nodded, and that won a small smile from her.

They both stood silently, unsure how to proceed.

"Now," she said after a moment. "You were saying something about getting my sea legs?"

"Yes." He had to stop himself from offering his arm, as he might have to a young lady. "Let's do that. Get you the lay of the land. Or the boat, as it were." Anything to change the subject.

Chapter Six

RUHI

Two days later, Ruhi was finally beginning to grow accustomed to the motion of the boat beneath her feet and the way it swayed back and forth in time with the waves. She was still trying to adjust to her new companion, however. Since the *Aden Star* wasn't large, particularly belowdecks, she found herself spending much of her time up on the main deck, usually close to a rail in order to keep out of the crew's way. That meant that she was often in close proximity with Sundra, especially since the two of them were the only passengers on this trip. It would've seemed strange for two young men of similar age and status to avoid one another, so she was forced to make herself agreeable and friendly to this stranger who already knew too much about her.

Not that he seemed like a bad sort, necessarily. Certainly, she'd met far worse in the warehouse. Whatever else he might be, this Sundra was clearly a gentleman, though, with his good looks, he'd hardly lack for companionship. Most importantly, he seemed willing to keep her secret.

She wasn't sure how long that prohibition would last, however.

They were out on the deck, having just finished the midday meal, when a man up at the top of the main mast shouted, "Sails to starboard!"

Ruhi had still not grown accustomed to the nautical terminology, but Sundra rushed to the opposite side. She followed, joining him and several sailors to peer out in that direction. Sure enough, some ways across the water she could make out a small, dark shape peeking up above the waves.

"Are they headed toward us?" she asked, remembering in time to deepen her voice. "Or just crossing our path?"

"More the former than the latter," Sundra replied, not turning away from the distant image. "They're growing closer with each second—and cutting across wind and wave to do it, which requires some effort and no mean skill. I don't think this is a chance sighting."

Sure enough, the captain shouted from up by the wheel, "Arm yourself and prepare for boarders!" Ruhi glanced up at him, to find him looking at her and Sundra. "Can you two fight?" the grizzled older man demanded.

"I can," Sundra answered quickly, his hand going to his side as if reaching for a sword, and Ruhi rolled her eyes. Did young men ever stop to think before they spoke or acted? It didn't seem that way.

Captain Mitra, however, looked pleased. "Good, good. Be ready, then. No honest ship'd be heading toward us at such speed, which can only mean one thing—pirates."

Pirates! This time the lurch in Ruhi's stomach had nothing to do with waves. She'd heard of the nautical bandits, of course—more than a few shipments had never reached her father on account of such scoundrels waylaying it at sea.

"What do we do?" she whispered to Sundra, who was making for the stairs down toward their cabins.

"We fight, of course," he answered, giving her a quick grin. "Don't worry, I'll protect you." Then he was gone. A moment later, he returned carrying a long, slim saber.

Ruhi jumped out of the way as sailors rushed by, following bellowed directives from Captain Mitra or Munda. Most of them carried short, stout clubs or large, wicked hooks she'd seen them use to haul in fish. A few had swords, though those were mostly short, wide blades, not the long silvery crescent Sundra carried.

The other ship was now close enough to make out its two sails.

"Can't we outrun them?" she asked whomever was nearby. "It looks like we're the bigger ship."

"Oh, we are," a sailor replied while emptying a bucket of water across the deck. "But size ain't everything. That's a dhangi, sure as sun-up, and in a straight race I'd back that over a baglah like ours any day. Sure, it's only got two sails, but it's got a lot less weight. And they've got a weather mage with 'em, to be running against the wind the way they are, so no fancy maneuvering on our part'll lose 'em."

"They're wetting it down so it won't burn," Sundra explained, keeping his voice down, hand resting on the pommel of his sword. "In case of fire arrows. You all right?"

Ruhi nodded. "Yes, thank you."

His quick grin made him look ten times more attractive, if that was even possible. "Don't mention it."

There was little to do after that besides wait. Ruhi noted that the captain had not entirely given up hope the way that one sailor had, and the *Aden Star* turned slightly, taking full advantage of the wind as all three sails filled, sending the boat speeding along. The other ship continued to grow in their sight, however, and it was soon clear the smaller ship was indeed gaining on them.

"What happens if they catch us?" Ruhi asked Sundra softly. She'd heard of pirates attacking ships but not the aftermath of such encounters.

He shrugged. "They'll board us." He didn't sound terribly concerned. "Then we fight them."

"And if we lose?"

Sundra flashed her that smile again. "I don't expect to lose."

Maybe you don't, and maybe you won't, personally, she thought, studying the men around them. *But you're just one person against who knows how many pirates. I can't exactly help in a fight, and who knows how the sailors will fare.*

A few more minutes passed. She could now clearly make out the men lining the approaching ship's front railing. Most of them looked to be shirtless, with only simple sadri worn open over their lightweight pants. Many had turbans or headbands holding back their hair and shielding their eyes from the sun. All of them bore weapons in hand, mostly long knives and short, heavy clubs but some swords and even a few bows. All in all, they presented a fierce, warlike aspect, and Ruhi could see several of the sailors around her shrank back at such a display.

"Here they come!" the captain shouted from the upper deck, drawing his own sword. "Repel all boarders!"

"Aye, aye, sir!" the sailors shouted back, though some with less enthusiasm than others. They all rushed to the starboard side and waited.

Ruhi and Sundra backed away, giving the sailors room.

She tugged at his sleeve. "What if we don't win? What happens then?"

He frowned, still watching the oncoming ship. "Then they take this ship and its cargo. They'll try to ransom back anybody they can." His frown became a shudder and then a look of shock and dawning horror as he thought that through. "I can't go back! I can't!"

"Why not?" she asked. "Surely your father would pay whatever they ask."

"That's not the point," he insisted. "I… Trust me when I say I can't go back. Which means they can't know who I am." He gripped her arm. "You've got to help me!"

"Fine." Ruhi thought quickly. It wouldn't do for them to discover her either, she suspected—not her true gender, at any rate. She didn't want to think about what a group of bloodthirsty pirates might do with a young woman, and one with no rich family to buy her safety. Which meant she had to help Sundra, since he knew her secret too. "Do you have any money on you?" When he nodded, she held out her hand. "Give it over."

"What? Why?" he sputtered, but finally extracted a heavy pouch from the larger pouch at his belt and thrust it into her hands.

Ruhi had a great deal of experience with coinage. She could often judge a bag's contents sight unseen, from its heft alone. This bag was heavier than most she'd encountered, and the sound of the coins within it told her that there were few coppers, if any. No, this was all silver and gold, and she'd guess that it was far more the latter than the former. She was holding a fortune in her hands and not a small one—there was probably more in her palm at this moment than her father's profits for an entire year.

It was with some reluctance that she turned and tossed the bag to the side, toward where a set of woven thatch doors covered the entrance to the ship's main hold. Doors that were currently sitting open, allowing the bag to disappear down into the depths of that dark space.

"Eldroi, are you mad?" Sundra demanded, grabbing her by the front of her jacket. "That's all the money I have, and my good jewels too!"

"And if we win, you can go retrieve it afterward," she pointed out. "But if we don't, the pirates'll never know you were rich. Speaking of which—" she had a small knife at her belt, less for defense than utility, and now yanked that free. "Hold very still." With a single deft slice she split his jacket up the back, then cut it along the seam of one shoulder and tugged until there was a noticeable gap there as well.

"Are you mad, wo—what?" came the angry cry.

"Your clothing was too fine by half," Ruhi replied. "They'd have known you for a noble at once. Now you look a bit shabby, like either you had money but have since lost it, or you got the coat after a noble discarded it."

Sundra sighed. "I hope you know what you're doing," he muttered.

Then the pirate ship reached them, lowering their sails and

turning so that their advance lost speed over the last few yards until their vessel's side bumped up against the *Aden Star* as gently as a babe nestling in its mother's arms.

"Ho, the ship!" someone called out. "Throw down your arms and surrender or prepare to be boarded!"

"To the pits with you all!" Captain Mitra shouted back, brandishing a sword of his own. "You're not taking the *Star* without a fight!"

"So be it," the pirate responded, and the battle was joined.

CHAPTER SEVEN

SUNDRA

Sundra felt his pulse race as he unsheathed his sword, holding it in a ready position, his every sense alert. This was it! He'd dueled before, of course, and sparred many times with his instructor, but this would be his first real battle.

He hung back, waiting for one of the boarding pirates to engage him, all too aware of Ruhi hovering cautiously at his back. He had to protect her at all costs—his honor as a gentleman demanded it.

The crew formed a bulwark against the invading men. And it was into that wall of flesh and metal and wood that the pirates crashed headlong with shouts of defiance. The air filled with the thud of body against body and the dull clatter of weapon on weapon with, here and there, the sharper, cleaner clang of steel upon steel. Sundra waited, legs slightly bent, balanced on the balls of his feet, sword held loosely but firmly, as he'd been taught, watching for the first to break through that human barricade.

It was utter chaos before him. Within seconds it was impossible to distinguish one body from another. He could catch brief images, that was all—here a sailor bashing a pirate over the head with a club, there a pirate returning the favor by stabbing a sailor through the belly with a wide, short sword, over there two men so tangled up in tussling and trading punches that he could not identify either's allegiance. *Blood and bones, was this what a proper melee looked like? It was so... uncivilized!*

Within a hundred heartbeats, the crowd had thinned. Half of the men laid out on the deck twitching and groaning—or completely unmoving. Sundra thought of Jivaka Pawari gasping out his last. This was different. That should have been just a silly duel over the sirdar's bruised ego. This had always been life or death.

One of the pirates emerged from the back of the tumult and spied Sundra. "Yield!" the stranger demanded, advancing upon him with quick, sure strides. His sword was heavier than Sundra's, but he wielded it easily. "You're worth more alive than dead."

"So are you, at least to yourself," Sundra shot back, raising his blade to cross his approaching foe's. "Walk away and live while you can."

That earned a harsh laugh as the pirate batted his blade aside, but his amusement disappeared instantly as Sundra simply rotated his wrist to bring his sword back in line on the other side of the pirate's weapon. The man's eyes narrowed, and his posture went from casual to wary.

A stirring came from behind the man, however, as several more crewmembers fell. "Throw down your arms and surrender or perish!" Someone shouted in a strong, clear voice. "This is your last warning!"

For a moment, no one moved. Then Sundra heard Captain Mitra. "Enough, lads. Ye've done well, but I'd not see you throw your lives away for naught. Lay them down." That was followed by the sound of a sword striking the deck, and Sundra knew the captain had tossed down his own blade.

A discordant clatter followed, as the rest of the crew disarmed. "Put it down, boy," the pirate facing Sundra warned. "It's over."

Sundra snarled and was about to retort when he felt a hand on his arm. "Let it go, Sundra," Ruhi urged behind him. "You can't win."

"I can still beat him," Sundra insisted, but the hand didn't retreat, and he felt his resolve weakening.

"Against him alone, perhaps," Ruhi agreed. "But against all of them? All you'd do is die. It isn't worth it."

Almost before he'd realized it, Sundra found himself disengaging, taking a step back, and then letting his sword dangle from his hand. He refused to dishonor the blade by hurling it to the deck, but held it out, hooked over his thumb. "Fine."

The man he'd faced straightened, sticking his own sword through his sash before executing a mocking bow and accepting Sundra's sword. "Many thanks, lad." Reaching out, he plucked the scabbard from Sundra's belt. "A fine weapon." He sheathed it, then added it to his sash as well with a broad grin that nearly had Sundra leaping forward to reclaim the sword. Ruhi's hand stopped him, however, and he could do nothing but seethe as the man chuckled and walked away.

"A wise choice, Captain," the one who'd called for their surrender said, and Sundra switched his attention to the crowd over by the main mast.

The man in question was tall and slim with long arms that seemed too long for the finely embroidered sherwani he wore over a bare chest and silk shalwar incongruously paired with sturdy leather boots. His dark hair was pulled back in a thick braid, unfashionable but undoubtedly practical; and atop that he boasted an impressive turban of a deep, rich blue with a large pearl set at the front. Between that and his neatly trimmed beard and mustache, he might've seemed a great noble if not for the odd fit of his garb and the pair of short swords sheathed at his side.

"Now I'll offer you another choice," the pirate leader continued. "Stay and be indentured—your skills will earn you a high price, and you could win your freedom before too long, even command of another ship. Or you may take the longboat and depart with enough food and water to last you five days."

It seemed a surprisingly fair offer, though not without its risks.

They'd been at sea only three days, but Sundra knew that there was a great deal of difference between a ship under full sail and a longboat powered only by the strength of one's arms. The captain might make it back safely, or he could perish at sea.

"I'll take the boat," Captain Mitra declared, head held high, and Sundra felt a fierce respect for the hardened sailor. "If I should die, at least I'll die a free man."

"So be it." The pirate turned to his men. "Ready the longboat for the good captain. And I wish you luck, sir." He turned away from Mitra to face the rest of the crew. "As for the rest of you, you will accompany us back to the Areyat Islands. Several of my men will take over command of this ship—cooperate and you won't be harmed. Resist or attempt sabotage and you will be dealt with harshly. Is that understood?"

There was a mumbling of agreement.

Sundra doubted any of them would try anything, not with Captain Mitra gone and with the pirates watching them so closely. Another good reason to offer the captain the longboat—it meant he would not be here to encourage resistance.

A figure suddenly blocked his view, and Sundra found himself facing one of the pirates. Only this one, he noticed at once, was like neither the man he'd nearly dueled or their strangely garbed leader.

For this pirate, as her short, open vest and simple choli made abundantly clear, was a woman.

"And what have we here?" she asked, hands going to her shapely hips. She wasn't unattractive, with fine eyes made bright from the recent conflict, and Sundra found himself smiling. Perhaps fortune had smiled upon them at last and he could charm their way out of here.

He opened his mouth to reply, already framing a suitable compliment to their would-be captor and potential rescuer, when a hand slapped him on the side of his head, hard enough to rattle his teeth as his jaw reflexively slammed shut.

"Quiet, you idiot, before you get us both killed!" Ruhi hissed as she slid in front of him to face the pirate, who was now laughing at his apparent plight.

"Apologies for my little brother," Ruhi explained, dipping her head in a short bow as his eyes widened in shock. "Sometimes he doesn't know when to behave. I'm Rawal Chera. This fool is Sundra."

She tugged her pouch from her belt and offered it—then snatched Sundra's from his side and held that out as well. "We have no family of note and little of value—indeed, most of our money went to book passage on this ship. We were off to seek our fortune."

"Well, you've found it, for good or for ill," the woman replied, still chuckling. She eyed them both, and Sundra saw her take in the copper studs in his ears and the tears in his coat with a nod before accepting the pouches and glancing inside. "You both look young and fit. Shame you're not rich or we'd simply ransom you back. But you're not causing trouble yet, which means at least it isn't over the side with you. Keep your heads about you and your mouths shut and you should make out fine."

Their money went into the pouch at her waist, never to be seen again, Sundra was sure. Then she called over her shoulder, "Two passengers here, Captain! Young men, little money, no family back home, but no trouble!"

"Two more for indenture, then," came the reply as the tall pirate strode over to join them. "I'll trust you two to behave. Do so and you'll not be harmed." Then, barely waiting for Ruhi's nod, he was gone again, seeing to Captain Mitra's departure.

The woman nodded at them both—pausing a second on Ruhi—then walked away as well.

"Why did you do that?" Sundra demanded as soon as they were left alone. "I could've talked us out of this!"

"You were about to flirt with her," Ruhi replied, her tone sharp but her voice low. "She'd have gutted you for it, most likely. Or tossed you overboard, from the sound of things, and me with you. These are pirates, not ladies at court. Use your head!"

Sundra grumbled at that, though he had to admit the woman had been nothing like anyone he'd known before. Still, he thought he could have swayed her.

Too late now. She was gone—and what had been left of his money with her—and two big, burly pirates took charge of them instead, watching them as most of the pirates returned to their own ship, leaving a handful here to keep the peace among the crew. Without his sword, Sundra couldn't have taken them all, and so he was forced to resign himself to whatever strange fate awaited them.

The pirate captain had spoken of "indenture—" what exactly did that entail?

Chapter Eight

RUHI

The next few days were stressful, to say the least. The *Aden Star* was both quieter and more boisterous than it had been—quieter in that the remaining crew was subdued, louder in that the pirates on board did their best to make up for that with shouts to each other and to their fellows on the neighboring ship.

The two vessels had now matched pace and traveled a mere ship's length apart, despite their differences in size and in the number of their masts and sails. Ruhi chalked that skillful sailing up to the weather witch the one sailor had mentioned. She guessed that to be the man standing at the pirate ship's prow, hands raised high as if reaching up to grasp the wind and force it to his bidding. Which was, perhaps, exactly what he did.

She and Sundra were still allowed to use their cabins and to come and go up on deck as they pleased. The pirates had searched their quarters first, of course, to make sure they had neither money nor weapons stashed within, and she'd been particularly relieved when they'd completely ignored her amulet, which evidently concealed itself from casual view, but otherwise they were left to their own devices.

On her apparent brother's part, that was mostly to sulk. He'd been in a grump ever since she'd stopped him from flirting with that female pirate. Which certainly fit in with his new role as the younger brother, for no one seeing his impetuous behavior would ever consider him the elder. She was just glad she'd gotten her hand on him before he'd opened his mouth because she was certain the woman's amusement would have turned to irritation quickly enough, and these people seemed likely to handle such annoyances with sudden bouts of violence.

They'd had some evidence of that shortly after setting sail for their new destination. One of the sailors, a short heavyset man with dark skin and a thick, woolly beard, had turned on their captors, bashing one over the head with a club he'd somehow kept hidden and hurling a coiled rope at another, knocking both men to the deck.

"Now, lads!" he'd bellowed, urging on the rest, but the other sailors had just stood and stared at this apparent rebellion.

Two more pirates had quickly tackled the man, disarming him and then hoisting him to his feet to face Jayant and Rohan, the two he'd attacked—the same two their captain had given charge of Ruhi and Sundra and of the *Aden Star* in general.

"You show some pluck," one of the two big men commented, rubbing the back of his head and wincing. "Shame you chose to spend it this way."

Then he reached out, wrapping one big hand in the sailor's vest. Lifting the struggling man off the ground, the pirate twisted—and tossed the would-be rebel over the nearest railing. They all heard the man scream as he soared through the air and then the splash and resulting splutter as he hit the water. The boat soon left him behind, awaiting what Ruhi could only assume would be his death.

There had been no additional resistance after that. And she thought perhaps Sundra appreciated her own interference more, seeing what could have been his fate as well.

★ ★ ★

She suspected the question of their fate would soon be answered, when the lookout shouted, "Land ho!" Rushing to the rail with her supposed brother, Ruhi saw that they were indeed approaching land.

"The Areyat Islands," Sundra said next to her. "Known as a den of cutthroats and murderers, a haven for pirates from all along the coast."

"If everyone knows that, why has no one done anything about it?" she asked, keeping her voice down.

Her companion shrugged. "There have been attempts, over the years. None of them succeeded. The pirates are too strong, and of course attacking those Islands means being days or weeks from home and any sort of support, whereas they have their bases right there at their backs." He sighed. "I wonder what they'll do with us."

"We'll find out together," she assured him, which earned her a brief smile. *So at least he wasn't still angry with her. That was something.*

"Welcome to the Areyat Islands," Jayant informed them. "And to Surpakat, our capital." He gestured grandly to where a manmade barrier was just beginning to be visible, nestled within a natural cove.

Ruhi watched, fascinated, as they approached. The city walls were impressive, made of rough stone piled high enough that she couldn't make out anything beyond them. Instead of gates between the wide opening onto the water, she saw massive chains, some low enough to dip beneath the surface and some high enough to reach just below the top of the ship's prow.

One of the men on the pirate ship brought out a large horn and blew a series of notes, the sounds carrying over the sea. After a moment, they heard an answering call from the land, and then the chains began to slacken, lowering until they all hung loose, vanishing under the waves.

"Clever," Sundra muttered at her side. "Sail into those when they're taut and you'd tear your ship to pieces, but now you can sail right over them without harm."

Their pair of boats continued on, the constant wind slackening so that their sails began to hang loose and their speed to fade even as they approached the docks ahead. By the time they reached the rough wooden piers, they were barely moving, and both prows bumped up against heavy rope nets that brought them to a halt right up against the dock.

Pirates leaped ashore and tied both boats in place. Then the captive sailors were herded forward and Sundra and Ruhi with them.

As they passed, Jayant held something out to Ruhi. "From Chhavi," he explained, and jerked his chin toward the pirate ship, where she saw the female pirate watching. The woman nodded once before joining the rest of her fellows in entering the city proper.

It was a small scrap of paper, carefully folded so it would not blow open. Ruhi unfolded it and read: "You don't need to conceal your true self here, but I won't expose you." So the other woman had seen through her disguise, amulet and all.

She'd worried about that—the magic was supposed to reinforce people's initial impression of her, based on the fake beard, but that wouldn't be enough if someone wasn't even remotely fooled right from the start. The pirate's words made Ruhi wonder, though—would it be safe to admit her gender here? Certainly if there were women among the pirate crews, they might not be as male-dominated a society here as back home. Still, she'd only seen Chhavi, and the fact she'd felt the need to send that message privately suggested it might still be safer to appear as a man. At least for now.

* * *

They were taken ashore, and Ruhi was both surprised and impressed to find that Surpakat looked much like a smaller, rougher version of her own hometown. The streets closest to the docks were still just hard-packed dirt, but there were raised plank walkways so people could move about without becoming mired in mud. As they moved farther inland, the roads transitioned to proper paved stone.

The buildings were mostly wood, stone, and even brick later on, but they all appeared solid and many had been whitewashed with lime, while roofs and doors were often brightly colored. Balconies appeared as well, wrought iron railings shaped to mimic climbing vines, complete with flowers or clusters of grapes and other fruits.

Men and women passed by, both on foot and on horseback and even occasionally on carts or in small carriages. While some of them looked much like the pirates who'd captured the *Aden Star*, others looked more like regular tradesmen and merchants and laborers and messengers.

Most of the less prosperous folk wore strange metal cuffs upon one wrist, but there were no chains or collars, and no one overseeing their activities. Ruhi did spot a few guards here and there armed with spears and swords, but on the whole, the pirate town seemed strangely peaceful.

Their path ended at a sturdy, stone building with a bright blue roof and a set of heavy doors painted the same hue. Their pirate escort ushered them all inside a wide, long hall with a high, beamed ceiling and a handsomely tiled floor. At the far end, rose a heavy wooden platform, atop which was a single, wide, high desk, almost a lectern. A woman sat behind that, and it was toward her that Ruhi and Sundra and the sailors were led. A smaller desk sat at one corner of that platform's base, and a man perched upon a stool there, quill in hand. He was scrawling in a large, bound ledger.

Ruhi and Sundra were pushed forward ahead of the rest. "Name?" the woman called down. The thick strands of gray shot through her long hair suggested an age comparable to Ruhi's father, as did the lines around eyes and mouth. Her tone and glance were both brisk and businesslike.

"Rawal Chera and Sundra Chera," Ruhi replied.

"Brothers?" came the question, and she nodded. "You wish to remain together?" Another nod. "Have either of you a trade?" Ruhi shook her head, and beside her, Sundra bristled but thankfully stayed quiet. "Money?"

This time it was Rohan, just behind them, who answered. "Three dirham, four falus between them."

The woman frowned, considering. "So seventeen falus each. Sahil, make a note of that."

Her scribe nodded. "Noted."

"Very well. Mark them down as general or household labor." The woman glanced past them toward the waiting sailors. "Next!"

Ruhi and Sundra were led over to the scribe. "Sign by your names," he instructed, handing Ruhi the quill and indicating a place in the ledger and then a second spot on the bottom of a sheet of parchment he had beside it.

She did so, trying to make them look natural. Sundra was next and wrote his first name with an easy flair but had to pause over the unfamiliar surname. If anyone noticed, they didn't comment. "Take this," was all the scribe said, handing them the document.

With that in hand, they were brought to a pair of men waiting against the far wall beside a little table—like an odd version of a cobbler's bench. "Nonwriting hand, please," the man seated by that bench requested, taking the document as well. Ruhi held out her left hand, and he took it and placed it palm up on the bench's surface, her wrist resting atop a broad metal strip laying there.

Then the other man reached out, hand held above hers, and the metal twitched, its ends rising like a waking cobra. The metal wrapped itself around Ruhi's wrist, as flexible as cotton and as cool as silk.

Ruhi almost jumped at the strange sensation. *How could metal behave like that?*

When it was in place, the man closed his hand into a fist, and she felt the band stiffen, all its pliability suddenly gone.

"Check the fit, please," the seated man instructed, releasing her hand. Ruhi raised it and twisted this way and that. The band wasn't tight, allowing room to shift so it didn't pinch, but it was close enough that it would not slip off. "Good."

The second man then applied something like a small, perfectly circular spoon to the cuff's handward edge, scooping out a small divot of metal which he then placed onto the document. The circle of metal spread like melted wax onto the parchment, sizzling and smoking, as if red-hot. "Next."

They repeated the process with Sundra. Then, with both of them now bearing those odd cuffs and Ruhi once again carrying the document now adorned with a pair of metal discs, the clerks guided them through a side door and out into an even larger room devoid of any furnishings.

Several others milled about around the edges of the room, all cuffed save for one who came over to them, hand out. "Contract?" he asked. Ruhi handed over the document, which he scanned before returning it. "Fine. Do you understand the terms?"

She must have looked blank because he continued, "This is your indenture agreement. You're indentured until such time as you pay off the full sum for you both, which totals ten dinar."

"Ten dinar!" Sundra exploded.

"Yes. Five apiece." The man went on, clearly unfazed by the outburst. No doubt he was used to it. "You will remain here in this hall until someone chooses to hire you. As standard labor, you're each entitled to one fals a week, plus room and board. If you're hired for household work, you'll typically earn two talus a week instead."

Ruhi did the math in her head. One fals a week for each of them meant just over one hundred falus a year, which was half a dinar. So one dinar every two years, which meant— "It will take us twenty years to pay that off!"

This time the look the man gave her was more appraising. "Very good. You may be able to command a higher price, with figuring skills like that." He gestured to an empty spot along the wall. "Wait over there."

There seemed little option but to do as they were told—there were guards stationed by both the door they'd entered through and the larger door at the front. A few were stationed at the corners as well. The pirates had remained behind in the first chamber, no doubt to make sure the sailors were processed.

"Ten dinar?" Sundra repeated, once they were leaning in their appointed spot, though he kept his voice down this time. "You know I had more than that in the pouch you threw away. We could have been free right now!"

"If they'd let us keep it," Ruhi shot back. "More likely they'd have taken that and ransomed us to your father instead." She did regret not taking out a few coins, but there hadn't been time. "At least we'll wind up together, wherever we go. And maybe we'll figure out a way to pay that debt off sooner." Her skills might indeed be marketable, but Sundra had clearly been raised as a gentleman, which meant, in Ruhi's eyes, he was all but useless. Still, it was nice to have the company and to know he would continue to keep her secret.

All they could do now was wait to see who purchased their contract and hope whomever it was proved a kindly employer. If there even was such a thing in this pirate nation they'd been dragged into.

CHAPTER NINE

SUNDRA

Sundra settled into a half-slumber, leaning against the wall with his head resting against it. He despaired over their current fate and the apparent hopelessness of escaping it, when the front door was thrust open with enough force to bang against the frame.

"Farhan!" a man bellowed as he entered, several larger men accompanying him fore and aft to make sure he had a clear path. "Where are you, my friend?"

Everyone turned at the interruption, which was clearly exactly what the newcomer wanted, for he paused just inside the doorway to pose and preen. He wasn't terribly tall, perhaps Sundra's own height, though it looked as if his elegant boots might have heels to enhance his stature. His churidars were properly tight-fitting, showing off legs that could have stood to have more muscle, and he wore both an embroidered sadri and a brocaded sherwani, as well as a beautifully woven sash done in the colors of the sunset. Atop his head was a turban of a matching hue, replete with a peacock feather in front. His mustache and beard were carefully oiled and curled, as was the dark hair showing below the turban. A long, slim sword was stuck through his sash, and an ornate curved dagger hung through the other side.

Sundra frowned. Everything about this man screamed excess and a desperate need to impress. Why wear both vest and coat, especially in this climate? Why churidars when shalwar would be far more comfortable? And why enter with such a fuss and with such a large entourage, if not to create a stir?

He'd known many such men back home, some of them his own age and some his father's. Men who, invariably, had less fortune and fewer merits than those who presented a more sober and dignified aspect.

"True quality doesn't need to demand attention," his father had often told him. "It will be evident to the discerning eye, and no one else's opinion truly matters."

He'd tried to live by that rule, dressing well but never ostentatiously, allowing word and action to build his reputation rather than seeking to form one himself. Here was a man who did the opposite.

"Ah, Raja Udayin!" the man who'd greeted them to this hall exclaimed, hurrying forward. He stopped a few feet shy of the newcomer and bowed deeply. "We are, as always, honored by your presence!"

Raja? Sundra turned away to hide a sneer. *This man was no king! But perhaps the title was used differently here?*

The overseer, evidently the summoned Farhan, was leading this so-called raja across the room—and directly toward him and Ruhi. Sundra straightened, and beside him, Ruhi did the same.

"These are the two I sent word about," Farhan was explaining in an obsequious tone. "Brothers and clearly well-bred." He turned a broad grin toward them that, as far as Sundra could tell, contained no actual malice. "This is the Raja Udayin Agarwal. He's one of the ruling members of these Islands and has a great interest in employing cultured young men such as yourselves."

Sundra executed a proper bow, any hint of his true distaste completely hidden from view. "Raja, it is an honor. I am Sundra

Chera, and this is my older brother Rawal, at your service." Ruhi did her best to match his bow, and he was glad he had thought to act first rather than relying upon her to know the proper forms and addresses.

The raja nodded back, the greeting of a noble to one of inferior rank, but that much at least was fair since they were penniless and indentured and he was some sort of ruler. "Well met, gentlemen. Please, you must call me Udayin. We're less formal here on the Islands."

His words were cultured, his tone somewhere between mildly interested and indifferent, but there was something in his gaze and his smirk that Sundra instinctively disliked.

"It seems you have fallen on hard times." Udayin's gaze went to Sundra's torn coat and Ruhi's intact but slightly shabbier one.

"We have, sir," she replied quickly, her voice deep enough to mask her gender. "Our father was taken from us a few years back and left more debts than assets. After settling those, all we had left was enough for passage on a ship we hoped would take us to new lands and new opportunities." Her gaze raked the hall. "And now here we are."

Sundra was impressed. He couldn't have come up with a fictitious history so quickly or made it sound so believable.

"Indeed! And I, for one, am very pleased you are!" the lord—Udayin, he'd insisted—assured them, his voice filled with a joviality Sundra felt did not reach his eyes. "You're educated, then?"

"Sir," she answered, dipping her head. "Reading, writing, mathematics, art—all the usual endeavors."

"Not to mention riding, sailing, dancing, and dueling," Sundra added in as offhand a manner as he could manage. Ruhi might not know to include such pursuits, but a proper gentleman certainly would.

Udayin nodded. "Of course, of course. Well, as good Farhan mentioned, I have a passion for assisting men such as yourself, men of good breeding who have fallen on hard times. I hope you will agree to enter my employ and join my household. I can promise you a fine home and fit company."

Now, this was interesting! Sundra hadn't realized they might have a choice as to who employed them. The question then became, what should they do? Take the offer on hand, or wait in the hopes of a better one? On the surface, Udayin's seemed good, or as good as they could hope in their circumstances. But there was something oily about the man, something Sundra mistrusted.

Ruhi spoke, however, while he was still considering. "We would be honored, lord," she said, bowing again, and Sundra had no choice but to bow agreement along with her.

Blast it all! He'd hoped for a chance to confer with her first. Still, she was probably right. For all he knew, they could wind up sitting there for days or weeks or more before another offer was made. Besides which, he suspected Udayin was the sort of man accustomed to getting what he wanted—and the kind who could make a deadly enemy if crossed or thwarted. Best to stay on his good side as much as possible.

"Excellent!" the man declared, all delight and happiness— and his dark eyes alight with victory. "Come, hand Farhan your contract, and we'll get you sorted and settled in your new home quick as can be!"

Ruhi gave the paper to the overseer, who quickly wrote the lord's name down at the bottom where it said "Employer" and put today's date.

Sundra noticed that was but the first of several lines and wondered how often people changed employment here. Over twenty years, he could imagine it happened a great deal.

He was marginally pleased, however, to see that, where it read "Employment," the man had written "household duties" and the rate read "2f/week."

The lord added his name with a flourish, his signature big and bold, and then accepted the contract from the overseer. "Excellent, you now work for me." And he swept out of the room, his men herding Ruhi and Sundra along behind him.

"I hope you know what you're doing," Sundra whispered to

Ruhi as they exited the building and took to the street among the raja's entourage.

"We were going to get hired by someone," she answered just as quietly. "And he seems eager to have us. Besides, he's paying us as household servants—or would you rather break your back hauling rocks and digging ditches?"

"No, but best be careful around him. I don't trust him."

"Oh?" Her tone was sardonic. "Too much like looking in a mirror?"

That irked him, to be sure. "I am nothing like that!" he insisted, offended she could possibly think so. This Udayin tried too hard, put on too perfect a face.

Chapter Ten

RUHI

This is, presumably, your first time in Surpakat," Udayin stated as they walked, laughing at his own joke. "I am sure you have many questions." He continued without waiting for a response or even glancing behind him to see if they'd given any. "Our Islands aren't unified except under the rule of the Rajas, the pirate lords who make up the *Parishad*—of which I am one."

Here he paused just long enough to give a small, superficially modest bow. "The Council oversees everything, but only insofar as enforcing certain basic rules. Such as no slavery."

"Hence the need for indentured servants," Sundra offered, and Ruhi didn't miss the momentary quirk of their new employer's eyebrow. It seemed Udayin didn't much appreciate having his monologue interrupted.

He continued after a moment, however, as brightly as if that interlude hadn't occurred: "Correct, young Sundra! Many of our residents came from slavery, and thus the Islands are adamant against it ever existing here."

From his tone, Ruhi picked up a clear distinction between "our residents" and the speaker. *Was the man some sort of island native, then?* "Beyond that, most of the Islands are divided into durga and khet. Khet, like Bahut Saare, provide much of our food, textiles, and other goods, but they're backwaters. The durgas are where you'll find most everyone of any real significance. You are, of course, in the most important durga right now. Surpakat is the meeting place of the Parishad, and every raja has a home here, making this the center of our culture." He spun in a loose circle, arms out to take in the buildings on either side. "As you can see."

Ruhi already had a slew of questions. If this was the stronghold where the Council met, what did that mean about the others? Were they somehow free of pirate influence? And what of these estates he'd just mentioned? Who controlled those? Plus, what were the other rules the Council enforced?

She held her tongue, however, having already seen the look Sundra had received for daring to speak. Instead she merely listened as the man carried on, now talking about this place's origins and naming the owners of some of the larger houses they passed.

"And here, at last, is my own humble domicile and now your residence as well."

The building before them could never have been thought "humble" except perhaps by some emperor somewhere, for it was at least fifty feet tall and a clean, almost stark ivory color. It had carved arches flanking a first-floor porch and a second-floor balcony with a far larger, grander arch over the enormous front entrance.

A railing adorned the flat roof, no doubt transforming that space into a rooftop terrace. The massive double doors were elaborately carved of solid teak, and the entire edifice sat upon a sturdy pedestal, as if the building itself didn't deign to share space with the street outside or with any of its neighbors.

One of the raja's men had already stepped out ahead of the group and banged his fist against the nearer door. It creaked open a moment later, along with its fellow, revealing a small but high-ceilinged entryway and another, smaller but equally grand set of doors beyond.

"Ah," Sundra remarked as they traipsed inside, and the second set opened to display a wide, handsome inner courtyard, its walls limewashed clean and bright, ringed by more columns, with a railed balcony around its upper level. "Your house is in the haveli style, I see."

"It is, yes," Udayin replied, shrugging out of his coat so that the man who'd appeared behind him could take it. The servant wore a sherwani not unlike Sundra's though his was more frayed and stained. Ruhi wondered why he was wearing it indoors rather than setting aside for any outdoor work or errands. "Do you note the floor? The tiles are all from the Empire of Makhaira, of course."

"Very handsome," Sundra agreed, and they were—done in classic geometric style with blue crosses at the center, cream outside that outlined in the same blue, and then a warm orange beyond.

"Good. That will be your task, then, to keep those clean." Their new employer gestured, and another man approached carrying a bucket of water in one hand and a small brush in the other. "You'll need to be careful, of course—I'll be quite cross if any of them are scratched."

The pirate lord frowned. "You will need to be lower down, of course. Shivaji?" The same man who'd pounded on the door, a big, brutish fellow in a black leather vest and a deep red turban, stepped up to Sundra and, without warning or word, punched him in the stomach hard enough to send the younger man stumbling to the floor, gasping on hands and knees.

Ruhi started to protest, but caught herself.

"There, that's better." Udayin's tone was bright, but there was no missing the glee in his eyes as he turned away from sputtering Sundra and beckoned the rest to follow.

"As for you, good Rawal—I did remember your name correctly?—perhaps you'd be so good as to oil the interior doors. All of them." Shivaji thrust a bucket into Ruhi's hands, along with a rag—she could smell the distinctive, bitter scent of shellac, and wrinkled her nose, which made Udayin giggle.

"I'm sorry, does that offend your delicate sensibilities?" he asked with a great show of false concern. Then he laughed again, the sound sharp and nasty. "Well, get used to it. You work for me now, and whatever horrible, smelly, demeaning task I set for you, that's what you'll do. Better get to it!"

He pranced off, and Shivaji gave Ruhi a dark look and a quick shove before following his master.

● ● ●

Ruhi didn't particularly mind the work. She'd used the resin-and-alcohol mixture many times on the panels, doors, floors, and furniture at home. It was tedious work, hot and smelly, but not particularly difficult. The drawback to shellac was that it scratched easily, requiring frequent touch-ups. However, for someone like Udayin, that clearly wasn't an issue. It was also clear he delighted in the idea they would be horrified by their assignments, so she was careful to look put out as she worked and to take a good deal longer at the task than she actually required.

She passed or was passed by other servants as she worked and noticed all of them wore former finery like Sundra's. Most were far better quality than her own but now in much worse repair. The other thing all of these men had in common was their look, which was that of a whipped dog. They looked beaten, and many of them trudged about, sunk deep in despair.

"Welcome to torture," a man told them when they were allowed to pause for a midday meal.

The fare was simple enough, rice and lentils with chopped up pieces of dried pear, plum, peach, and mango mixed in, but it was fresh and filling and adequately prepared. They were all brought into the long dining hall to eat together—minus Udayin and his crew of followers—allowing them their first proper look at their fellow workers.

"Veer Babu, at your service." The man who addressed her was a tall older gentleman, or at least middle-aged. His curls were mostly gray, as was his beard. Those were neatly trimmed, but his nails were ragged, his hands chapped and battered, and what had once been a fine pair of churidars now had holes worn through at both knees.

"Rawal Chera," Ruhi replied, bowing in return. "And this is my younger brother, Sundra."

Her supposed brother bowed as well, evidently recovered from the earlier blow. "Babu," Sundra said upon straightening. "I remember… seeing a Babu back home. That was a Maha Babu, though."

Their new acquaintance smiled. "My son," he explained. "I am glad to know that he, at least, is well?"

"He is," Sundra promised. "At least, when I saw him—from a distance—he appeared it. But he's a thakur."

"As was I," Veer agreed. He spread his arms, indicating his ruined attire. "Look at me now. All because I chose to accompany a wedding gift I was sending a cousin. We were set upon by pirates, and I was taken, but my family lacked the money to ransom me, so I was indentured instead. And hired on by Udayin." He spit on the ground at his feet. "A thousand curses upon the man!"

"He seemed decent enough when we met," Ruhi said slowly as they sat to eat. "I am beginning to suspect that was a ruse, however."

"Oh, he's as foul a master as you could ever imagine," another man nearby offered. "Tejas Dhar, at your service. I was a merchant, and a successful one, until our boat went off-course in a storm and we wound up being found by a pirate ship." Tejas was short and round, and his hair and beard were still mostly dark, peppered with gray. He sighed. "I have been stuck here five years already, and would throw myself into the ocean if I could, just to end the daily torment."

"He does seem to enjoy bullying people," Sundra noted.

"Gentlemen, specifically," Veer corrected. "One can only assume he was slighted by men of noble birth and good breeding at some point in his life. Now he delights in hiring such men as us and then debasing us as much as possible." He indicated his still-tidy facial hair. "We're required to keep our beards and hair properly cut and arranged. And when he hits us, he does mostly keep to those areas easily concealed, torso and chest and back, beneath what is left of our own clothes, which we're also expected to wear at all times."

"This is unacceptable!" Sundra declared, smacking the table's well-lacquered surface. "Surely we can do something about it? Revolt? Quit? Run away? Appeal to the authorities?"

The two other men both laughed, though there was no merriment in the noises. "No one cares, as long as he can deny the abuse and as long as he's still capable of paying the contracts he signs. And as far as run—" Tejas held up his wrist, displaying the silvery cuff. "Impossible with this."

"Why?" Ruhi asked. "What happens if you try?"

Veer nodded. "It's tied to the piece of it attached to the contract. The farther apart the two are, the heavier they become— unless you were specifically sent on an errand by your employer and have the chit to prove it. If you were to get as far as the docks, it would be dragging upon the ground with each step. Make it to the water…" He shuddered.

"There was a man once who did," Tejas finished for his friend. "He was even able to buy passage on a boat—but the second he set foot onto the ship, he sank right through it, tearing a hole in the hull from the force of his descent. Don't try to run."

Ruhi nodded quickly, as did Sundra. She could feel the young man's glare, though, and when they rose to clear their places— handing their dishes to one of the other men, who took them back to the kitchen to be washed—he was quick to hiss, "I knew we shouldn't have taken his offer."

She ducked her head, acknowledging the truth in that statement. She was the one who'd accepted, so the blame was squarely on her. But what else could they have done? Who knew if anyone else would've even offered them employment, especially since it'd been clear, even then, that the man in charge, Farhan, had an arrangement with Udayin. At least this way they were earning money toward their eventual release.

She said as much, and one of the others passing by laughed bitterly. "Don't expect to win free," he warned. "One of the others, Shray, was here nearly ten years. He was within months of buying his freedom." The man shook his head sadly. "He 'took ill' and died before that could happen. Udayin will never risk any of us being in a position to make him look bad to the other raja."

Fortunately, Sundra wasn't dissuaded by such news. "We'll find a way," he promised. "Somehow."

Ruhi could only hope that, for once, his unbounded optimism wasn't misplaced.

Chapter Eleven

SUNDRA

The next two days were the worst in Sundra's life. He'd been raised to privilege—taught about responsibility and duty and instructed in all the proper gentlemanly arts, but other than caring for weapons and horses, never expected to actually lift a hand to do work himself.

Now, however, he found himself scrubbing floors, washing dishes, hauling water, and every manner of menial task. Udayin took great delight in ordering them all about as if they were the meanest household drudge, and any time anyone dared speak back to him, he had them savagely beaten, a task Shivaji and the other bullies took clear pleasure carrying out.

Ruhi didn't seem to suffer in the same way. Sundra wasn't sure of her actual family history, but it was evident she was no stranger to work, and she seemed unfazed by the chores they were given. So much so, he noticed her reminding herself to sigh and scowl and groan whenever their employer or his men were near, in case they should suspect how little she minded and come up with some other, far worse punishment for her.

And if any of them discovered her true gender! That had caused

Sundra—and no doubt her—a good deal of concern when they'd first arrived, lest someone suspect the young woman in their midst. He shuddered to think what depravations Udayin might've subjected her to then.

Fortunately, although the servants were all quartered in a single long room fitted with rows of bunks, there'd been a spot at the very end that lay unclaimed, and the "brothers" were able to select that for their own. Ruhi took the top bunk, which was tall enough that someone walking by couldn't easily see her face while she slept, and she made sure to rise earlier than the others in order to wash in peace with Sundra standing guard outside the washroom door.

How long they could maintain this subterfuge, he didn't know. It was difficult to see how they could continue in this new and awful situation of theirs. At their current rate, it would take them a good decade to pay off their indenture, and if what they'd heard was true, they would never be allowed to reach that point anyway.

In the meantime, Sundra did his best to grit his teeth and bear the insults, the sneers, the giggling, and the work.

This was made more difficult by Udayin's deliberate attempts to goad all of them, and Sundra in particular. The raja insisted they all break their fast together each morning and dine together in the evening unless he was occupied elsewhere.

Each day the man was dressed in new finery, each outfit elaborate and expensive and incredibly garish in its clash of colors and designs, too much ornamentation overlaid one atop the other with no real sense of style and grace but a clear counterpoint to the ragged state of his employees' attire and persons. Whenever they were all together, Udayin made a point of commenting on how low the mighty had fallen, how awful their clothes looked now, how poor their work ethic and quality of work were, how useless they all were, how blessed they were that he'd taken them in, and so on.

Most of the men had long since been broken in spirit, but Sundra bristled at each and every insult, and several times only Ruhi's warning hand upon his shoulder had kept him from leaping up and confronting this horrible, egotistical fool who styled himself a pirate lord.

They'd heard the truth about that from Veer and the others. It was Udayin's great-great-grandfather, the first Lord Agarwal, who'd been a fierce and ruthless pirate, amassing much treasure and an entire fleet of ships loyal to him alone. He was among the half-dozen who'd originally decided these Islands needed to be more than just rough hideouts and had formed both the original Parishad and the first of the durgas. His son had been equally powerful, consolidating their position here.

But *his* son—Udayin's father—had wanted to distance himself from his bloody family history and humble beginnings as much as possible. It was clear the current lord took after his own father in that regard and spent all his time trying to convince the world he wasn't rich and powerful only because his ancestors had brutally sacked ships by the hundreds.

Then there was Shivaji. The man enjoyed his work a great deal, and like his master, was clearly determined to break down any resistance Sundra and Ruhi might have. His methods were more direct, however, and more brutal.

And since Sundra couldn't allow the thuggish pirate to lay hands on a young woman—or risk him learning the truth—he stepped in whenever Shivaji was threatening her and diverted the attention to himself. Which earned him her gratitude and an extra share of bruises with it, but at least the big man seemed content with watching him groan and wince and left it at that.

Matters came to a head one day, as Sundra had known they must. Ruhi was elsewhere, washing the dishes from the midday meal. He was polishing woodwork on the top floor, taking a rag and the foul-smelling oil to the beautifully carved door of the mansion's small but cozy puja. He wished he could slip into the prayer room himself and just close the door, shutting out this strange and terrible life for even a short while.

One of the other men, an older fellow named Nalan Anand, was scrubbing at the floor, using that same small brush Sundra had been handed his first day. Nalan was a decent sort, a minor noble who'd fallen on hard times even before winding up here, battered and broken but still kind to all.

They both jumped as the door to Udayin's bedchamber banged open and the lord emerged, still tugging on a pair of elbow-length, elaborately decorated black leather gloves that clashed horribly with both his handsome crimson silk turban and his midnight blue-beaded sash.

"Out of my way, you old fool!" the raja impatiently ordered Nalan, who was indeed right in his path to the grand staircase that dominated the building's central hall, but though the old man scurried to the side, he wasn't quick enough to avoid a solid boot to his midsection. The impact lifted Nalan off the ground, sending him crashing back down on his back, curling up in pain.

"Hey, there's no call for that!" Sundra declared, dropping his rag and rushing to the other man's side. "He was trying to move!"

"Silence, you pathetic cur!" Udayin snarled, but Sundra bounced to his feet, anger washing over him and clouding all other sentiment and reason.

He lunged forward, and only Nalan desperately grabbing at his ankle and nearly toppling him prevented Sundra from barreling into the astonished lord and slamming him to the ground on the freshly cleaned tiles. As it was, he was brought up just short, face to face with the shocked raja.

His employer's surprise quickly changed to outrage. "How dare you try to lay hands on me!" He backhanded Sundra full in the face, the pearl beads across the glove's back catching Sundra's cheek. "I'll deal with you when I return."

"Give me a sword and I'll deal with you now," Sundra shot back, tugging his leg free at last and straightening to face his tormentor, his cheek stinging where he'd been struck.

"A sword?" Udayin tugged off his glove and sucked on his knuckle, where he'd apparently bruised himself on Sundra's cheekbone, but paused to regard Sundra as if he had suddenly sprouted two heads. "And what would you do with such a thing, young lordling? Challenge me to a duel?"

"That's right," Sundra replied, then added offhandedly, "if you're not too cowardly to accept, that is."

He watched the man's face redden. Clearly the jab had struck home. "You aren't worth the trouble," the raja hissed and turned away, glancing down to where Shivaji was now waiting at the bottom of the stairs. "Shivaji," he called down, the usual façade of good cheer absent from his voice for once, leaving it sharp and brittle with rage. "Have this one beaten badly for me, will you?" His eyes glittered with malice as he added, "Oh, and break his hands afterward. Wouldn't want to risk him getting his hands on a sword someday."

"You don't even dare do it yourself, do you?" Sundra raged, struggling against the urge to just attack the man now and be done with it all. "You coward! You're not a raja! You're barely even a man! Without your thugs you're nothing!"

Udayin spun back to glare at him, his foot already raised to take the first step of his descent. "Shut up!" he hissed at Sundra, his eyes bulging. Sweat was beginning to trickle down his face. "I don't have to prove anything to you!" His lips twisted into a sneer. "And soon, I think, you won't be able to speak so to me—or anyone—ever again."

"You spineless excuse for a man!" Sundra shot back, taking a step forward but knowing that, for Ruhi's sake if nothing else, he could go no farther. "You're nothing, do you hear me? I wouldn't sully a blade on you! You should just curl up and die! By the Eldroi, I wish you would!"

The pirate lord opened his mouth to retort again, clearly determined to have the last word—but suddenly doubled over instead, clutching his stomach. He teetered there at the top of the stairs, straightening again but too much, completely rigid, as nothing except a strange, gasping cry emerged from his lips. His face began to purple as he grabbed for his throat, his limbs shaking so much he punched himself in the jaw in the process.

Then he lost his balance and toppled, twisting and writhing

like a hooked fish as he fell down the stairs. Halfway down there was a loud thunk when his head collided with one of the sturdy balustrades, and a softer but more chilling snap.

His body went completely limp, sliding and rolling the rest of the way to land at the bottom, sprawled out on the tiles with limbs and neck bent at improbable angles. Udayin Agarwal, Raja of the Areyat Islands, stared up at the mosaiced dome high overhead, his eyes glazed and unseeing.

"No!" Shivaji had been frozen in shock, but now rushed to the dead man's side again, falling to his knees beside him. "Master?" He shook Udayin with a surprisingly gentle hand, but the lord didn't respond. Nor would he. It was clear he'd passed on, his spirit gone to whatever eternal reward it had earned.

Sundra was still trying to make sense of the sudden event when Shivaji twisted about, glaring up at him where Sundra had unconsciously moved to the top of the steps to look down. "You did this!" the red-turbaned pirate accused, rising to his feet and crossing to grab the banister as if he could tug the entire stairs down at once, and Sundra with it. "You killed him!"

"What? No!" Sundra wanted to back away but couldn't. "You saw, he just fell! I didn't touch him!"

"You cursed him, and he died," Nalan offered from behind, his voice fearful but also filled with awe. "You must be Touched! You carry a Gift!"

"No," Sundra insisted. "Well, yes, but not like that! I can't kill someone with a word!" Nalan was pulling back, though, and peering at him with something like uncertainty on his lined face.

Shivaji was quick to recover his voice, though he appeared loath to climb the steps now. "Who do you work for?" he shouted from below instead, gripping the railing so tightly Sundra was surprised it didn't snap. "That bitch Kosala? That fool Vihaan? That villain Chetan? Someone put you up to this. Who was it?"

"I don't know what you're talking about," Sundra insisted. "I don't even know who any of those people are! I didn't do this!"

"I'll get the truth out of you," Shivaji snarled, looking like he'd finally overcome his fear enough to confront Sundra up close, but several of his men had gathered around him and their dead master. One of them grabbed his arm.

"Don't," the man insisted, his words rising to reach Sundra as well. "If you kill him, it'll just be your word he did it. Let the city guard take him. Then everyone will know what happened."

For an instant, it looked like Shivaji wasn't inclined to listen, and Sundra tensed, readying himself to try fending off the big man. Then the thug grunted. "Maybe. But if they don't finish you off after—" he pointed up at Sundra "—I will!"

"Seems fair," Sundra muttered as the big man turned and stalked away, ordering his men to stay by the stairs and to guard the other servants as well so Sundra couldn't try to run. And, truly, Sundra had considered it. But where would he even go if he did? And what would become of Ruhi in that case?

Instead he did as he'd wished to before, stepping backward into the prayer room and sinking to his knees on the rich rugs covering the floor there. At least if he had to await some gruesome fate, he could do so in peace and some modicum of comfort.

CHAPTER TWELVE

RUHI

R uhi found Sundra still ensconced in their dead master's prayer room. "What are you doing?" she hissed, throwing open the doors and wincing as they clattered against the walls. "We need to get out of here!" Downstairs, there was utter chaos, but she'd finally managed to pick up the fact that their master was dead—and that everyone thought her "brother" had killed him.

"And go where?" Sundra asked, surprisingly calmly. "We can't run, remember?" He held up his wrist, displaying that damnable cuff. She'd already gotten so used to the thing she'd practically forgotten about it.

"Well, that doesn't mean you have to just sit there waiting to die!" she told him, stepping into the small chamber and grabbing him by one arm. "Come on! At least face your fate on your feet."

Sundra shrugged. "What's the difference whether I sit or stand?" But at least he let her haul him to his feet and drag him out of the small room, back into the hall beyond, and to the top of those fatal steps. Already Ruhi could hear noises outside, what sounded like a mass of people approaching. *Eldroi, they were quick around here!* There wasn't any time, but she had to know.

"Did you do it?" she demanded, keeping her voice down, standing only a foot from him and watching his face closely. "Did you kill him?"

"What? No!" He certainly looked startled enough, irritated enough, disgusted enough for Ruhi to believe him. She let out a little sigh. Not that she'd liked their employer at all, but it was still a relief knowing that her only friend here hadn't suddenly become a murderer.

Now they just had to prove it. Unfortunately, from what little she'd seen, the Areyat Islands were much like anywhere else. Money could buy you all manner of things, including safety and forgiveness—but not having any money opened you up to accusations and assumptions with no way to defend yourself.

The front doors shifted open, too ponderous to bang and clatter, moving with a slow creak as several of the men put their backs into the task in response to a shouted command from the street. Light streamed in from outside—it was dark and cool inside the building, at least when you were away from the inner courtyard, but the sun was high and fierce beyond—and silhouetted against that harsh glare, Ruhi saw several figures waiting to enter.

As they marched forward, she could make out what looked to be long tunics or pullover jackets, flared below the waist, made from overlapping scales that gleamed like metal but moved more like cloth. On the newcomers' heads were circular metal caps that tapered as they rose to a point, with fine chain links hanging down along the sides and across the back of the neck. They carried tall spears with long, chiseled tips, and each one wore a sword or dagger or both through their sashes.

The one who headed straight for the stairs, brushing aside Udayin's men as she passed, wasn't as tall as some of the others, though broad-shouldered enough, and Ruhi could tell from the fit of the scaled armor that it was a woman.

"You two," she called up from the base of the stairs, her voice deep and clear. "Who might you be?"

"Rawal and Sundra Chera," Ruhi answered promptly. No point denying when the cuffs would surely reveal that much, if not more.

The woman nodded. "Thought as much. I don't recognize you, and your clothes aren't in tatters yet. Come down here so I don't have to shout, please." She glanced over toward where someone had mercifully thrown a sheet over the deceased. "That him?"

"Yes." Descending the stairs, Ruhi watched as the woman went over, knelt down beside Udayin's body, and gently lifted the sheet.

"Huh. Looks wretched. I'm guessing he died in agony." Her tone was neither sympathetic nor gloating, merely matter-of-fact. "Who saw it happen?"

"I did," Sundra replied. "And Nalan. Shivaji. Maybe others." His own eyes were glued to the dead man but snapped up when the guard woman let the sheet fall, covering the contorted corpse once more.

"Indeed? Tell me about it." She rose to her feet and moved away from the body to join them, and Ruhi saw that this confident woman couldn't be much older than she was. She was tough, though—this close you could make out the outline of strong muscle beneath that armor, and she wore it and bore those weapons like they weighed nothing. Ruhi didn't see any hatred in her, though, or even animosity. Just a genuine interest in knowing what had happened. And presumably finding someone to blame.

Still, she had to ask—"Sorry, who are you?"

That earned her a quick glance, but not an angry one. "Ahilya Pillai. I'm captain of the town guard. Now, about what happened?"

Sundra shrugged. "It was up there. He came out of his bedroom and into the hall there. Nalan was scrubbing the floor, and he kicked him out of the way. I was oiling the doors and said to leave him alone. Udayin shouted at me. I went to hit him, but Nalan held me back." He indicated his cheek, which had a large, angry welt across it. "He hit me instead. I challenged him to a duel. He refused. I called him a coward. He ordered me beaten. I told him to drop dead." A small smile flickered across his lips for an instant, then was gone. "Then he tripped and fell down the stairs."

"So—what—you cursed him?" Ruhi noticed that this woman—Captain Pillai—didn't seem overly frightened by that notion. She was wary, careful, alert, but not scared.

The question wrung a short laugh from Sundra. "Believe me, I would've if I could've. I'm no mage, though. No, just my dumb luck to say something like that and then have it happen. But I had nothing to do with it."

"What about you?" That question was directed at Ruhi. "You're brothers?" Ruhi nodded. "So your master picks on your brother—you just gonna stand around and let him?"

"Not much I could do about it," Ruhi pointed out. "He always had all his pet thugs around, making sure none of us could ever try anything. Anyway, I wasn't here when it happened. I only heard about it from some of the others."

"Sure, maybe you couldn't and didn't gut him here in the hall, but you've got access to the kitchen, right? Maybe you could whip something up there. Serve it to him while he's distracted. Then just wait for it to take effect, like when he's walking down the stairs."

"Maybe," Ruhi agreed. "But so far the only time I worked in the kitchen was to clean up, not prepare meals. And what would I use on him, even if I could? Chilis and mango? Scary stuff!"

That earned her a small scowl. "I don't know, I'm not an herbalist or a baker, but for all I know, maybe you are."

"There're dozens of us in this place. Why don't you pick on any of them? Why just me and my brother?"

"Because all of them've been here a while," the guard captain answered. "Whatever goes on around here—and believe me, I've heard rumors—they're used to it. So why wait until now to kill him? No, something changed. And the one obvious thing is you two being hired." She frowned and pulled a small notebook from a coat pocket. "You came in on the *Kalinga* a few days ago. Got hired by Udayin right away. Household work for both of you." She frowned at them, tucking the book back away. "Where were you from before that? Who were you before you boarded whatever boat Khandereo captured?"

"Just two men seeking their fortune, Captain," Sundra offered bitterly. "Nearly broke, hoping to see the world and improve our luck. Guess that didn't turn out so well."

"And you'd never been to the Islands before now?" Pillai stressed. "You didn't know anyone here?"

"Who would we have known?" Ruhi demanded, now annoyed enough to lose some of that instinctual respect for authority that had kept her polite. Why were they even being interrogated like this? Just because they were new here? "And if we had, why would we ever have let ourselves get hired by a man like that?"

"To get close enough to kill him, of course," a deep, husky voice cut in. All three of them spun about, glancing toward the still-open front doors—and the woman now slipping in between them. She was shorter than Ruhi, though taller than Pillai, and powerfully built, her broad shoulders filling out her black-and-red sherwani nicely, the jacket open to show off a beaded black choli beneath, over charcoal-colored gharara. Tall, black leather boots and short, black leather gloves completed the picture, as did the handsome talwar slung through her belt.

The woman herself was equally impressive. Her features were strong, firm chin and slightly hooked nose, widely spaced eyes under a stern brow, thick black hair pulled back in a tightly woven braid.

"Raja Kosala." Pillai bowed deeply. "I certainly wasn't expecting to find you here."

"You didn't," the newcomer corrected. "I found you. And them." A jerk of her head indicated Ruhi and Sundra. "I came to… bring them home with me."

Pillai frowned. "You're claiming their indenture for yourself? Do you have their contracts? Or some sort of proof to indicate they should now work for you? A missive from Udayin agreeing to this, perhaps?"

The pirate lord gave the guard commander a flat, chilly look. "Is my word not good enough?"

"Not for something like this, no."

The two women glared at each other. Ruhi could already see they didn't like each other—which, considering she was annoyed with the guard captain herself, only made her like this fierce raja even more.

"I don't have their contracts—yet," Kosala admitted slowly. "But I will." A nasty, smug smile spread across her face. "It's not like Udayin is in a position to stop me, is it? And I know you'd never interfere with the activities of a Council member unless they were breaking one of our few laws—which I'm not." Then, with a short, sharp laugh, she walked away.

"You were talking about your luck a minute ago?" Pillai asked them after the pirate lord had departed, her lips twisted into a grimace. "Believe me, it just got worse." The grimace became a scowl. "But how convenient for you, that a new master should swoop in just as the old one—one of her bitterest rivals—dies. Almost like it was planned that way."

"We didn't plan anything," Ruhi protested. "And we didn't do anything. We don't know why he's dead, but it wasn't anything to do with us."

"I suppose we don't have to take her offer, whatever it turns out to be," Sundra said, still looking where Kosala had gone. "Though, to be fair, we need to be employed by someone. Otherwise, it's back to that hall again, waiting for the next rich, crazy person to offer us jobs." Suddenly he grinned, if sheepishly. "Besides, what are the odds of that happening to us twice?"

"Better than the odds of a healthy man suddenly dropping dead in his own home," Pillai reminded him sharply. "Go with her. But this isn't over, not even close. I'll find out what happened here, and when I do, you'd best hope it truly did have nothing to do with you."

CHAPTER THIRTEEN

SUNDRA

A few minutes later, while Captain Pillai and her men were still walking the house but giving him and Ruhi space, Raja Kosala—not Rani, Sundra noted with some interest—returned. "Here," she stated without preamble, holding out a document Sundra recognized at once. It was their contract.

He and Ruhi both reached for it, but before their fingers touched the parchment the pirate lord pulled it back. "Did you kill him?" she asked bluntly.

So much for social niceties.

"No, of course not!" Sundra responded, recoiling at both the suggestion and the effrontery. "Not that I mind him being gone, but if I'd killed him, he'd have a sword sticking out of his chest."

She nodded, turning her gaze on Ruhi next. "And you?"

"Absolutely not!" She was red-faced with indignation. "I'd never do something like that!"

"Fine." Just like that, Kosala thrust the paper and quill at them. "Sign and let's leave this place. It feels like a tomb, and not just because of the body festering over there under that sheet."

Sundra saw that she'd already filled in her name and the date and copied "Household work" and the rate from the line above. He took both document and writing implement and hastily scrawled his name, remembering at the last to use their shared fiction of a surname instead of his true one.

Ruhi scowled but signed as well before returning the paper to their new employer. "Any personal effects to collect?" Kosala asked, and both of them shook their heads. "Good. Sanga, we're leaving." That last was called to a man who'd been leaning against the hall's front arch. He pushed himself off the frame with a nod. He was tall, taller than Sundra, and lean, but his open sadri showed muscle under tanned skin, and his eyes were sharp and bright as he fell into step just behind the three of them.

"What about the others?" Ruhi asked as they headed for the front doors, gesturing at some of the other servants who'd gathered to watch them go.

"What about them?" the pirate lord replied. "They're useless to me. None of them have skills worth a damn."

"And you assume we do?" Ruhi pressed. That earned a small, satisfied little smile, but Sundra didn't think it was anything to do with their supposed skills. Because he'd just remembered that he'd heard her name before she'd arrived.

"You're not taking us in for any skills we might have," he guessed aloud. "You're doing it because the guards think we killed him—and, if we work for you, they'll think you sent us to do it. You were the first name Shivaji shouted at me, when he was accusing me of working for someone. So you were Udayin's biggest rival, and now he's dead, and you're leaving his house with the two people everyone thinks did it."

"Very good," Kosala complimented. "Now, quiet." She'd slowed just inside the front entrance, and Sundra heard the clatter of rapid footsteps behind them. He turned to see Captain Pillai headed their way at something approaching a run, her men behind her.

"Stop right there!" the guard captain called, racing after them. "You can't just leave!"

"Why ever not?" Their new employer's eyes were wide in mock-innocence, but her tone was simply mocking. "Were you accusing me of something, Captain?"

Pillai came to a halt almost on top of them and was so out of breath it took her a moment to respond. "No, Raja," she admitted. "But these two are still of interest to me in all this."

"They are interesting," Kosala agreed with deliberate disingenuousness. "And if you wish to speak to them at any point, you know where they'll be. But unless you're leveling charges at them, I am taking my new workers with me. In order to put them to work."

The guard commander fumed, but there was little she could do to argue and everyone there knew it. Sundra was impressed. He had watched his father calm and cajole and mediate and had seen the other sirdars and thakurs similarly working to manipulate—most of them with far less finesse and usually less success. His father, however, had never enjoyed the game, it had simply been a necessity, given his rank and responsibilities.

It was clear, however, this woman thoroughly enjoyed dancing rings around people like Captain Pillai. And she was good at it, which was why the guards did nothing to impede them as the pirate lord led the way out of the front doors and back onto the streets of Surpakat.

"That went well, I think," Kosala commented after they'd walked a minute or three, heading farther from the indenture hall and the docks. She made a show of brushing imaginary lint from her jacket.

"I think the good captain would disagree," Ruhi argued, and Sundra caught the grin that flashed on his new mistress's face before she hid it away.

"Pillai is not a bad sort," Kosala offered. "And honest to a fault. That's rare around here." She frowned. "She'll have her hands full with this one, though. Are you sure you have no idea what killed him, or who?"

Sundra took a second to catch up with the sudden shift in

topic, but finally it sank in, and he shook his head. "No, none. He was just shouting and hitting, and then suddenly he started flailing about. Then he fell down the stairs and died."

"Sounds unpleasant." She didn't sound disappointed in the notion. "And not at all within the code."

"What is the code?" Sundra asked. "We heard about there not being any slaves. What else is there?"

"Of course Udayin didn't tell you," their employer muttered. "Typical. No backstabbing, no stealing, no sabotage. That's the bulk of it, along with 'no slaves.'"

Ruhi was already shaking her head. "No stealing? You're pirates! And no backstabbing or sabotage? I bet you fight amongst yourselves all the time."

Sundra worried that her outburst would upset their companion, but evidently not.

"No stealing amongst ourselves," Kosala explained. "And as far as backstabbing and sabotage, it's an honor sort of thing. You can duel all you want or attack each other's ships—but openly. No sneaking among us. We have to trust each other to fight fair."

"If you trusted each other, you wouldn't need a code," Sundra commented quietly.

"Aye, you've got the right of it there. We're pirates, after all." She grinned before putting on a stern face once more. "Now, less talking, more walking. Come on."

The road twisted and turned, curving around rocky outcroppings and small depressions or equally slight rises. Clearly the architects of this stronghold had preferred working around nature's obstacles to forcing compliance from them. For all that, though, the road was wide and fairly clean, and the people they passed all moved quickly, as if on urgent business. Many nodded at Kosala or tipped their hats. Some sidled away when she approached. She didn't react outwardly, but Sundra suspected that particular response gratified her more than any mere pleasantry.

The buildings were more spread out the farther they went, and at last they reached an impressive lawn, rich and green with mango trees planted all around, and a large, handsome house at the center. "Welcome to your new home," Kosala declared, gesturing broadly with both arms. "Be it ever so humble."

Sundra laughed at that, as did Ruhi. The building had been built in the Nalukettu style, Sundra saw at once, fashioned from wood for the most part, with stone at its base. Widely spaced columns supported a shingled roof over a broad front porch, and a second roof rose above that one, with smaller awnings cut at the corners and at intervals along the sides to allow light and air to reach the interior. For all that, it was less grand than Udayin's haveli. There was something far more comforting about a home like this, which was clearly less about ostentation and more about practicality, stability, and comfort.

"Sanga will get you settled," the pirate lord told them as they stepped up onto the porch. "And find you suitable work. I'll call if I need you. Otherwise, do as you're told, and you'll be fine." And with that she disappeared into the house proper. Sundra could hear her calling for a drink and the sound of people rushing to comply.

"This way." Sanga led them around the side. "The servants all bunk over here. You're brothers, so I'm assuming you can share." They entered a long hall with doors on the far wall, and he stopped at one, rapping on it once before pushing it open.

The room beyond wasn't large, but it had a bed on either side with a chamber pot beneath each, hooks on the walls for garments, and a running shelf above that for small items. An open window looked out onto the greenery beyond. The floor was rough stone rather than fine tile, but it was clean, as were the whitewashed walls, and the whole space seemed inviting, almost cozy, in much the way his cabin on the *Aden Star* had.

"Meals at morning, midday, and evening, in the courtyard," he went on. He favored them with a quick, sharp grin. "You can hang your finery up, and if you need simpler garb, we'll get you some. Kosala doesn't stand on ceremony."

Then he was gone, leaving them to study their quarters and this strange new situation.

"Well, she doesn't seem horrible," Sundra offered first. "Abrupt, tactless, manipulative, but not horrible."

"No," Ruhi agreed. "Which means she probably is, right? Since Udayin seemed good and then turned out to be a beast?"

"Maybe." Sundra chose a bed and sat on its edge, scuffing his boot soles across the floor. "Still, it beats where we were. By miles and miles."

"I suppose." She didn't sound convinced as she stepped over to the window and gazed out, hugging herself tight. "But she wants something from us, and I don't think it's just the reputation that comes from hiring us to kill her rival. There's something more going on. I just don't know what yet."

"Well, when you figure it out, let me know," Sundra instructed swiveling his legs up onto the mattress so he could stretch out. Ah, that was better! Unlike at Udayin's, these were real, decent beds. "For my part, I figure right now they haven't found any chores for us yet. Might as well take advantage of it."

He shut his eyes to her grumbling but had to swallow a laugh a few minutes later when he heard the other bed sag, followed by a long, deep sigh.

After that, the room was quiet, save perhaps the faint sounds of someone snoring.

Chapter Fourteen

RUHI

Ruhi woke to a knock on the door. "Coming!" she called, still waking up. Her jaw and cheeks felt scratchy, and when she lifted a hand to them she found hair there, thickly clumped into rough braids. That woke her the rest of the way, and she repeated "Coming!" but in a deeper, raspier voice as she rose from the bed and stumbled toward the door, checking to make sure her amulet was in place as she went.

A young woman was standing there, probably about her own age, short and sturdy with a thick plait of dark hair draping over one shoulder and a round, open face. "Hi," she started, offering a shy smile. "I'm Meera. Sanga sent me to tell you that there's food and to show you where."

"Rawal," Ruhi replied, wondering yet again if she'd made the right choice in sticking to this male guise once they'd reached the Islands. With Udayin, she figured it'd probably been for the best—he might not have been interested in her at all, since she wasn't noble-born, but then again he might've decided to teach a young, well-bred woman some harsh lessons. But Meera was the fourth woman she'd met since arriving here, counting that pirate woman on the ship, and none of them looked to be suffering any from their gender.

She was also finding it a bit uncomfortable here, and not because of the bed. Back at Udayin's they'd all been lumped in together, but here it was just her and Sundra in this room. Her and a man. Not her husband, not actually her brother, yet they were sleeping together, albeit in separate beds.

True, he continued to be a gentleman—when she'd needed the chamber pot he'd rolled over and practically shoved his face into the wall, covering his head with his pillow for good measure to give her as much privacy as possible. She appreciated that, but it still made for awkward quarters, even though having grown up around warehouse workers, Ruhi wasn't as squeamish about sharing space with a man—or about bodily functions—as her aunt might have wished. It was still awkward, but manageable.

Besides which, this fake beard itched like crazy.

Still, time enough to worry about that later when her stomach wasn't reminding her that she'd barely eaten today.

"Sundra, get up," she called over her shoulder, and her brother groaned, sitting up and then shifting to swing his legs around so he could set his feet on the floor. "Food," she continued, and that got him standing in a hurry. His hair was pressed flat on the side he'd been sleeping on and puffed out on the other, and Meera smothered a giggle, as did Ruhi herself. "Come on or there won't be any left," she warned.

"Right," he answered, nodding at the girl waiting for them, a smile blossoming on his face. "Hi, I'm Sundra."

Ruhi rolled her eyes at his tone and then sighed when she saw the girl's eyes widen and her cheeks flush. Yes, even completely disheveled he was still too good-looking by half.

"This is Meera," she explained, elbowing him in the ribs hard enough to make him grunt in surprise. "She's being kind enough to show us the way."

He nodded, but evidently couldn't stop himself from executing a lofty bow. "Delighted to make your acquaintance." That earned another giggle which made him grin in return.

"Stop fooling around, I'm hungry," Ruhi said, shoving him out the door and shutting it behind them. "Sorry, Meera, just ignore him."

The other girl laughed and led them down the hall.

"How long have you been here?" Ruhi asked as they walked.

"Oh, only a few months now," came the reply. "In Kosala's employ, that is. I was born here on the Islands, though I grew up on a plantation with my mother's family before this."

"Still, nice. I know who to ask about local customs, then." That could prove useful—assuming they were ever allowed out of the house.

They came to a wall screen done in a grid pattern and stepped around that to enter the house's inner courtyard. It wasn't as big as Udayin's had been, and much of it was taken up by the long, rectangular pond at its center. Columns lined that, supporting the edges of the roofs where they leaned in to shade the pond's sides. Benches lined the walls on one side, a set of long tables the other, and there were already men and women milling about the area, some already seated and eating. But Ruhi's attention was on the table and the food presented there.

Again she found herself comparing things to what they'd been at their last employment. Udayin had been careful to keep them fed, since he wanted them around long enough for him to torment, but the food had been extremely simple and fairly bland. In the evenings, when he'd insisted the entire household dine together, his own dishes had been far more complex and spiced, with larger quantities of meat or fowl or fish, so they'd have to watch him eat finer fare while they had only lentils and rice. Here there was a large bowl containing stewed goat in a rich tomato sauce, another with grilled fish in lemon and herbs, and a third with chicken shredded in lentils and spinach. Then there were cheese balls in a spicy green sauce, dates and mangos and melon, rice, lentils, and roti. All of it looked and smelled good, and Meera smiled, handing Ruhi and Sundra plates.

"Help yourself," she told them, taking a plate herself and dishing some food onto it. "We're not formal, especially not morning and midday. When the raja is home, we dine with her in the evenings in the dining room, so that's more a matter of waiting for each dish to be passed around, but it's still pretty relaxed."

Ruhi nodded, filling her plate. She poured some juice from a tall pitcher into one of the empty mugs waiting beside it. "What do you do here?" she asked their guide. "I mean, what kind of work?"

"Housekeeping. Mostly washing linens." Meera smiled. "I don't mind—I've been doing that sort of thing all my life, and it gives me an excuse to go outside some."

"Speaking of work—" Ruhi hadn't heard the tall man, Sanga, approaching, but suddenly he was there at her elbow. "What kind are you best at, hmm?" He reached out and squeezed her arm, then checked her hand, and she was glad she'd often pitched in at stacking bales or hauling boxes. Auntie Rudra had always despaired at the state of her nails, but it meant she didn't have a typical lady's hands, at least. "Not bad, some muscle on you," was his verdict.

"I can haul things," she agreed. "I'm good at tallies and figures too."

"Hmm," was the only response to that before the man turned to Sundra right behind her. "And you?"

"I'm good at all the gentlemanly pursuits," Sundra answered, his mouth half full of roti.

"I'll be sure to keep that in mind next time we need one." It was clear Sanga wasn't impressed by the claim. "For now, we'll keep it simple. You can both help with household chores, carrying linens and foodstuffs and sweeping up. After that, we'll see."

Sundra looked like he was about to protest, and Ruhi readied herself to step in, but then he nodded instead.

She let out a sigh of relief, and her "brother" turned to her as Sanga wandered away to speak to some of the others. "What? You thought I was going to say that sort of thing was beneath me?"

"Isn't that what you were thinking?" she countered.

He shrugged. "Maybe. But I guess it's not, is it? Besides which,

I already made one employer angry enough to beat me. I figure, this one doesn't seem as bad, why provoke her?"

The comment about beating made Ruhi glance at his cheek, which was still an angry red, the skin raised in small, irregular bumps. "How does it feel?"

"Not great, but better than before—I splashed some water on it earlier. It'll be fine." He stuffed the rest of the piece of roti in his mouth, making her laugh, and then ambled over, plate in hand, to find a seat on one of the benches.

Ruhi followed. A few of their fellow servants made room, and she soon found herself chatting with some of them. Most had been captured off ships, just like her and Sundra, but one or two were native-born like Meera—which meant they didn't have these horrid bracelets. "We don't have to earn our citizenship the same way you do," one of them explained when she asked. "So instead we get to keep our wages. And we could leave any time if we wanted. But why would we?"

Meera had a valid point, Ruhi decided. They might as well make the best of it.

Chapter Fifteen

SUNDRA AND RUHI

Sundra lasted three days before he couldn't take it anymore. "Stop!" he shouted, throwing down the armload of branches he'd been carrying and stomping across the back yard. "Just stop!"

Three sets of eyes turned to stare at him, one of them larger and higher than the other two. The horse shied at his approach, but despite his irritation, Sundra was careful to slow his pace and soften his steps, relaxing his posture so the animal would no longer be upset by his visible anger. His voice was low and quiet as he stopped beside the man there, Angad, and carefully but firmly removed the horse's reins from his grasp, ignoring the glimpse his Gift provided of those same reins from earlier. "You're going about this all wrong," he explained, doing his best not to raise his voice again. "All you're doing is upsetting her and making things worse."

"Excuse me!" Angad bristled—and not just his short, jutting beard. "Who do you think you are talking to me like that? I'm in charge of the stables here! You're just manual labor!"

"You may be in charge, but you have no idea what you're doing, do you?" Sundra shot back. Then he deliberately turned his back on the other man and focused on the horse instead. "It's fine," he told her, speaking soothingly, her reins held loosely in his grip. "He won't be mean to you anymore. I'm here now."

The horse, whose eyes had been wild even before he'd intervened, began to calm, and she stopped rearing, standing steadily on all four hooves. Her sides were still heaving though, and her tail swished about.

"She's got a temper," Angad insisted behind him. "It has to be broken before she can be ridden, otherwise she'll kick and bite."

"She doesn't have a temper," Sundra disagreed, still keeping his voice low and his back to the stablemaster. "You do. She's just scared and unsure, and your yelling and yanking and hitting were making it worse."

"I'm going to tell Kosala about this," the other man threatened.

"Good. Go do that."

The sound of rapidly receding footsteps suggested Angad had done exactly as promised, but he couldn't worry about that right now. He had to concentrate on the horse he was holding instead.

"What's your name, pretty girl?" he asked, and her ears swiveled toward him, those big eyes watching as he took one slow step toward the horse, then another. Good, she was paying attention to him, and her breathing was slowing a little. She was starting to calm down. "What's her name?" he asked over his shoulder, still not raising his voice much.

"Chaaya," came the answer from the young woman—barely more than a girl—watching from the stalls. He'd seen her before, helping clean the stalls and groom the horses, but she was clearly young and deferred to Angad. More's the pity. At least her tone was more curious and interested than annoyed or offended, so that was something. Her name, he remembered, was Naaz.

"Chaaya," he tried, and the mare's eyes flicked again. "That's a pretty name for a pretty lady. It suits you."

Which it did—her coat was a dappled gray, shading to black around her mouth and rump and hooves, much like the shadows her name suggested. He took another step or two, and she nickered at him, but her hooves stayed put, and her tail was moving gently. Good, good.

"Do you have an apple or some grapes around?" he asked the girl watching.

"Some grapes," she confirmed.

"Good. Bring them to me, please. But slowly."

She approached, her footsteps soft on the dirt, and he noted that Chaaya watched her but didn't grow agitated again. "She likes you," he commented, and the girl was now close enough that he could see her smile from the corner of his eye.

"I don't think she's mean either," the girl said softly, handing him the grapes. "That's just Angad."

"You're right," Sundra agreed. "Thank you." He took another step, and now he was right next to Chaaya, close enough to feel the warmth coming off her and smell that rich, heady scent of a horse that was being fed well and kept clean and healthy. "Hello, girl," he slowly raised his empty hand with the palm slightly cupped and facing her. "I'm Sundra."

She sniffed his hand, then whickered as he gently rubbed her nose, her eyes half-closing. No, not mean at all.

"You're a very good girl," he assured her and gently lifted his other hand, offering the grapes cradled there. "Would you like some grapes? It's fine, they're for you." After a second, she leaned in, baring her teeth, but Sundra didn't flinch at the sight, as he suspected Angad might have. Instead he just waited, keeping completely still except for the other hand that was still stroking her nose as she extended her neck and carefully, gently, captured a grape from his palm. "Oh, you have lovely manners," he told her, and the horse snorted softly so it seemed more a chuckle than a retort.

He heard a door open behind him, and he said, "Please ask Kosala not to rush over here or shout; she'll spook Chaaya." The girl, Naaz, didn't reply but there were steps away from him, and then a low, rushed voice saying something. No further sounds came from that direction, so he could only assume the pirate lord had agreed.

For the next few minutes, Sundra just stroked Chaaya's nose and murmured to her as he fed her grapes. Finally he turned, his hand still resting on her neck. Kosala was standing there, Angad fuming beside her, but the raja didn't look angry. More thoughtful.

"Naaz, will you walk her a bit?" Sundra asked, and the girl, who'd been off to the side, glanced to Kosala for confirmation. Kosala gave a short nod and Naaz hurried over, taking the reins from him.

"Don't worry, Chaaya, you can trust her," he promised the mare. "I'll be right here."

The horse bobbed her head twice, nibbled at his hair, and then let herself be led away, allowing Sundra to join Kosala by the house's back door.

"You know horses," the pirate lord said when he was standing before her.

"Yes. I was taught to ride as a small child, but my father insisted that a proper gentleman also knew how to care for his steed rather than assuming others would do it for him. So I learned how to muck a stall and groom and feed and even shoe a horse, and then how to train them." He frowned at Angad, and the other man actually shrank back. "She was frightened, as you would be if someone was shouting at you and telling you to do things you didn't know how to do. That's no reason to be mean to her. You need to be patient and gentle. If you can win her trust, she'll want to please you, and that makes everything easier."

Kosala was considering him carefully. "From now on, you're in charge of the horses." She raised a hand as Angad opened his mouth to object. "You're still in charge of the stables," she assured him. "But leave the training to Sundra. It wasn't fair of me to assume you would be able to do that as well as you keep the place clean and maintained."

The compliment clearly drained any anger the man had been feeling, and Sundra filed away that excellent technique for later.

"It's true, I don't have any formal training at teaching horses," the stablemaster agreed instead.

It was an olive branch, and Sundra wasn't slow to notice or to accept it. "I can teach you," he offered. "It's not hard, it just takes patience, attention, and care." The other man managed a half smile and a nod, still embarrassed at being found wanting before his employer. But at least he was no longer obstructive, and Sundra hoped with the help of some praise here and there, he could mend that potential conflict and the two of them would work together smoothly.

For the first time since setting out from home, he actually felt like he was starting to enjoy himself and to have a sense of what his life might be like.

◆ ◆ ◆

Ruhi was dusting one of the many window alcoves around the house—bright, sunny spots with pillows so you could sit and enjoy the sunlight and fresh air filtering in through the elaborately carved wooden screens—and humming to herself as she worked. She'd never minded getting her hands dirty and actually enjoyed the process of taking something from dirty to clean, and the humming helped both to the pass the time and to provide a rhythm for her motions, a trick she'd picked up from one of the warehouse workers years ago.

She stopped both the humming and the dusting, however, when she heard the cursing.

"Hello?" she called out, keeping her voice down in case the anger was from her causing too much noise. But the cursing continued unabated, and she edged closer to the slightly ajar door it was emanating from. Ruhi pushed the door further open and saw a small office, bright and clean with colorful paintings and tapestries hung on its whitewashed walls and light streaming in from windows on both outer walls. A heavy desk of beautifully carved teak took up much of one wall—a handsome, bronze lamp set at each end to provide light when it grew dark. A man sat the desk, cursing as he stared at a large ledger laid open before him. He glanced up at her, and she was surprised to see it was Sanga, Kosala's second-in-command.

"Sorry," she said quickly. "I heard…"

To her surprise, he laughed, pushing the book away from him with both hands. "I'm sure you did. It's just this…" He gestured toward the ledger. "It makes my head ache! Give me someone to fight, that's fine. A problem to solve, absolutely. Bargaining, mediating, of course. But tallies?" He sighed and shook his head. "You might as well ask me to weave a rug."

Ruhi found herself stepping into the room and approaching the desk before she even realized. She considered resting a hand on Sanga's shoulder, using her Gift to make this easier, but decided that would be presumptuous and could easily backfire.

"May I?" She waited for his resigned nod before reaching out and tugging the ledger toward the desk's edge, turning it so she could get a better look.

It took her a moment to figure out what she was seeing, exactly. "Are these expenditures?" she asked, pointing to one set of numbers stacked one atop the other.

"That one is, yes," Sanga confirmed, indicating the first number. "And that one." He tapped the third. "This one—" the middle number "—and this one—" the last of the four "—are monies we brought in by selling some of the produce we grow."

"That's—" She stopped herself, took a deep breath, and started again. "You can't jumble cost and gain together like that," she explained slowly, carefully, aware that this man was still a pirate and could hurt her badly if he chose, and with little effort. Yet he sat and listened as she went on, "You need to set up two separate columns, one for profits and one for expenses. Then you'll be able to just run down each column to see things more clearly. Here, like this." She flipped to the next page and, reaching across to grab the quill that sat in its rest above the book and dipping its tip in the inkwell, quickly created a basic chart, adding "Item," "Quantity," "Date,"

"Profit," and "Expense" across the top. She used the edge of the inkstand to draw straight, neat lines between them running down the pages. Then she filled out the first two or three items from memory, flipping back to the previous pages to confirm she'd remembered the details correctly and then adding the next few as well.

"You see?" she asked when she'd copied all of it over. "Now you can tell which is what at a glance. They're all organized by date so you can also keep a running tally—" She added "current total" at the top on the right side with another column divider and used the number he'd had at the top of the previous page as her starting figure to add and subtract each row as she went. "This way you'll always know how much you have after each sale or purchase."

Sanga stared at her. "How did you do that?" he asked, and there was something uncomfortably like awe in his voice.

Ruhi shrugged as casually as she could to disguise the way her heart was suddenly beating ten times faster. "I've always been good with numbers, so my father—*our* father—taught me how to handle the business's finances."

Sanga was studying the ledger again, tapping his fingers on the desk as he read.

Finally, he looked up and nodded. "From now on, you're in charge of all this," he said, rising to his feet and offering her the chair. "I'll check over it, make sure you're not trying to cheat us somehow, but I don't think you will." He frowned, though not angrily, and nodded. "Yes, I think this makes the most sense for you to work here instead. It'll let me concentrate on other matters." He gave her a smile. "Thank you."

And then he was gone, as if he needed to exit the room quickly before the book itself somehow prevented his escape.

"Well, I suppose I'm the estate's bookkeeper now," Ruhi said to herself. She was good with that.

Now she just had to remember to give Meera back her feather duster.

Far less pleasant for either of them was the follow-up visit from Captain Pillai. "I just wanted to see how you both were settling in with your new employer," the guard commander claimed, glancing back behind them where Kosala leaned against a pillar, arms crossed over her chest, not scowling but not welcoming either. "Horse trainer and bookkeeper, eh? Those are some impressive promotions in just a couple days."

"I believe in putting people where they'll be the most use," Kosala declared. "And in promoting talent."

"Yes, they certainly have proven useful to you, haven't they?" Pillai pointed out.

That made the raja laugh. "Did you find any new evidence about Udayin's tragic death, Captain?" she asked pointedly.

When the other woman scowled and shook her head, Kosala's smirk widened. "So this is simply a fishing expedition, hoping someone will say something you can use? Good luck with that." She pushed off of the pillar to get in the commander's face. "You say you came to see how they're doing here. As you can see, they're quite well and happily employed. Will there be anything else?"

"No," Pillai admitted through gritted teeth. "Thank you for your time." And, with terse nods to both Ruhi and Sundra and another to Kosala, she turned on her heel and marched out, her boots clacking angrily on the tile floor.

"That woman takes her job much too seriously," the pirate lord stated once Pillai was gone. "But no matter." Her nod to them was equally terse, but they were beginning to realize that was just her way. "Back to work, you two." Then she was gone as well, leaving them to return to their individual occupations.

"She's not going to stop, you know," Ruhi commented.

"No, probably not," Sundra agreed. "But we didn't do anything, so she won't be able to find anything, right? Right?"

"Of course not," Ruhi agreed. But neither of them was entirely convinced by her answer.

Chapter Sixteen

RUHI

Shortly after the midday meal the next day, Meera came and found Ruhi in the office Sanga had turned over to her. "The raja is asking for you," the younger woman reported, and Ruhi rose at once, setting quill and ledger aside. She'd already realized that Kosala wasn't someone who enjoyed having to wait for anyone.

Following Meera out, she took a second to pat her beard and hair, making sure everything was still in place for her disguise.

Their path took them to the front hall where Ruhi found not only Kosala but Sundra and Sanga waiting. "Good, let's get a move on," the pirate lord announced once they were all together. Meera retreated as Kosala led the way outside, the other three drifting back slightly so that Sundra and Ruhi wound up right behind their employer with Sanga bringing up the rear.

"Where are we going, exactly?" Ruhi asked. She worried that this might seem presumptuous of her, but at the same time felt it was worth making sure they weren't being taken back to the Indentures Hall to wait for whomever might wish to employ them next.

As if divining her thoughts, Kosala laughed. "Don't worry, I'm not getting rid of you two. Yet. There's a meeting of the Parishad. I thought you might be interested to see it."

This time it was Sundra who laughed. "You mean you thought it might prove useful to show us off to the other rajas," he corrected with just a touch of bitterness, Ruhi thought. "Your pet assassins."

"Something like that," the woman leading them agreed easily. "It never hurts to keep your enemies off-balance—make them upset, confused, angry, and they're more likely to make a mistake."

"I'll remember that," Sundra promised, and behind them Sanga chuckled. All in all, it was an odd conversation and one that Ruhi felt typified their burgeoning relationship with their new employer.

Back home, her father had always been careful not to get too close to the workers—he was a good employer, considerate and supportive and never demanding more than was reasonable, but he maintained that careful separation between himself and his employees, so that no one could ever forget he wasn't their friend but their employer.

Ruhi's relationship had been more fluid—she was his daughter, yes, but she also worked on the floor with the men, rolling up her sleeves and getting dirty right alongside them. During the first few days, when most of the workers had been too afraid to speak, Ganath had told a very old, very funny in an awful way, very adult joke, loud enough for everyone around him to hear. Including Ruhi.

The entire warehouse had gone deathly silent, not even a breath stirring the thick, dusty air—until Ruhi had burst out laughing.

From then on, the men had treated her like one of them. Not in a bad way—in fact, they'd been oddly protective of her, and the one time a new worker had dared get overly familiar with her, he'd wound up with a broken arm and had quickly found other employment—but just that they'd known they could talk to her, laugh with her and not have to worry about it. As a result, she'd known them far better than her father had.

Even when she'd switched from loading and unloading to

tallying and then to overseeing and bookkeeping, she'd managed to retain that connection. And her father, rather than reprimanding her for being "too friendly with the help," as Auntie Rudra so often did, had come to rely upon Ruhi's bond with the workers to keep him informed if there were any problems. Not in the sense of gossiping on them, but in case someone was sick but didn't want to admit it for fear of losing their job or someone was slacking and forcing the others to work extra to cover for him, things like that.

It had taught Ruhi that different people handled being in charge in different ways. Udayin had been a monster and a bully, buying the loyalty of his thugs and terrorizing his indentured servants, making sure no one ever forgot who was the lord and who were the hired help. With Kosala, she could see that there was a certain familiarity allowed behind closed doors and even some out here in the open. Never disrespect, though—Ruhi could already tell that was a quick way to get on her employer's bad side. But asking valid questions, making astute comments, those were all well within allowances.

They'd been walking as she'd pondered this, and now she found that they were back near the heart of Surpakat. They passed the Indentures Hall without slowing and continued toward the docks but veered off just before reaching them to head across a wide, empty stretch of sand and stone toward a long building with a first floor of stone and three more floors above that of whitewashed wood or plaster or perhaps also stone between dark, heavy wooden beams. The second floor had a wide balcony and a row of glass doors opening onto that while the two top floors had more standard windows. The first floor looked like a taproom of some sort.

Kosala slowed a second, just long enough for Sanga to slip ahead of her. "Stay close," she instructed as the four of them marched up to the building's wide front doors which Sanga tugged open and led the way through. The place was indeed a taproom, smelling heavily of spices, flatbread, grilled meat, and rum, with a long bar against one wall and tables spaced about the rest of the single large room. He ignored all of that, cutting a path through the place's patrons toward a wide staircase in the center. They headed up that, the heady aroma dissipating as they rose, and then turned off it onto the second floor where Ruhi was surprised to find four of the city guard posted outside a pair of handsomely carved wooden doors.

"Weapons," one of them instructed, angling his long spear to the side to cross that of the man on the other side of the door, effectively blocking Sanga from proceeding.

"This is the Raja Kosala," Sanga replied, managing to sound a trifle haughty and a smidge bored.

"Yes, we know," the guard agreed. "And we still need your weapons. Just like we do every time."

Sanga grumbled but in a good-natured way, and he was laughing as he handed over his sword and dagger. Kosala passed them hers as well, then—at a raised eyebrow from the guard—a dagger from each boot, another from the back of her jacket, and two more Ruhi didn't even see emerge from hiding places. After which, at last the guards stood aside and let them enter.

The room they entered was one of the most beautiful Ruhi had ever seen. The floor was covered in a massive carpet that, though faded here and there, was still deep and rich and intricately woven. Inscribed gold tiles formed the ceiling. The broad band below that, where the ceiling sloped down to meet the walls, was a bright mosaic of white and blue and gold. A carved wooden frame ran beneath the mosaic, all gilded a deep gold that was nearly bronze, and that rested atop scalloped arches supported by sturdy but still graceful columns. On the two side walls those arches were wide and stood over otherwise blank white walls, but on the side they'd entered the arches were more numerous and formed a small waiting area between the outer doors and the inner chamber. And opposite them were matching arches before the row of glass doors she'd seen from outside, allowing a view of the harbor beyond with all its ships bobbing against the docks.

The room itself was dominated by a massive table, its top

clearly a single slice of an enormous oak, the edges smoothed but still irregular, the surface sealed and varnished and polished to a mirror shine. Ten chairs were placed at even intervals around the table, each a tall-backed gilt object with plush, red cushions. Other, less grandiose chairs sat in double rows lining the two side walls. The whole space smelled faintly of furniture polish and wood mixed with the salt air scent of the sea, mild but pleasant.

"Sit there," Kosala told Ruhi and Sundra, indicating seats in the front row on one side. Then she stepped forward and claimed the seat at the table directly in front of them, though she didn't yet sit down. Sanga followed her, placing himself behind her chair with his legs braced apart and his arms crossed in a clearly protective stance.

Their employer barely had a chance to set a hand upon her chair when a man of middling years and average height approached her. "Raja Kosala," he all but simpered, bowing deeply. "Always a delight to see you again."

"Shri Khatri," Ruhi heard Kosala reply and could already tell from the tone that she wasn't overly fond of the man whose rounded build suggested a life of leisure rather than exertion. His clothing was expensive and even gaudy, though nowhere near as outrageous—or as badly mismatched—as Udayin's had been. He clearly wasn't a raja, so who was he?

The man was still speaking, and Ruhi caught something about a package, but little more. That was because she saw how Kosala's attention suddenly transferred to the man approaching the table directly across from her.

"Chetan." If her tone had been cool toward Khatri, it was downright frigid now.

"Kosala." His was no warmer, and his glare was chilled as well, his scowl fierce enough to terrify a flame into snuffing itself out. His clothing wasn't as handsome as Khatri's but looked both sturdy and well-used, much like the newcomer himself. And he must also be a raja, given that he'd just settled unceremoniously into his chair.

Sundra leaned in toward her and said quietly, "Oh, I've heard his name before. When Shivaji was threatening me, he asked who

I was working for. Kosala was the first one he mentioned, but he said Chetan too. And one other—Vihaan, I think?"

"Well, anyone Udayin didn't like shows some promise," Ruhi replied just as softly. "But he and Kosala clearly don't like each other, which is a mark against him for me."

Others were filtering in, some alone and some with companions or even small groups. A few men and women also took seats at the table, marking them as fellow raja, and Ruhi was intrigued to see that Kosala wasn't the only woman there. The rest all went to sit in the rows of chairs on either side, except for a few who, like Sanga, stayed close to their master, ready to render assistance as needed.

Many of those entering went around the table before seeking seats themselves, saying hello to this lord and that one, and Ruhi found it fascinating to watch both the variety of greetings and the range of reactions. Chetan, she saw at once, was brusque with everyone and downright rude to many. Kosala wasn't much better, to be fair—she never openly spurned anyone, but there was a noticeable difference between those she considered worth her time and all the rest.

She was most respectful to an older woman who also sat at the table, her hair all turned silver and her face deeply lined but her blue eyes still clear and her hand firm for all that she'd used a sturdy silver-topped cane to make her way through the room. She barely acknowledged one of the other lords, a younger man in well-appointed and tasteful gear that, to Ruhi, seemed a bit too clean and fancy to have seen any real use.

There was a stir throughout the room as one woman entered, flanked by two men who both peeled off from her to take seats as she joined those at the table. "Falguni," Ruhi heard the fancy raja call out. "I'd not expected you to grace us with your presence."

The woman snorted in return. "It's not every day one of us dies, Vihaan," she replied. She had sharp features and eyes, but her voice had been so soft Ruhi had strained to hear it.

The comment sent another ripple of whispers around the chamber, and Ruhi felt many eyes upon her. Kosala was glancing about as well, and the little smirk upon her lips suggested she was well pleased with the chaos she was sowing.

"Perhaps we should come to order," one of the other raja suggested, a large man with an impressive beard and a booming voice. "We're all here, after all—all of us still alive, that is." He laughed at his own joke, and there were a few scattered chuckles but no other response.

His first statement had been directed particularly at a gentleman who'd taken the final seat at the table, a short, heavyset man with dark hair over a round, ruddy face. His fine clothing suggested wealth, and his pudgy form suggested he earned it without personal exertion. That individual nodded now, rising to his feet and giving a polite cough before speaking.

"As host to the Council, I, Nayak Laghari, hereby call this meeting of the Parishad to order."

So, this was the governor of Surpakat, Ruhi thought as the man sat, looking almost embarrassed to have dared address such an august assemblage. Interesting. It was clear that his role here was largely ceremonial, but at the same time, she suspected his presence—and the reminder that they didn't control this town entirely—might occasionally help keep the pirate lords in check.

"We do need to talk about Udayin's seat," a tall, slim pirate lord suggested quietly once the governor was seated. "He had designated no heirs, correct?"

That immediately launched a discussion that quickly rose to a debate—and from there to a full-blown argument—about how the dead pirate lord's property should be divided. Voices were being raised, people jumped from their seat, a few were even shouting from the sides, and it might have escalated further except the silver-haired raja rapped her cane upon the tabletop.

"Before we start fighting over his belongings," she stated, her voice quavering but clear, "perhaps we should make sure none of us will be next, hmm?" She'd half stood to be heard and now collapsed back into her seat, the effort having taken a visible toll on her.

"A good point, Jasleen," the raja Chetan agreed, and beside her Sundra whistled.

"That's Jasleen Lal?" he whispered. "My granddad told me stories about her. She was one of the fiercest pirates on the ocean." He shook his head. "Of course, that was a long time ago."

"Shhh," Ruhi urged, intent upon the main conversation. One of the pirate lords had gestured, and a man stood from the front row to approach the table. He was neither short nor tall, fat nor thin, and his hair was graying at the temples and chin. Small, wire-framed glasses sat perched upon his wide nose, and he pushed them up as he cleared his throat.

"Tell us, Vaidya Dara," the burly, jovial, giant of a raja asked loudly, "have you examined our fellow raja's body?"

"I did, yes, Raja Koliya," the doctor confirmed. He frowned.

"And could you determine cause of death?" Jasleen wanted to know.

"Yes, well, he died from a broken neck," the doctor answered. "His injuries were consistent with a fall down the stairs. There were some strange secondary—"

"Did someone push him?" Chetan demanded, glaring at Kosala, who spread her hands wide as if to declare her innocence. Ruhi shifted in her seat, aware that people were looking at her and her brother yet again. *So nice of Kosala to bring us to be examined like caged pets.*

"I—" Vaidya Dara frowned again. "I have no way of knowing that," he answered. "I don't see anything to suggest it, but I'm not—"

"There, you see?" Jasleen announced, banging her cane on the table again. "An accident, plain and simple. Tragic but that's all it was."

The room erupted into conversation, some of it too loud and emotional to be called polite, and Ruhi was aware that some were defending Kosala's innocence—and thus hers and Sundra's—while others were insisting they'd killed Udayin anyway. Several people were shouting for quiet, including the governor, though his protests were far too soft to impinge upon the din. Ruhi began to worry that violence might erupt with their neighbors resorting to fists and feet and chairs if nothing else.

"Enough!" the big pirate bellowed, cutting through the din. "Quiet down!" Everyone did, and after a second he nodded. "Right. Moving on. We should discuss Udayin's ships, homes, and other goods. We can—"

"If I may." The voice was smooth, oily, and Ruhi recognized it at once, even before its owner stood and executed a graceful bow to the room. It was the man who'd greeted Kosala first, Khatri. "Perhaps now would be a good time to bring up yet again the matter of representation for the various estates scattered across our fair isles. Really, there is—"

"None of that nonsense right now, Khatri," the fancy raja, Vihaan, declared in an airy voice that nonetheless cut the man off completely. "We have more important matters at hand than your precious little farm."

"But I really think—" the man tried again, only to be talked over once more. Defeated, he returned to his seat, his face red and his expression murderous.

"Thank you, Vihaan," the big pirate said, receiving a bow from his well-dressed young counterpart in return. "Now I think, as the one with the most ships, it only makes sense if I—" He got no farther before half the table was screaming at him, including Kosala. The shouting continued for several minutes and by the end of it most of the pirate lords were glaring at everyone and refusing to speak further.

"I suppose we must adjourn until our next meeting," Vihaan suggested smoothly, rising to his feet as graceful as a snake and just as slippery. He looked pointedly at the governor, Laghari, who took the cue and also rose, though with far less poise.

"I hereby declare this meeting of the Parishad to be at an end," the stocky little man declared formally. "Thank you all for coming," he added, addressing the crowd beyond the tables before excusing himself and heading toward the door with as much dignity as he could muster.

Vihaan nodded as if to approve the decision he'd prompted, then turned back to his fellow pirate lords to say, "Take care, all. I look forward to our next meeting." Then, with a small bow, he slid away from the table and was halfway across the room before anyone had even realized he was leaving.

"Damn it, we won't get anything more done until the next meeting now," the big pirate groused, and Jasleen chuckled and poked at him with her cane.

"Serves you right, getting all greedy," she said with a laugh. He grumbled and swatted the cane away before standing and stomping out without any farewells. People in the crowd began to filter out as well, but Kosala was still seated, so Ruhi kept hers as well, reasoning that they were less likely to be run over if they had the chairs as bulwarks.

A few people stopped by to exchange a quick word with their employer on the way out, but finally the last of those left, and Kosala pushed back from the table to stand and stretch. "Home," she ordered, and Sanga led the way once more, Ruhi and Sundra hurrying to follow. They stopped to retrieve their weapons just outside the chamber, then it was down the stairs and back out onto the street, which sounded blissfully quiet after all that shouting and arguing.

"And that," Kosala told them as they headed back, "is the ruling Council of the Areyat Islands." Her expression was half grin, half grimace, as if aware she was also at least partially the butt of her own joke. "Are you impressed yet?"

"Impressed the place is still standing, absolutely," Sundra agreed. "I've seen meetings of sirdar and thakur before, and those were perfectly tame, civil, and productive compared to that."

"It isn't always as bad," Kosala argued, then stopped herself with a sigh. "No, that's a lie. It's always that bad, but you work with what you have, I suppose."

That, at least, Ruhi could agree with.

CHAPTER SEVENTEEN

SUNDRA

The next day, Sundra was walking Chaaya. The mare had now accepted him fully and allowed him to lead her in a circle around the yard—the first step to getting her used to the reins—when a shadow appeared behind him.

"Handsome beast," a voice declared, and he placed it at once as belonging to the young raja from the day before, the one with the good clothes and smooth manners. Vihaan.

Sure enough, when he glanced over his shoulder he found the pirate lord standing there at the entrance to the practice yard, hands on his hips, watching Sundra and Chaaya—and it was hard to tell which of them the man was more interested in.

"She is, yes," Sundra agreed, choosing to take the comment that way and no other as he stopped their walk, moving in to pat the horse's nose and stroke her neck. She snorted and snuffled at him affectionately in return. "She's a very good girl too."

"You were at the Parishad yesterday." The raja approached. He was sensible enough to not rush forward but moved at a calm, steady pace, his voice low and even as well. Chaaya flicked her tail, and her ears swiveled to track him, but she didn't retreat or bare her teeth. "You were the one who was there when Udayin died. You and your brother."

"I was, yes," Sundra admitted. There didn't seem much point in lying about it. "The raja tripped and fell down the stairs."

"How tragically careless of him. Though, truth be told, he won't be much missed."

Up close, Sundra saw that Vihaan was probably no older than him, making him young to have a seat on the Islands' ruling Council. He was roughly Sundra's height as well, though of a leaner build. He had a thinner face, and his eyes seemed too bright and more than a bit bloodshot. His clothes were fine, clearly of the highest quality, but tasteful and all paired beautifully from his boots to his sash to his gloves to his coat to the band keeping his long curls out of his eyes. A talwar in an elegant, black leather scabbard chased in silver was stuck through his sash, and a matching dagger protruded from his belt at the small of his back. Sundra guessed from the angle of the weapons and the way he moved to accommodate them that the man knew how to use both and better than most suspected.

"What is her name?" Vihaan asked, reaching up to stroke Chaaya's neck, but now she did shy away, and it took all of Sundra's strength to hold onto the reins and keep her from bolting. "That's all right," the pirate lord said softly, keeping his hand high and visible as he backed up a pace. "I didn't mean to frighten her."

Though he acted calm, Sundra saw that he was sweating, even though the weather was mild and there was a pleasant breeze to cool it further.

"Is your master in?" From Vihaan, the term didn't emerge as an insult, which was a pleasant change from the late and unlamented Udayin's way of stressing the difference in their positions.

"I believe so, yes." Sundra stepped away, murmuring to Chaaya to calm her. When he'd finally gotten her to settle again, though her ears were still pinned back, he turned back to their visitor. "Did you want me to take you to her?"

That earned him a bright smile and a handsome bow. "That

would be most kind, and I'd be much obliged."

Naaz was nearby, as always. The girl spent more time in the stables than in the house, perhaps because she appeared more comfortable with horses than with people, although Sundra had been able to earn enough of her trust for her to relax some around him. He beckoned her over. "Would you finish walking Chaaya for me?"

She nodded quickly, a smile blossoming on her face, and the mare relaxed and nickered a hello as the girl took the reins, leaving Sundra free to bow in return. "If you'll follow me."

"You have excellent manners," Vihaan remarked as Sundra led the way in through the side door, down the hall to the central courtyard, and then along its one side toward the door that fronted Kosala's private study. "What were you before you came here, if you don't mind my asking?"

"Poor and desperate," Sundra replied with what he hoped was a convincing air and a self-deprecating laugh. "Our father raised us to be gentlemen but didn't have the money to allow us such a life. We hoped to fare better elsewhere, and—" he waved a hand around him "—here we are." He rapped on the door.

"Yes?" came Kosala's shout from within.

"Apologies, raja," Sundra called back loud enough to be heard through the sturdy wood. "But you have a visitor. Raja Vihaan is here to see you."

A few seconds passed and the lock opened with a loud, solid click, and the door swung open. Kosala stood there, and her eyes went straight to her fellow raja. "Vihaan," she said. "This is a surprise."

"But hopefully not an unwelcome one," he answered, sweeping into a far deeper bow than he'd offered Sundra. "I'd hoped to discuss a few matters with you away from the chaos of the Council. This way we might actually be able to hear each other."

She nodded, though her expression remained guarded, and stepped back, allowing the door to swing open further. "Come in."

He slid past Sundra, murmuring, "Thank you for your assistance." The door shut again, sealing the two raja in and Sundra out. Not that he wanted to be trapped in there with those two, but still he burned with curiosity to know what they were saying. Alas, the door was far too thick for much sound to carry through it.

At least, until the shouting started.

Reasoning he would need to show their visitor out again, and thus it made no sense to go away only to have to come back later, Sundra found an unobtrusive spot to stand, leaning in a corner with a pillar casting him in shadow. From there he couldn't make out words, just that the voices within had become raised and that it was definitely both of them. And neither sounded happy.

"What's going on?" It was Ruhi, emerging from the office she'd been given by Sanga.

Sundra quickly motioned her over to join him. "It's Vihaan," he explained quietly, though there was no one else there but them. "He came to see Kosala. They're arguing about something."

"Do you think it's about us?" she asked, and he could see the worry on her face and guess what it meant.

"Don't worry, Kosala isn't going to sell our service to him," he assured her. "Not as long as it's still useful to keep us around." He hoped that with Ruhi's bookkeeping skills and his talent with horses that their usefulness would become more about what they could actually do and less about their roles as Udayin's possible killers until the latter faded away completely. "I'm sure he's here on some other Council business, something they didn't get a chance to discuss in all that madness yesterday."

She nodded, but still looked unconvinced. They both jumped when the door was flung open and Vihaan came storming out. The young pirate lord only made it out into the hall, however, before he spun about.

"Why must you be so stubborn about this, Kosala?" he demanded, his voice somewhere between a scream and a whine. "This could work, I know it could! But only if you're part of it as well!"

Kosala emerged as far as the doorframe. "That will never happen, Vihaan," she snapped, her voice as loud as his but her features and posture far more controlled while he was sweating and nearly manic. "Don't waste any more of my time or yours trying to convince me otherwise."

"Ah, you make me crazy!" he insisted, reaching up and tearing at his own hair with his bare hands—at some point he'd evidently removed his gloves and thrust them through his sash beside his sword. "Think, woman! This is the chance of a lifetime!"

"My lifetime has thus far been a good deal longer than yours, and I have already seen far too many such chances lead to awful ends. It simply isn't worth the risk, and when you're a bit older, you'll realize that yourself." He started to argue further, but Kosala held up a hand. "This conversation is over, Vihaan," her tone making it clear she would not be swayed in the slightest. She glanced over at Sundra. "Kindly see our guest out," she ordered.

Sundra nodded, straightening and stepping away from the wall. "This way, if you please," he stated, gesturing not the way they'd come but the opposite direction, toward the home's front doors. Vihaan, after one last furious glare, stomped after him.

"That woman is infuriating!" the raja declared as they marched down the hall and out the front doors onto the wide porch. It was nearing noon, and the sun was high enough overhead that even in the shade of the porch roof Sundra could feel its warmth after the cool shadows of the inner hall. "Do you have any idea what she's passing up? Do you?" His face was flushed and his eyes wild as he turned to face Sundra.

It seemed that the man did in fact want an answer, so Sundra shrugged. "Not really, no, but I'm just the horse trainer."

"She's—We could—If only she—Oh!" Vihaan was so worked up he could barely speak, the disjointed words emerging in short bursts from between spit-speckled lips. "I could just—Aaah!" He reached up as if to tug at his hair again, the curls there already damp and disheveled, but his fingers froze halfway there, shaped in rigid hooks. His back arched, and his arms began to wave about in almost a flapping motion but more disjointed and haphazard. All the while his face had grown redder and redder, and his breath came in ragged gasps, his eyes bulging as he stared at Sundra. His lips worked as if he were trying to speak, but only a shuddering wheeze emerged.

Then those curled hands flew to his chest, slapping against the flesh there, as the Raja Vihaan toppled backward, as inflexible as a statue. He hit the porch's polished wooden floor with a loud bang, all the breath whooshing from him in a single wavering groan before he collapsed, going from stiff to limp in an instant even as the brightness faded from his eyes.

Sundra stared down at the dead raja. "Oh, hells. Not again!"

CHAPTER EIGHTEEN

RUHI

After the young pirate lord stormed off, Ruhi realized she was left standing there with Kosala, who was watching her as if waiting to see what she might do next. Deciding to chance it, Ruhi ventured, "It sounds like that didn't go too well."

The other woman sniffed. "Not as well as he'd have liked, certainly." She shook her head and returned to her office, waving for Ruhi to follow. She did and found herself in a space similar to the one where she now worked, if slightly larger and with more windows. Kosala settled into the large, heavily carved teak chair behind the equally ornate desk against one wall. Papers, rolled parchments, and folded maps covered Kosala's desk. A flat box that looked like a gift sat on the floor.

"Did you want this?" she asked, picking the box up and offering it to her employer, who snorted.

"Not likely," the woman replied. "A pathetic attempt sent to me a couple of days ago to bribe me by an equally pathetic man. As if I'd accept a gift from someone I loathed or be swayed by such a thing. He's almost as big an idiot as Vihaan."

Ruhi laughed, setting the box atop the stack. "Is he actually so bad? Raja Vihaan, I mean."

Kosala, however, remained unamused. "He's a fool. A young, impetuous fool. He relies upon his wit and his charm, both of which are considerable. But me—?" Here she bared her teeth, suddenly looking ferociously deadly. "I've had to fight my way to the top. I know smiles and soft words only get you so far. Sooner or later you have to get blood on your hands. He doesn't believe in that, which means, push comes to shove, I can't rely upon him to actually step up and do what needs doing." She shook her head. "I won't ally myself with someone like that. Someone I can't trust."

Her gaze went straight through Ruhi, who felt as if her soul had been bared. *Could that last comment have been about her somehow? Did her employer know her secret?*

Her thoughts were interrupted by a heavy thud from the front of the hall. "What was that?" Kosala demanded, already on her feet and headed for the door. Ruhi found herself right behind as they raced out into the hall, through the front doors, and onto the front porch—and came to a sudden stop, staring at the mess before them.

"I didn't do this!" Sundra insisted, looking up from the undoubtedly dead man at his feet. "He just keeled over!"

"Like Udayin just fell down the stairs?" Kosala asked, but her tone was oddly not accusatory.

Ruhi wondered at that, as she'd certainly have suspected Sundra if she'd been in Kosala's shoes.

But the raja just sighed. "Well, there's little to be done for it now. Sanga!"

He appeared behind them almost immediately and let out a string of low curses when he saw the dead raja on their front step. "Send someone to the guard at once."

Sanga stopped spewing obscenities to glance at her. "You sure? This isn't gonna look too good."

"It'll look even worse if we try to cover it up and someone finds out," she replied, still without any real anger.

It was one of the things Ruhi liked most about her employer—Kosala was strong-willed, certainly, and set in her ways, but she was also willing to listen to different opinions. That was something she couldn't have said about Udayin—or her aunt.

Sanga clearly knew not to argue further. He simply slid through the doorway past them and headed out onto the walk and from there to the main street beyond.

"What am I going to do?" Sundra pleaded, pounding his fist into his hand. "That's twice now. They'll never believe I didn't do this."

"You're not convicted yet," Kosala countered. When his whining continued, she stepped forward and slapped him hard across his cheek—the same one that was still red and puffy from Udayin's blow. Sundra gasped, his head rocking to the side from the impact, but at least it quieted him.

"Are you listening now?" the raja asked, her own voice steady. "Good. You haven't been found guilty yet. But you're right, they'll think you did this. It is the easiest explanation." She frowned, tapping her fingers against her hip as she stood there thinking. "I could send you away, and that may be the best course. But not yet."

"Why not?" Ruhi asked. "If you don't want the guards to take us in, wouldn't it be better if we weren't here when they arrived?"

"Except how would it look if you ran now?" Kosala queried in return. She seemed to want an answer, and Sundra had one at once.

"Like we really were guilty," he admitted. "There's no way they'd believe us then." It was interesting that both he and Kosala—and even Ruhi herself, she realized—had been assuming that his fate and hers were tied together. But, as supposed brothers, it made sense. And, in reality, they had too many secrets between them to not stick together, especially when they still knew hardly anyone here.

Kosala nodded slowly. "You'll need to stay for them to question," she decided. "After that, we'll see what happens."

"And him?" Ruhi looked toward the dead man, splayed upon the floor, and quickly turned away.

"Find something to cover him with," their master instructed. "Let's grant him at least that much dignity."

Sanga had clearly impressed the gravity of the situation upon the guard because when he returned an hour or so later he had Captain Pillai and several of her guards with him.

"Again?" was the first thing she said as she approached the porch, her sharp eyes going from the covered body to Sundra and back again. "This does seem to keep happening around you, doesn't it?"

"I am fabulously unlucky," he agreed, though without much of his usual flippancy. "That truly is all it is though. Honestly."

"Um hmm." She knelt and lifted the sheet, whistling when she saw the man beneath it. "Two raja dead," she said softly. "That's a serious blow to the Parishad. Did this one fall down the steps too?" She tilted her head. "Only, I'm not seeing any steps nearby. Unless he fell up these?" That last with a gesture toward the handful of broad steps leading onto the porch.

"No, no steps," he answered. Ruhi, standing nearby to provide at least support, felt he sounded both confused and sad by these strange events. "He just fell over."

"Walk me through it," the guard commander instructed, leaving the body behind to stand and face Sundra fully. "From the start."

That left him looking even more bewildered. "The start of the day? The start of... this?" He gestured vaguely toward Vihaan's body. "What?"

"This," she replied, her tone sharp but not nasty. Yet. No doubt she was trying to decide if Sundra was merely playing the fool.

"He's really shaken up," Ruhi offered in his defense.

"I can imagine." Was Pillai's tone a little less angry, a touch less judgmental? Perhaps. Ruhi hoped.

Sundra, meanwhile, shot Ruhi a grateful look, then took a deep breath. "Right. I was training Chaaya—she's a horse, a lovely mare, very sweet—" A cough from Ruhi brought him back. "Right. I was training her when Raja Vihaan showed up. He walked right up to me, told me how pretty Chaaya was, and tried to pet her." He frowned, evidently remembering. "She didn't like that much. I asked him what he wanted, and he said he was here to speak with Kosala. So I left Chaaya with Naaz and showed him the way to Kosala's study. She answered the door, told him to come in, and they talked."

"Shouted, actually," Ruhi put in.

"Yes, shouted—louder and louder," he agreed. "Then the door flew open, and he came charging out. He was extremely angry, all sweaty and red in the face. He told her she needed to agree; she told him no and then asked me to lead him out. So I did. We came out here; he ranted about her and how stubborn and shortsighted she was, then he started choking, turned bright red, and fell over." He shrugged. "That's it."

Pillai turned her sharp eyes on Ruhi, who nodded. "I didn't see the whole thing," she explained. "I heard the shouting and came out into the hall to see what was going on. I was there when he stormed off after Sundra. We heard a loud noise and came rushing out here to find him dead right where he is now."

"So that's twice someone dies near your brother, and both times you're nowhere in sight," Pillai pointed out. "Convenient."

"How?" Ruhi demanded. "Wouldn't it be more convenient, at least for us, if I claimed I was there both times and could confirm he didn't do anything? Seems dumb of me to not give my own brother an alibi."

"True," the guard captain acknowledged after a moment. "But maybe you aren't that bright. Or maybe you're just more concerned about saving your own neck than his." She'd already turned back to Sundra. "I don't suppose anybody else was around to see all this?"

He shook his head glumly. "It was just us out here." He brightened. "What about his men? They must've come here with him, right? Maybe they saw something."

But the look on Pillai's face said otherwise. "Vihaan never

traveled with an entourage," she explained. "He said he didn't need anyone to protect him."

Because he felt he was invincible, Ruhi thought sadly. She'd seen young men like that before. They couldn't conceive of ever getting hurt, of ever losing. That made them careless. She'd seen one get crushed under a small mountain of rice bags once—he'd been crossing the warehouse floor while some of the other men were hoisting the bags to the upper level and had ignored their warnings to hurry up or least steer clear. Then the rope had snapped, and all that weight had come pouring down, burying him before he could do much more than look surprised. They'd rushed to get him out, but it was already too late—all those bags together were nearly the weight of an elephant, and they'd all slammed down atop his empty little head. Foolish young men sometimes grew into wise or at least sensible men, provided they got the chance. That worker hadn't—and neither had Vihaan.

Pillai sighed and beckoned to her men, who approached and moved to flank Sundra. "I'm afraid you're going to have to come with me," she started but got no further as a shadow detached itself from the open doorway and stepped outside. A shadow in black and red.

"Raja," the guard captain stated, bowing.

"Captain." Kosala's answering nod was curt but not quite rude.

"I have to take him in," Pillai insisted, her tone slightly pleading. Ruhi thought that was less a wish for Kosala to confirm her decision than a hope that the pirate lord would allow it.

"No," the raja stated bluntly. "He is not going anywhere."

"Two dead, Kosala. With Udayin, people were willing to believe that story that he fell down the stairs. This? There's no way this was natural or an accident."

"I know, but you're still not taking him in." She lifted her chin, staring at Pillai as if daring her to argue. "You're taking me instead."

"What? No!" Sundra yelled. "I didn't do anything, and neither did you!" he insisted, turning then to Pillai. "She wasn't even out here when he died!"

"It doesn't matter," Kosala answered, looking at the guard captain instead of him. "It's my home, my lands, and you're my servant. Therefore, the responsibility is mine."

"You know how this will look," Pillai pointed out, neither upset nor gleeful. To Ruhi, the woman sounded matter-of-fact.

"Like I had two of my biggest rivals eliminated," Kosala said. "And, with the second one, that I was so careless as to kill him on my own front steps. Yes." She shook her head and laughed bitterly. "Not terribly bright of me, was it?"

"You were angry," the guard commander supplied. "He confronted you in your own home. Maybe he found something proving you killed Udayin. Maybe he was trying to blackmail you with it." She shrugged. "That's not for me to decide."

"No." If anything, Kosala straightened even more. "There will have to be a full trial. With two raja dead and a third suspected of their murders, there could be nothing less." She was looking at Ruhi when she said this, and Ruhi felt there was a message for her in there somewhere. But, curse it all, she didn't know what it was!

"All right," Pillai agreed at last. "You're right, I suppose. If not now, the Parishad—what's left of it—would demand I take you into custody later." She looked torn. "I should bind your hands. You're clearly dangerous. But—" It was obvious she was loath to subject a raja to such indignity.

Kosala graced her with a short bow in return. "I promise I'll go quietly and cause no trouble." Then she tugged her sword from her belt, still sheathed, and handed it to Sanga, who'd appeared behind her. The dagger followed and then the other ones Ruhi had seen her surrender before the Council meeting. "May I have a moment or two to consult with my second?" she asked when that was done. "He'll need to see to my affairs while I am in your custody."

"Of course." Pillai retreated a few steps back down off the porch, and her men followed her without a word, leaving Kosala, Sanga, Sundra, Ruhi, and the deceased Vihaan with some privacy.

Kosala murmured a few things to Sanga that Ruhi couldn't catch, but a glance from the woman toward her and Sundra suggested they weren't merely about standard household matters. Then she swiveled back about to face the two of them.

"I am counting on you two," she said seriously. "Don't disappoint me." And, with a single short nod, she marched past them, down to where Pillai waited. "I am ready."

The guard commander nodded and turned to go, Kosala walking beside her. Two of the guards fell into place behind the two women, while the two other guards clambered back up onto the porch and took up positions on either side of the covered corpse there.

Ruhi watched until Kosala was out of sight. Then she spun around to study Sanga. Somehow he'd moved soundlessly to the porch's far end, as distant from the corpse and its guards as it was possible to be and still be on the same surface. Ruhi marched over to him, and after a quick glance from her, Sundra followed.

"All right," she said softly once they were all clustered together at that end. "What does she want us to do?"

CHAPTER NINETEEN

SUNDRA

Sundra didn't know their employer's second particularly well. To be honest, the man scared him a little, far more than those who blustered and boasted and bragged.

Sanga was quiet, calm, and unnerving. But to Sundra's eye the pirate looked like he was trying to pretend a calm he didn't actually possess, particularly since he seemed unable to meet Ruhi's eyes when he replied, equally quietly, "Oh, nothing much. She just needs you to prove her innocence."

"Us?" Sundra yelped. He couldn't help it. "Why us?" he continued in a near whisper. "We've barely been here a week."

"That's exactly why," the pirate answered quietly, though it sounded as if he were trying to work through the rationale himself even as he voiced it. "Everybody else here, the whole town knows we work for Kosala. Like me—I'd never be able to go anywhere in Surpakat that people didn't know my name, my face, and my raja. You two, you're still unknowns to most. Unless they were at the Council meeting or specifically informed, they won't make the connection between you and her."

Ruhi nodded. "So you think people would be more likely to

open up to us—or at least not close off—if they didn't realize we were working for her."

Sanga sighed. "She's not exactly the best at making friends, all right? You saw her at the Parishad. She keeps her own counsel, only talks when she wants to and then only says as much as she feels she needs, and half the time she's laughing at everyone around her. Not exactly the type to inspire help. Plenty would love to see her go down for these deaths, whether they think she did it or not."

"But she didn't," Sundra insisted. "She didn't have any more to do with it than I did." He was absolutely certain of that too. Oh, with Vihaan one could easily claim she'd done something to him when they'd been arguing in her study, out of sight from everyone else. But Udayin? By the time she'd shown up, he was already dead on the floor, and Sundra hadn't seen her there previously.

The other two stared at him.

"Don't forget, a lot of people—possibly including Pillai—think you *did* do all this," Ruhi reminded him. "And since we're working for Kosala, that would mean she did it, just through you." She frowned. "There's got to be more to her picking us for this than just because nobody knows us yet. What aren't you telling us?"

The tall pirate squirmed a bit under her gaze. "She didn't tell me everything. Just that it had to be you two, that you were the only ones who could do it." He shrugged. "I guess she just really believes in you. She's always been remarkably good at finding people's real talents and putting them to use."

"So she wants us to prove she didn't do this," Sundra cut in, pacing the length of the porch while he spoke and ignoring the two guards by Vihaan's body, who didn't even pretend they weren't listening in. But he was too worked up to care. "How exactly are we supposed to do that? The whole 'we're new here' thing cuts both ways, you know—sure, nobody knows us yet, but we don't know anybody else either. We wouldn't have the first idea where to go, who to talk to, even what to look for."

If he'd hoped Sanga would be able to tell them what to do, he was sadly mistaken.

The pirate just shrugged again, looking miserable about it. "I don't know what to tell you," he said, shuffling his feet. "You want to know where to get the best beer and wine in town? I can answer that, sure. Where's the easiest place to get into a fistfight? Absolutely. Which ships' crews get sloppy drunk and can be outmaneuvered the next day on the water? You bet. But how to figure out something like this? I don't have a clue."

"Well, let's start with those enemies you mentioned," Ruhi suggested, waving Sundra over to join them again. "Who are the biggest ones?" She was leaning against one of the pillars, and he envied her ability to keep still even as he continued pacing, albeit in a smaller circuit.

"Udayin was one," Sanga answered right away, not even having to think about it. "Vihaan was another. And Chetan's the third."

Sundra nodded, remembering the Council meeting. "He was the one with the rougher clothes."

"Yes. He and Kosala butt heads all the time." Sanga shook his head. "I can't see him pulling something like this though."

"You never know," Sundra offered. "At the very least, it's someplace to start."

Ruhi stood straight and said quietly, "Speaking of places, we should probably clear out of here. There may only be these two guards here now, but sooner or later Pillai's going to realize that anyone here potentially could have killed Vihaan, if not Udayin." She grabbed Sundra's arm and started back into the house, all but dragging him through the front doors and down the hall to their shared room.

"Pack what you need." She matched deed to word, shoving clothes Kosala had given them on their arrival in a bag.

"Pack? With what?" Sundra asked, but almost before the words escaped his lips there was a knock at the door. He answered it to find Meera there holding a well-worn, much-patched shoulder bag done in a handsome gray striped pattern with black elephant silhouettes in rows across the body and interlocking white elephants along the upper border below black straps.

"This is all I could find on such short notice," the young woman said apologetically as she offered the battered satchel. "I made it myself, and it's seen some wear, but it should still serve."

He took it and gave her a smile in return, recognizing she was handing him a treasured keepsake. "Thank you. I promise I'll take good care of it."

Once they'd both gathered their few things, they returned to the inner courtyard, where Sanga handed Ruhi a small drawstring bag. "Here."

She weighed it in her hand before adding it to her belt pouch, and Sundra could hear the sound of coins sliding against each other.

"That should help." Then he gave each of them a strange little chit the size of a small coin but carved of bone and bearing the same seal that marked the front doors. "These will let you roam freely, all the way to the water's edge."

"Thanks," Ruhi told him.

Sanga nodded, already starting to turn away, but Sundra stopped him as something occurred to him. "I need a sword."

Both Sanga and Ruhi stared at him as if he were mouthing nonsense words. Still, Sundra wasn't about to back down on this. They were after someone who'd already killed twice. It was important to be able to defend themselves against whatever threats might appear, and Sundra could tell Ruhi had never been in a real fight in her life. Which was fine, he was happy to protect her as well—but he needed a sword to do it.

"I'm not giving you a sword," Sanga argued, crossing his arms over his chest and frowning down at Sundra. "No way."

"It's not like we can fight our way off this island with one sword," Sundra pointed out. "But if whoever killed Vihaan comes after us as well, what're we supposed to do, fend them off with stern words and maybe some finger-wagging?"

Sanga looked as if he might even agree with Sundra, but he still shook his head. "Can't," he told them as firmly as before. "Council finds out I gave you a *sword*, it'd be hanging or keelhauling for all three of us." He hesitated a second longer, then pulled the heavy, curving dagger from his own sash. "Here, take this." He offered the sheathed weapon to Ruhi, who accepted it as hesitantly as if it were a live cobra rearing up and preparing to strike. "Now go."

Ruhi handed over the dagger as soon as they'd stepped out into the front hall away from everyone else. "Sorry about the sword," she told him.

He did his best to shrug. "I can see his point, I suppose," he admitted, sticking the dagger through his belt, angled for a quicker, easier draw. "I'd just feel a whole lot better with a proper weapon in my hands."

They'd reached the front door, but Ruhi peered through the ornamental, carved screen built into the wall alongside the frame and stopped Sundra from opening it. "Two more guards," she warned softly. "Just joining those first two."

"Any sign of Pillai?" he asked, and she shook her head.

"Not yet. But it's only a matter of time before she comes back, right?"

He nodded. "Come on." He led her back through the courtyard and then to a hall running sideways from it. The door at the end of this one was smaller, less elaborate, but also far more familiar to him, as it opened out onto the stables. Just as he'd hoped, Pillai hadn't stationed men here yet.

Chaaya nickered a greeting as they passed—and went into the fields beyond.

CHAPTER TWENTY

SUNDRA

They stayed close to the side of the house as they walked toward the street. Another building stood to their side, forming an alleyway, and across the street were several other structures with people milling about. Once they reached them, Sundra reasoned they could blend in with the crowd in case anyone was looking for them.

Just as they reached the corner, he stopped in part from surprise and in part because of the horse blocking his path.

And what a horse! Tall and slim with almost delicate legs and features and a long, graceful neck. Its coat was a gray so pale as to be nearly white, and its large eyes were dark and alert. It snorted as he and Ruhi stood staring and regarded them a second before pointedly turning its head away.

"What is that doing here?" Ruhi demanded beside him, but Sundra shushed her absently, his mind already working.

"He's Vihaan's," he answered and didn't miss the flicker of the horse's ears at that name. "He has to be." Because it wasn't just the horse's quality. There was also the gear.

The stallion had a handsome bridle of dark leather decorated in strips of beaten gold with a snowy plume jutting up over the top of his head. The reins were braided leather woven with gold wire and had been left loosely draped over the animal's long neck across his perfectly trimmed white mane. A row of golden disks affixed to leather straps ran across his chest like a collar, and a gold-edged crimson blanket covered his back beneath a black leather saddle.

His saddle blanket was adorned with golden baubles that matched the ones across the top of the animal's halter. Strings of small gold beads were affixed around each of his front legs above the knee, and his hooves had been dusted with gold. All in all, it created a breathtaking display, but somehow the overall effect was grand rather than gaudy, the size of the decorations keeping it from crossing that line into garish. The steed's master was a man of both wealth and taste. He had to be Vihaan's.

"I suppose he would've ridden over here," Ruhi agreed after a moment. "Especially if he came on his own."

"Exactly. And the horse is well-trained enough to wait on his own and no one would dare mess with him," Sundra pointed out. "But Vihaan didn't bring his horse into Kosala's yard. Maybe he thought that'd be rude?" He felt a pang at that. The young raja had seemed a decent sort—a bit overexcitable, perhaps, but not bad—and now his horse was waiting for a master who would never return.

"We should take him," he decided, and beside him Ruhi's mouth dropped open.

"What? Are you mad?" she started, lowering her voice when a man passing by turned to stare. "No stealing from citizens, remember?"

"We're not stealing," he replied confidently. "First off, his master's dead, so there's no one to steal him *from*. Second, we're not taking him, we're returning him. He can lead us back to his home."

"That's—" She stopped as what he'd said sank in. "Huh." He grinned, waiting, and after a few seconds, she was forced to admit, "that's... not the worst idea ever."

"I know, right?" He was getting excited about the perfection of the plan himself. "We don't know where Vihaan lives, right? We need to start somewhere. So why not there? Maybe whoever killed him did whatever it was there at his house, and we can find something to prove it."

She nodded. "All right, let's try it. But how?" The way she was eyeing the stallion, it was clear she'd never done any sort of riding. That was all right though. Sundra was expert enough for the both of them.

"Just stay here, stay still, and keep quiet," he instructed. "I'll take care of this." Then he shifted his attention to the stallion, who'd been steadfastly ignoring them since that one glance. "Hello, boy." The swiveling of one ear said the horse was listening, at least. "I'm Sundra. What's your name?"

The horse didn't answer and didn't turn to look, but he also didn't move as Sundra took a single slow step closer.

"You're a handsome fellow, aren't you?" he said, continuing to talk as he edged nearer. "I know your master, you know. You could say we're friends." That was stretching the truth a bit, but the young raja had at least been friendly toward him. "I bet you're tired of standing around out here, aren't you?" he added, taking another step. "Why don't we take you home so you can have some oats and some water? How does that sound?"

This time the horse whinnied, shuffling his feet, and swiveled his head around to watch Sundra's approach. He wasn't alarmed but he was restless and unsettled for some reason. Perhaps just because he wasn't Vihaan—any horse well-trained enough to be left on its own like this with its reins just loose probably only responded to its master and perhaps the stablemaster. Sundra wasn't either of those.

He took another step, and the animal reared back slightly, baring large, square teeth. No, definitely not fully comfortable with him yet. "It's fine, boy," he promised, but the stallion shook his head side to side. As he did, the light caught his neck, and Sundra frowned, seeing two thin red streaks there. What was that?

"I won't hurt you," he said softly, holding his hands well out from his body and up to shoulder height, fingers splayed. But the horse snorted and stomped a foot, tossing his head and fixing him with a gaze that was still semi-curious but also wary, frightened, and even a touch angry.

And, this close, he could confirm that those red lines were welts.

He paused, and behind him Ruhi called, "What's wrong?"

"Someone's beaten him," Sundra answered over his shoulder, still keeping his voice low. "So he's skittish now."

That didn't make any sense though. He'd seen Vihaan with Chaaya—true, she'd pulled away, but not because of any particular move he'd made. Nor had he been angry about the apparent rejection. Nothing about the young man Sundra had seen had suggested the sort who would hurt an innocent animal—especially a horse, when he clearly admired them a great deal.

Where had the marks come from, then? Had someone been trying to upset Vihaan by harming his beloved steed?

Whatever the reason, Sundra knew that an animal as smart as this one, once wronged, tended to distrust everyone. Given time, he could work past that. But they didn't have time. Already he saw a few people stopping to see what was going on in the alley. Soon enough word would spread of the horse there and the man trying to talk to him. If that word reached the guard, they'd be trapped.

He risked another step forward, and the horse shied away, eyes going wide and neck taut as he reared, pawing the air with his front hooves.

"It's no good," he said finally. "I'm not going to be able to calm him enough for us to ride him."

"What's our other option?" Ruhi asked from a few steps behind him. "I'm starting to feel a little hemmed in here."

"There's only one I can think of," he admitted. "Get ready to run." He glanced up at the horse and sighed. "Sorry about this." Then he took a deliberate stomp forward and flailed his arms at the same time as he shouted, "Go home!"

Startled, the horse reared again, whinnying loudly. Then the stallion twisted about, managing to extricate itself from the alley.

When its front hooves landed on the ground out in the street, it kicked back, bunched its muscles—and bolted.

"After it!" Sundra shouted, taking off down the street as people threw themselves out of the way of the charging horse. Ruhi rushed after him, and the two of them raced after the fleeing animal until they both ran out of breath and had to stop, gasping for air.

"Lost it," Ruhi stated, but Sundra, still doubled over, shook his head.

"Not really." He pointed ahead of them. They could hear the sound of the horse's passage in the distance. Sundra grinned at her. "Shall we?"

Chapter Twenty-one

RUHI

Ruhi was tired and footsore by the time they finally slowed to a stop. "That must be the place," she said. She was panting a bit, but no more than he was.

Beside her, Sundra nodded.

Together they stared at the house across the street. It was large, though not as massive as either Udayin's or Kosala's, and done in a somewhat different style with gleaming white walls offset by gold trim and a narrow front porch barred along the front by towering white columns that threw the arched doors and windows into deep shadow. A railing along the flat roof protected a walkway, and directly over the front door—with its protruding smaller porch and columns—rose a golden dome above a handsome cupola. All in all, she thought it was more elegant than Kosala's and more tasteful than Udayin's, making all three raja's homes she'd seen thus far accurate representations of their owners' public personas.

There was no sign of Vihaan's horse—it had left them in the dust both literally and figuratively some time ago—but a path looping around the side most likely led the way to the stables, and the trail of destruction had definitely led to this building.

Plus, the town guards standing outside were a likely indicator as well.

"They got here ahead of us." Sundra sounded so despondent about it, Ruhi had to struggle not to laugh.

"Well, they did know where they were going from the start," she pointed out as gently as she could. "That's a pretty hefty advantage."

He nodded, but still seemed glum. "So, what now? We can't exactly barge in and start asking questions with them around."

She considered. "We could linger and try to listen in," she suggested. "Maybe we'll learn something that could help."

To be honest, she'd no idea what that might be. Short of someone saying, "Oh, Raja Kosala had nothing to do with our master's death, it was clearly..." and the speaker having some sort of proof to back that up, at best they'd get some rumors and theories. Still, it could give them a place to start, which would be something now that they couldn't get into Vihaan's house.

Sundra evidently agreed with her proposal, because he retreated a step or two and moved to the side of the road, finding a spot to lean against one of the buildings there. Then he did his best to look nonchalant.

Unfortunately, the spot he'd chosen proved to be beside a merchant's, within arm's reach of open bins holding a variety of fruits and nuts and vegetables and grains for sale.

"Hey," someone called, and Ruhi glanced over to see a heavyset man with a large, curling mustache lumbering toward them. "You can't park yourself here. Either buy something or move on."

Ruhi fumbled in her pouch for the money Sanga had given her and withdrew a dirham which she held up for the merchant to see. "All right, calm yourself," she urged. "We were just about to look through your excellent wares and decide what we wanted."

"Well, see that you do," he grumbled, mollified by the sight of the coin and retreating to his previous post, a stool near the center of his display. That had bought them time, Ruhi knew, but not a lot—the merchant would be watching them and coming over again if they didn't make good on her promise soon enough.

"Anything useful?" she asked Sundra, who'd only been paying half attention to the exchange, the rest of his focus on the house across the street.

"Not much, no," he replied. "Looks like the staff are all upset about their master's death and not just paying lip service. Can't say I'm surprised—he seemed like he'd be a good employer. Except for those marks on his horse's neck." He was frowning as he recalled those. "I still can't match that with what I saw of him, but I guess you never know. Anyway, the guards aren't doing much more than keeping an eye on everyone and trying to calm them down at the moment."

Ruhi thought on that. "Why wouldn't they be questioning them more and searching the place?" she wondered aloud. "If I were Pillai, that's what I'd be doing. Oh, by Ganesh's nose, look."

Because no sooner had that thought crossed her mind then she turned to check the street—and saw a familiar figure in guard's armor approaching. The guards hadn't started a search yet because they'd been waiting for their commander, and here she came.

And here stood Ruhi and Sundra, already high on her suspect list, directly across from the latest victim's home. Which was nowhere near their own master's house.

"We need to go," she whispered, and Sundra straightened, pushing off the wall. "Now."

He followed her gaze and winced. "Definitely."

But as they turned to go, the merchant spotted them. "Hey!" he shouted. "You said you were here to buy. You can't just loiter and then run off without purchasing. You're wasting my time and blocking traffic!"

Ruhi rushed to quiet him, but it was too late. "The guards are looking our way," Sundra warned. "Now two of them are heading over here." His voice was tense. "What do we do?"

"We need to get out of here before Pillai sees us," she replied quickly.

"Fast. Right." Sundra studied the merchant's wares nearest them. "Get ready to run. Again." And, without any further warning, he snatched up a pair of mangos and took off down the street—in the opposite direction from the approaching guard captain.

"Stop! Thief!" The merchant shouted, leaping to his feet. "Don't just stand there," he bellowed at the guards, who'd stopped midway and were staring in confusion. "Get them!"

Ruhi took off after her Sundra with only an instant's hesitation and a pair of muttered curses that would've done old Ganath proud—and left Aunt Rudra speechless with horror. Then she was concentrating too much on running to spare any breath for such imprecations.

Sundra sped straight down the street then abruptly turned and dove into an alley. Chasing after him, Ruhi was aware of pounding feet behind her, but the sound faded as she slid through the gap and emerged on another, smaller street beyond. She caught a glimpse of Sundra ducking around a corner and darted after him. That alley was wider and had shop entrances along it, and she almost didn't stop in time as he called, "Over here!" from a door. She covered half the distance to the next establishment before her brain registered the words and she skidded to a stop.

He was leaning against the doorframe, looking completely casual, except for the way he was panting heavily and the two large mangos clutched guiltily to his chest. Ruhi walked over, trying to calm her own racing heart and gulping for air. He grinned at her.

"What in the heavens was that about?" she demanded, reaching him and snatching one of the pilfered fruits from his grasp. "We had money, we could have paid for these properly, you know."

"Yes, but then the guards would've reached us," he replied,

still breathing hard but slowly getting that under control again. "And we would've looked suspicious if we'd paid quickly and tried to duck them."

"So you thought stealing was a better, less conspicuous choice?" she demanded, lowering her voice as she followed him into the shop, which proved to be a small restaurant, dark and cozy with low, heavily beamed ceilings and thick cushions at low tables spaced around the room. The strong smell of spices, grilled meats, and boiling rice hit her almost like a punch, then wrapped around her like a hug, warm and inviting and nearly suffocating.

A young woman seated them at a table toward the back. She smiled broadly at Sundra, who smiled back, and placed cups of water, a small pot of tea, and a bowl of nuts and dried fruit in front of them, along with a list of the day's specials, then retreated to give them time to order.

Sundra took a long gulp of water. "Not less conspicuous, maybe, but utterly unconnected. Those guards, all they saw were a pair of thieves making off with some fruit. I'm sure Pillai shouted at them to get back to their post, because obviously a murder is a lot more important than some petty theft, especially when the victim's a raja. They'll completely forget about us within the hour."

He grinned. "Much better than 'those two young men who were obviously watching the dead raja's house,' don't you think?"

Put that way, Ruhi had to admit it did make sense. "You could have clued me in on the plan," she muttered at last, drinking some water as well. She wasn't ready to tell him he'd been right just yet.

He waved off that complaint. "No time. Sorry. Besides, I knew you could keep up." He flashed her that grin again, all boyish confidence and exuberance, and she had to laugh. *Sundra was a difficult person to stay mad at. Especially when, as he'd pointed out, his impulsive plan had actually worked.*

"Fine," she said at last. "So we got away with it. This time.

But we still don't know anything more than we did, and we can't exactly go back there right now."

"No, but at least we know where it is now," Sundra pointed out. "We can try again tomorrow or something, once the guards are done with whatever they're doing. In the meantime…" He waved the server over. "What're you having?"

Chapter Twenty-two

SUNDRA

Sundra stretched, stifling a yawn as they exited the little restaurant. *Ah, that felt better.* "So, what now?" he asked, patting his belly. He'd have to remember this place—the food was excellent, and their server had been a pleasure to behold too!

Ruhi scowled at him, running her fingers through her fake beard to comb out any last bits of rice or lentil or roti.

At first, he'd thought she was oddly vain about the false facial hair, but eventually he'd realized that she was just being careful—if it were real, she'd feel it when the hair was tangled or dirty, so leaving it messy or filled with crumbs might make people suspect its authenticity.

She said, "You were the one who said we should eat and then figure out what to do next. Well, now we've eaten—and I've paid. You come up with the next part."

"Fine," he replied, crossing his arms over his chest. "I will."

A part of him wanted to tell her "to the winds with this" and go back inside to see if the serving girl might be up for some light dalliance, but he knew that this wasn't the time. Besides which, he didn't like Ruhi's tone, dismissive—as if he couldn't come up with a plan. It'd been his idea to follow the horse home, hadn't it? And his idea to steal the mangoes—which they still had tucked away in Ruhi's bag. Admittedly the first one hadn't worked out so well, but that had only been because Pillai had beaten them there...

Which made him realize, if she was there, it meant he also knew where she was *not*.

"I know where to go," he told his grouchy companion. "And this is one we can find on our own, no horses necessary."

"Where—?" she started to ask, but then her eyes widened. "Oh, no!"

"Yes," he argued. "Come on, it makes perfect sense. There've been *two* deaths, right? And they're busy looking at the home of the second victim. But they've already been to the home of the first one. Which means they aren't there now. So it's the perfect time for us to go back there and poke around ourselves." He started walking, and sure enough, Ruhi fell into step beside him after only a few paces.

That didn't mean she'd given in yet. "What do you hope to find there?" she demanded as Sundra turned them down one street then another.

He didn't know the layout of this strange pirate town yet, but he did know to keep the water on his left and to angle them toward what was either a lookout tower or the top of an enormously tall building.

"We were there when it happened, remember? If we didn't see anything useful then, what makes you think we will now, especially when the guards have already been all through the place?" she asked.

But he already had answers to both those questions. "We weren't looking then. We were just trying to get through the day with Udayin constantly tormenting us—or me at least—and then shocked at what happened. Now we're going back there knowing he was murdered somehow and that whoever did it has since struck again with Vihaan. And the guards didn't know what they were looking for either. They could've walked right past something important without even realizing it."

Ruhi stewed on that for a bit as Sundra took a few more twists and turns, trying to stay on or near the main road as much as possible. He spotted a house he was sure he recognized when she finally sighed. "All right," she agreed with obvious reluctance. "We'll go. But at the first sign of trouble, we're out of there."

"Of course, but there won't be any trouble. Udayin's dead, remember? What've we got to worry about?"

"Besides the fact you're going the wrong way?" she shot back. "Udayin's home was back that way."

"Well, I got us this close, didn't I?" he grumbled, twisting around to follow her directions.

⬠　⬠　⬠

The house didn't look any different from the outside, an ivory cube with arched openings carved all along the front and fine detailwork on every surface. The doors were shut, and Sundra was relieved not to see any guards stationed outside. That was a good sign, and he grinned at Ruhi as he led the way up to the doors and banged on the right side with his fist. "Hello, the house! Anyone home?"

After a minute, there was a creak and a groan from the other side, and the door began to open slowly. It took what felt like forever before the two sides were far enough apart for him to see the person standing on the other side.

When that individual's face was finally visible, however, Sundra broke into a broad smile. "Thakur Babu!" he bowed deeply to the older man, who was still blinking against the bright sunlight outside. "How are you, my friend?"

Veer Babu stared, then started. "Sundra? And Rawal? What are you doing here?" He twisted sideways to struggle through the opening and join them outside. "You must leave at once!"

Ruhi stepped up to join them in the high but shallow overhang of that exterior alcove. "We aren't here to cause trouble, sir. We're just looking for answers."

"It doesn't matter what you're looking for," their friend insisted, grabbing each of their hands. "It is not safe for you here. You must go and quickly!"

"But why?" Sundra shook his hand free. "Veer, talk plainly. What is the trouble? We thought you'd be happy to see us—and that you'd all be much happier in general now that Udayin is gone."

"If only it were that simple." The older man sighed then motioned them to step inside into the short entryway between outer and inner doors. "We must be quiet and quick or he'll hear, and then you'll be in for it."

"Who?" Sundra asked. "Is someone bothering you? Who is it?"

That brought a laugh out of the former thakur, though it was a bitter one. "Who do you think? Shivaji! And if he catches you here, well, I wouldn't want to be you."

"Shivaji?" Sundra remembered how the big pirate had threatened him right before Pillai's arrival, and he shivered. "But what's he even still doing here, with his master gone? I thought he'd, I don't know, find a new home or something."

Ruhi was thinking, arms crossed, one hand cupping her chin. "Is he the new master here?" That was a terrible thought and might explain Veer's obvious terror, but their friend shook his head.

"No, in some ways it's worse," he told them. "If he was the master, he'd probably be content, and that would be that—he's a bully, of course, and a savage, but at least he wouldn't take such glee in tormenting us. But everything is still uncertain, and that means he's prowling around like a hungry tiger, just looking for an excuse to pounce."

Sundra sighed. "I don't understand. He's not the master, but he's in charge? And it's worse than if he *was* the master?"

"They don't believe in the same rules of inheritance here," Veer explained. "When you die without a designated heir, your belongings get divided up and handed out by the Parishad."

"Which is why they were talking about who would get Udayin's ships at the meeting," Ruhi recalled. "And his home and whatever else."

Veer nodded. "Exactly. Now, from what I've seen, most of them get around that by gifting things to their heirs while they're still alive. If you've already given someone else all your ships, they aren't up for grabs when you die. You can still be in charge, head of the household, but nothing actually still belongs to you."

Sundra nodded. It made sense, in the twisted and raw logic of this place.

"But that didn't happen here," he guessed.

"Correct. Udayin didn't trust anyone enough to give them anything," Veer said, which certainly sounded like their first master. "Shivaji was his right hand, but he was an enforcer, not an heir. And now, with Udayin dead, he's got nothing—except that he's here and no one else is yet, so he's trying to claim possession by force, hoping if he plants himself deep enough, the Council won't bother to dig him out."

"That's… a plan," Ruhi said slowly. "And he's inside right now?"

Sundra knew what she was thinking and had to agree. He had no desire to run into the big, brutal man again, especially if Shivaji still blamed him for Udayin's death and his own fall from grace.

"He is." Veer glanced back through the partially open inner doors, toward the interior courtyard. "I need to get back," he pleaded. "Before he notices and comes to see who's out here with me."

"We'll go," Sundra promised. "But first, we came here to see if we could figure out what really happened. Have you any idea? Was there anything strange that day, anyone around, anything?"

But the older man shook his head. "It was quiet," he recalled. "Just the usual chores. I was one of the first up, as always. I had to answer the door at dawn." He frowned. "It was a package of some sort. I brought it in and handed it off to one of the men who took it to Udayin."

"Hm." Sundra tapped a finger to his lip. "Do you know what was in it? Or who it was from?"

"The messenger didn't say, and of course I didn't open it. It wasn't large though." He held his hands perhaps two, three feet apart. "No more than that—and slim. Nor did it weigh much." He shrugged. "That's all I remember."

"Thank you," Ruhi told him, reaching out and putting a hand on the older man's arm. "We'll go so as not to cause any more trouble. Take care of yourself though."

That earned her a smile. "I will," Veer told her. "You two as well." There was a clatter from within and the sound of shouting, and he turned pale. "Go," he urged. "And don't come back. For your own sake." Then he slipped through into the house proper and shut the door behind him.

"We need to go," Ruhi said sharply, tugging at his sleeve. They could hear footsteps approaching the inner door and more shouts, angry ones—some of them in an all too familiar voice. "We need to go *now!*"

CHAPTER TWENTY-THREE

RUHI

Ruhi wasn't sure how long they ran. Nor was she entirely sure where they ran *to*. Every time one of them slowed down to catch their breath, the other would grab their arm and urge them to get moving again, and they would stumble back into motion. It was less running than staggering, gasping, and panting, and they must have been a sight as they lurched along, the pair of them, bumping into each other every few steps, weaving like drunkards but somehow staying on their feet, dripping with sweat, gasping for air.

It wasn't even entirely clear *why* they were still running. Oh, there was Shivaji, of course, he of the cruel sneer and the powerful arm and the vicious nature, but he was all the way back at Udayin's house. That building was now somewhere well behind them, lost in a haze of twists and turns and alleys and side streets. She doubted even that pirate would've pursued them this long. No, more likely he'd have given up the chase after only a few minutes.

And that was assuming he'd even discovered they'd been there. For all she knew, the pirate was still unaware of their abortive visit.

Finally, however, her legs could carry her no further. She tripped on nothing more than her own feet and tumbled to the ground, rolling across the hard-packed dirt before fetching up against the side of a building. Sundra managed a few steps more before his legs buckled as well, driving him to his knees and then to his hands as he pitched forward and nearly got a face full of dirt.

"I think…" Ruhi managed after a moment, finally recovering enough breath to speak, "that we're… safe."

Her friend shook his head, slowly like some great beast, but after a second's irritation she realized he wasn't so much arguing her statement as attempting to calm his own thoughts enough to reply. "Maybe." The single word spilled from his lips like overcooked leeks, limp and soft, and he coughed, giving the rest of his statement more volume and structure. "I don't… hear anyone… after us."

She sat up, leaning her back against the wall. The street they faced was wider than the one Udayin's house faced and appeared newer, made of larger, flatter stones, and the buildings were larger and farther apart than any she'd seen besides the rajas' homes and places like the Indentures Hall. Only a few people were out and about, and none of them spared her and Sundra more than a curious glance as they passed. No shouting reached her straining ears—nor the pounding of feet.

"I think we've lost him."

Sundra glanced about, a small smile quirking his lips. "Actually, I think we've lost *us*," he corrected, sounding calmer and more controlled.

Ruhi considered their surroundings as well. "No, you're right. We've come south a considerable ways, and I can smell the ocean, but I don't hear the sound of ships at all."

Sundra nodded and tried to stand but gave it up after a moment. Instead he crawled over beside her on his knees, twisting around to sink down against the wall as well. He groaned as he stretched his legs out before him. "What now?"

She frowned, peering up at the sky. The sun was already beginning to set. Had they been fleeing their former tormentor for that long? "We'll need to find someplace to spend the night. Get some rest and figure out our next step in the morning."

"Maybe get a drink while we're at it?" he suggested.

Ruhi started to snap at him, surprised he could think about something like carousing at a time like this, but then he pointed over their head with a grin, and she craned her neck to peer up. "The Quiet Fire" she read off the worn wooden sign hanging there from a sturdy iron arm and had to laugh. Apparently she'd landed them at a tavern.

"Why not?" she agreed, planting her hands on the ground to either side of her and using them and the wall to lever herself to her feet. She offered him a hand once she was standing, and he nearly pulled her back down but finally managed to rise as well, the two of them leaning against each other like two old men. It took them another minute before they could straighten, separate, and move slowly and gingerly toward the establishment's front door.

Tugging the door open and stepping inside, Ruhi stopped in surprise. She'd expected someplace similar to where they'd eaten lunch, low-ceilinged and dark and cozy. This place was the opposite. The varnished wood ceiling towered high overhead, supported by thick columns spaced even down the center of the single large room. The walls were whitewashed, and the floor was pale gray stone, making the space feel both airy and bright despite the only windows being small ones spaced across the front and on the sides just below the ceiling. Although it had been warm outside, the air here was cool and pleasant, and although several of the tables were occupied, she could barely hear people speaking, the sounds muted by the room's sheer size and height.

"Table for two?" the voice emerged from right beside her, and Ruhi stifled a yelp as she jumped back a pace, colliding with Sundra. The speaker was a short older woman, sturdily built, with gray hair in a thick braid and a vivid blue dupatta draped across her broad chest over a sari of a milder sky shade.

"Yes, thank you," Ruhi replied after recovering, and the woman smirked slightly, her dark eyes twinkling as she nodded and led them to a spot midway down one side.

"Sit," she commanded, and Ruhi obeyed automatically, as did Sundra. "Menus," came the next instruction, stiff sheets of paper thrust at them both. Then she'd turned and stomped away, though Ruhi had the impression that was simply the woman's standard mode of travel rather than any indication of temper.

"Strange place," Sundra commented, leaning back in his chair and looking around them. "You'd expect it to have large windows open to the breeze, but I suppose we're too far from the water for that."

Ruhi nodded, not trusting herself to speak since she could already see the woman returning.

This time she had a tray up on one shoulder, and on that was balanced a water jug, two earthen cups, and a woven basket filled with roti. "Here," she announced, swiveling the tray about with the ease of long practice and setting its contents out on the table. "What do you want?"

When they'd entered she'd felt that she must still be full from lunch, but now Ruhi realized that had probably been hours ago, and they'd run a great deal since, because suddenly she found she was actually ravenous. She quickly consulted the menu. "I'll have the crab with coconut rice, please."

"Same," Sundra agreed. "Thank you." The woman grunted, swiping the menus from their hands, and marched off once more. "Not as graceful as our last server or as friendly," Sundra observed, watching her go before returning his attention to Ruhi. "Now, what're we going to do? I know you said we should plan in the morning, but I'd feel better if I had a general idea now, even if we didn't act on it until morning."

That was fair, and Ruhi pondered, absently pouring them both water and taking a piece of the roti, sipping the cool liquid and shredding the soft, fresh bread with her fingers as she considered their predicament. "We can't go back to Udayin's," she said finally. "And we didn't have any luck getting into Vihaan's either."

"We could try again though," her companion offered. "Maybe

by morning, Pillai will have finished whatever she was doing there and moved on."

"Maybe, but I wouldn't want to count on it," Ruhi argued, and Sundra sighed in what sounded like agreement. "So we may not be able to search either home. Where's that leave us?"

He frowned, then brightened. "What about searching them directly? Udayin and Vihaan, I mean. Maybe if we can get a look at them, we could figure out what happened to them."

"Their bodies, you mean?" She shuddered at the thought but had to admit he had a point. She could see several problems with the idea though. "Pillai's sure to have Vihaan under guard," she pointed out. "And Udayin must have been buried already, don't you think?"

"Probably," Sundra admitted. "Damn." They both quieted as the old woman returned, this time carrying two large, copper bowls. The steam rising from them was redolent with the scent of broiled crab, roasted coconut, rice, mango, ginger, and several other spices, and Ruhi found her mouth watering as the woman set the dishes down in front of them. But something had occurred to her, and before the woman could turn away, Ruhi spoke.

"We're trying to find out about an associate of ours," she said carefully. "The Raja Vihaan."

The old woman eyed her. "He's dead," she replied brusquely. "This morning."

"Yes, we heard that," Ruhi confirmed. "We were wondering what was being done with him now. We'd like to pay our respects."

"Funeral's at dawn, along the docks. They always use the dock across from Council Hall for rajas."

"Thank you." She set aside further questions and plans as the aroma of the meal took away all other thoughts. Sundra was already digging into his, making small happy noises as he devoured mouthfuls of tender crab, delicately seasoned rice, and flavorful spices, and Ruhi wasted no time following his example. The food truly was excellent, far better than anything Aunt Rudra had ever taught her, better than Kosala's cooks had produced in their short time there. For a while, Ruhi just let herself enjoy it, using pieces of roti to scoop up the mixture and gulps of cool water to wash it all down.

By the time they'd finished, each of them scraping their bowls clean, many of the other patrons had finished, paid, and filtered out, leaving the large room even quieter. "Anything else?" the old woman asked as she gathered up the empty dishes.

"Do you rent rooms for the night?" Ruhi asked, and the woman glanced her way, those sharp eyes piercing.

"One bed or two?" she asked, and Ruhi nearly choked on the water she'd just sipped. "Two, then." That smirk was back, even more knowing than before.

"We're brothers!" Sundra protested, and the woman dismissed him with a sniff.

"A dirham a week," she declared at last. "Meals included."

Ruhi nodded, unsure if that was a fair price but afraid to argue and risk being tossed out with nowhere else to go and night closing in fast. She handed a coin over, and the woman beckoned them to follow as she carried the tray of dishes over toward the back of the room. There she set the tray aside and started up a set of broad stairs which led to a wide upper hall overlooking the dining area— Ruhi hadn't even realized she'd been seeing a balcony that whole time. Set back from the front was a row of doors, and the woman unlocked one with a key from a ring at her waist, pushing the door open and offering Ruhi the key itself.

"Fresh water in the basin," she told them, indicating a large copper bowl set atop a tall dresser beside the door. "Pots under the beds. Bath at the end of the hall." That smirk resurfaced. "One person per bath." Then she backed out, tugging the door shut behind her.

"What was that all about?" Sundra asked, plopping down on one of the two beds with a sigh of relief.

Ruhi could feel the flush on her cheeks. "She knows. Somehow she knows." The snide comments made no sense otherwise. *But how? No one else had seen through my disguise.*

Her companion watched her, even as he tugged off his boots. "Do you think she'll tell anyone?"

Ruhi considered that, but finally shook her head. "No. I think she just thinks it's funny or something. Who knows?" Sitting on the other bed, she soon found herself swiveling about to bring her legs up and stretch out fully. "I'm too tired to worry about it right now," she admitted, yawning widely. "Figure it out first thing in the morning."

Chapter Twenty-four

RUHI

When Ruhi woke, it was still dark. Which wasn't surprising—despite the exertions of the day and the good food and the fact that the bed was comfortable, she'd tossed and turned all night. Her mind had continued to turn over their current conundrum, and not even the broader picture of "How do we prove Kosala didn't kill Udayin and Vihaan?" No, what had kept her up was the smaller, more immediate question of "How are we going to attend that funeral?"

Sanga had been correct in arguing that, to most of the people of Surpakat, she and Sundra were nonentities, just two among the many teeming about the busy place. They could walk with anonymity, secure in the knowledge that, even if someone had heard the rumors about them and their lethality, those individuals would never connect such stories to the pair of unassuming young men walking beside them.

That logic fell apart, however, when you switched from "most of the town's residents" to "people who might attend a raja's funeral." Like the other rajas. All of whom had been present at the last Parishad meeting where Kosala had made a point of seating her and Sundra front and center for all to gawk at. She had little doubt any of them would have trouble recognizing her and her supposed brother.

Then there was Captain Pillai. The head of the town guard already knew them, not just on sight but from actual conversations, and would certainly be present at such an event and be on the lookout for her two star suspects that had mysteriously gone missing after the second suspicious death. A few of her guards might recognize them as well. Plus any of the others who'd attended that Council meeting could remember seeing them there and, at the very least, inquire as to their identities—at which point Ruhi was sure she and Sundra would wind up sharing a cell with their employer.

A part of her considered just avoiding the funeral altogether. Certainly that would be safer. But it was also the best chance they had to learn more about what had happened, more about Vihaan in general and to see if any of the other attendees—many of whom might've had cause for wanting the impulsive young pirate lord out of the way—did or said anything that could help piece this mystery together and find the true culprit.

The problem then was how they could attend and not get caught.

When sleep finally fled for good, it was because a single, crystal-clear thought had shoved its way into Ruhi's brain and taken up residence there, shouting until she'd no choice but to acknowledge the notion:

She'd been thinking "how can we attend" all along. But if she changed that to "how can *I* attend," the answer was blindingly simple.

It was also something she really didn't want to do. She didn't want to wind up in prison either. And she couldn't see any other solution.

Accordingly, she sat up and set her bare feet on the floor, moving slowly and carefully so as not to cause any creak to the old, worn floorboards. Then she stood and, pausing only long enough to dip her fingers in the washbasin and rub the wet digits over her eyes, nose, and mouth, Ruhi moved to the door. The latch clicked as she opened it, sounding as loud as a thunderclap in the otherwise still room, but Sundra barely stirred in his bed.

There were several other doors along the hall, and she had no idea which one might be her goal, but Ruhi decided to start with the first one, closest to the stairs. That would be the noisiest spot, she reasoned, but also the one with quickest access, and so the most likely for an employee or owner to claim in case there was trouble downstairs and they needed to move in a hurry. Walking silently, she reached that door and, screwing up her courage, raised her hand to knock.

She managed only a single soft rap on the wood panel before she heard the latch. The door slid open enough for a pair of wise old eyes to peer out at her.

"I need your help," Ruhi explained simply, and the old woman nodded, stepping back and letting the door open wider in invitation.

It wasn't until the portal had been closed behind her and she'd looked around quickly to make sure that they were truly alone that Ruhi took a deep breath, unclasped the amulet from around her neck, and began.

"My name is Ruhi Naidu. I am traveling as a man, Rawal Chera, because it is easier to escape notice and unwanted attention this way. Sundra is my friend, nothing more, but he maintains my secret."

The old woman nodded, and for the first time, the hint of a smile cracked her face. "I am Padmini Bhatt," she replied, bowing slightly. "I knew what you were the instant I saw you."

"How?" Ruhi demanded, momentarily sidetracked from her objective. "No one else has." Well, except for that pirate, Chhavi. But Pillai hadn't, nor Meera, nor Kosala, so it wasn't that the disguise didn't work on women.

That got a snort from her audience. "I was a mother long before I came to these Islands. Two boys and two girls, and all of them still healthy when I left. I know the difference, and it's more than a fake beard alone can hide." Her eyes turned shrewd. "Is that why you're here? You want me to help you perfect your disguise?"

"No." Ruhi paused and considered. "Well, yes, if you would, that would be wonderful. But first I need to undo it all, at least for one morning."

Padmini nodded. "The funeral." It wasn't a question, but Ruhi answered it anyway.

"Yes. I have to go, but I can't be found out." She shrugged, a small chuckle slipping from her lips. "Fortunately, no one else has been as observant as you. So—"

"If you go as a woman, they won't recognize you," the old woman finished for her. She considered, and finally nodded. "I don't know your business, and I don't need to, but you seem decent, and that young fool with you too. I don't think you're out to hurt anyone. And I can respect your wish for privacy and protection. So yes, I'll help you." She smiled more broadly, turning toward an old, heavily carved chest under the window, its surface thick with old varnish and fading paint. "Luckily for you, what I lack in height I make up in girth."

A short time later, Ruhi slipped back into her own room. This time she was less quiet about it, deliberately so, and Sundra stirred, blearily opening one eye to peer up at her.

Then he sat bolt upright, both eyes wide, sleep forgotten.

"You—" he started, that one word sputtering off. He tried again, with marginally more success. "You're—" He rubbed at his eyes, lowering his hands to stare at her more. "You're a girl!"

"A woman, thank you," Ruhi retorted, drawing herself up straight. "And yes, thank you for noticing." A part of her was pleased at how flustered her presence was making him, but the rest reminded that she didn't have a great deal of time. "Listen," she said, casting aside all teasing to sit on the edge of his bed, a fact that made him curl his legs in under himself and wrap his blankets more tightly around his middle. "There's no way we can both get into the funeral, not without being spotted. But like this—" she waved a hand at herself "—no one will recognize me."

"That's for sure," Sundra muttered, eyes still wide and cheeks flushed.

Ruhi pushed down a happy little flutter at the implied compliment. Padmini had been a tremendous help. Her cholis were all much too broad for Ruhi's narrower frame, but they'd fashioned one out of a shorter, emerald-hued dupatta instead, and a dhoti out of a shorter sari that had once been black but was now faded to ash gray. Now she appeared to be wearing a bodice and trousers beneath a much longer sari of a muted blue-green and a dupatta of deep green.

The old woman had helped her peel off the false beard, using oils to soothe the reddened skin. She had braided Ruhi's hair into a short but serviceable knot. Makeup had followed, far more than she would've worn back home, but it seemed appropriate here, both for the occasion and for her current attire. Besides which, it was clear Padmini had been enjoying herself—she'd commented while braiding Ruhi's hair that she hadn't been able to do such things since her own girls were small—and that had seemed a small price to pay for her aid. She even loaned Ruhi some jewelry, dangling earrings of sapphire and moonstone, a necklace of the same, rings and bracelets of worked silver with tiny aquamarines and iolite. All in all, when she'd looked in the older woman's mirror Ruhi had been pleased. There was no chance anyone seeing her would think of Rawal Chera now.

"I'll go and see what I can see, listen in, try to find anyone we might need to look into, any place we might need to go," she continued doggedly. "Padmini—that's the innkeeper's name—has offered to go with me. You wait here, out of sight."

That did make him blink past his current daze. "But what if there's trouble? I won't be around to help."

He seemed genuinely concerned for her, and she smiled to let him know she appreciated that, even as she shook her head. "I know, but it can't be helped. If just one person recognizes you, they'll toss you in jail. And how am I going to figure all of this out on my own?"

"Fine," he agreed with a scowl. "I'll wait here. But only until noon. If you're not back by then, I'm coming to find you."

It was a gentlemanly thing to say, and she could see he meant it. At least he wasn't as self-centered as some young men she'd met. He was even quite noble, in his way. And handsome.

She cut that thought off quickly and rose to her feet for good measure. "I'll head there now. Stay out of sight and out of trouble until I get back."

◆　◆　◆

Getting there proved to be a simple matter. In their twisting and turning to escape Shivaji and anyone else chasing them, it seemed that Ruhi and Sundra hadn't traveled as far inland as she'd thought.

It turned out the Quiet Fire was only a handful of buildings over from the coastline, they were simply tall enough and the road curved enough that she hadn't seen the water from here. With Padmini guiding her up between a pair of pillars and then over slightly before continuing north and east following the shore, Ruhi found herself at the pirate lords' council space soon enough.

The problem would be getting into the funeral service itself. People had already lined up in the area between the meeting hall and the docks, waiting to be allowed onto the long central pier. Guards checked each and every entrant.

Seeing them there, she froze. True, there was no way they'd

recognize her, but that meant she'd appear as a random resident who had no business attending a raja's funeral rites. And it wasn't like she could tell them she was here on Kosala's behalf—that was likely to get her into more trouble.

Padmini was still standing beside her and now took her elbow gently but firmly. "Come with me," the older woman declared and led the way with a resolute step, sliding between a pair of what looked like merchants and an older gentleman on his own. Ruhi didn't know what the tavern owner was up to but had no better idea, so she went along without complaint.

She did, however, remember her manners enough to turn back to the man they'd just cut off. "I'm so sorry, do you mind?" she asked

He smiled and responded with a surprisingly smooth bow. "Not at all, dear lady," he insisted, his voice rough with age but his eyes still bright. "Please."

"Thank you." Turning back around, she proceeded forward with Padmini. So, they were in line at least. But she now had a clearer view of the guards and saw that they were checking people's waists and wrists in particular. The first had to be for weapons—but the second would be for indenture bracelets, like the one glittering on her own arm. So servants weren't being allowed, at least not without their masters. *What was she to do about that?*

An idea came to her, and she leaned into her companion. "Go along with whatever I do," she whispered, and the older woman nodded.

Then, just as the pair in front of them reached the guards, Ruhi stumbled, giving a low cry as she pitched backward.

Padmini moved to help her—but the gentleman behind them was quicker, stepping forward at once and catching her by the arm to keep her from pitching onto the rough rock and sand. "Are you all right?" he asked with genuine concern.

"Oh, yes, thank you," Ruhi replied, leaning into him slightly but not so much as to be improper. "I just became dizzy all of a sudden. It must be the sun, it's so bright." Which it was, in fairness, the day having dawned clear and warm.

The merchants ahead of them were gone now, and the guards had turned their attention to Ruhi and her two companions. What they saw, however, was an older man, clearly wealthy—Ruhi took him to be a merchant or landowner rather than a pirate, both because of his fine manners and because his clothing, skin, and gait all spoke of someone more accustomed to land than sea—and an older woman, both hovering protectively over a younger woman.

The gentleman's bare arms were clearly visible, as were Padmini's. Ruhi's were curled around her middle, her shawl conveniently draped over the bracelet, but the guards had no reason to think she would be wearing such an item when her two companions clearly were not, and when she was of an age to be their daughter. Since the man was also obviously unarmed, the guards simply waved them past and proceeded to the next people in line.

"You must allow me to assist you," the gentleman was saying with a slight bow, proffering his arm. Then, out of courtesy, he extended the other to Padmini.

"You're too kind, sir," Ruhi told him, straightening and resting her hand gently on the crook of his arm.

He smiled back in return. "Not at all. A gallant gesture on my part, and in return I am gifted with the company of two lovely ladies."

She smiled—it was purest flattery, as she was no beauty and Padmini even less so—and the three of them stepped forward as a trio, onto the worn wooden beams of the dock.

Once past the guards' checkpoint, the crowd thinned, spreading out across the broad wooden platform even as they all made their way toward the far end. Padmini was now engaged in a conversation with the gentleman, who evidently owned a plantation on this island somewhere outside town, leaving Ruhi free to observe without having to participate.

Most of the people here were well dressed, and the majority looked much like their escort, not at all piratical. She wondered if that was because they'd all trotted out their best clothes for the occasion or if it meant Vihaan had more connections with townsfolk than with sailors. She did spy one familiar face—Chetan, the gruff, weatherbeaten pirate lord who'd argued with Kosala at the meeting. Then, over the heads of a small group, she spotted a second—Koliya, the big, burly raja with the loud voice. Each of them had brought a few pirates with them, and both groups were headed for the end of the dock where she could just make out an empty space.

As they moved closer, she saw that a small boat bobbed in the water just beyond the dock's edge. A figure was stretched out atop it, and soon enough she could see Vihaan's features. The dead raja looked calm and composed, not at all the way he had when she'd been near him last, with his face and body contorted in pain. Now he looked as if he were sleeping peacefully, though dressed in all his finery—the gloves he'd worn that last day were once more adorning his hands, the pearls across their backs showing hazy reflections of the sun beginning to rise above the horizon.

Ruhi, Padmini, and their new friend had only just settled into a spot a few rows back from the front but still with a clear view of the proceedings when there came a stir through the crowd. Gasps were heard in back, and then a path slowly parted, allowing a quintet to approach. In the lead was Captain Pillai, and at her side, flanked by guards and followed by another, was Kosala herself.

"What are you doing here?" Koliya demanded loudly, stepping forward to confront Ruhi's employer. Kosala was still wearing the same clothes as when she'd gone into custody, Ruhi noted, but her face and hair were clean. Nor was she shackled, though with the guards so close there was little chance of escape even had she tried.

She did not, of course. Instead Kosala straightened, meeting her fellow raja's glare with a steady gaze of her own. "I am here to pay my respects," she replied, pitching her voice loud enough to be heard by all. "Vihaan may have been a young fool, impetuous and careless, but he was a fellow raja, and he could be both kind and charming when he wished. He and I didn't always get along, but I didn't hate him, and even if I had, I would wish to say goodbye to one of my peers."

She gave a grateful nod to a short man standing not far away who Ruhi recognized as the town's governor. "I petitioned Nayak Laghari to be allowed to attend, and he graciously agreed." But she evidently couldn't resist adding, "After all, I am still a member of the Parishad."

"For now," Koliya sneered, his face inches from Kosala's own. "We'll strip you of your rank and possessions for this."

"If I'd wanted Vihaan dead, I'd have challenged him and run him through. This—" she waved her hand at the dead man in question "—is beneath us, and I'd never stoop to it."

"Not you personally, perhaps," someone called from the crowd—Ruhi didn't see who, but it was a man's voice. "But what of your two pet assassins? Are they in custody too? Or roaming free, ready to kill again?"

That caused a stir, and people looked about anxiously. Ruhi mimed such motions so as not to stand out, though she was bristling inside. *Pet assassin indeed!*

This time it was Pillai who responded. "They've evaded us so far, but we'll find them. And then we'll find out the truth about who did what to whom." Her glare, sweeping over the crowd, made it clear that whoever had done this would pay, and Ruhi barely dared breathe as that fierce gaze slid across her without pause. "For now, however, I suggest we proceed with our purpose, which is to see Raja Vihaan off with all due honor and respect."

That sharp reminder quieted the murmurs, at least for the moment, and a pujari emerged from the crowd, walking to the edge of the dock before turning back to face everyone. "Let us give thanks," he instructed, and all heads bent in prayer as he began the ritual service.

Ruhi peeked at the other attendees as best she could from that posture. Kosala appeared completely calm, her face betraying neither anger nor satisfaction at the death of her young rival, nor irritation at her current circumstances.

Chetan was scowling, but that looked to be his standard expression, and his glare wasn't aimed directly at Kosala but rather at poor, dead Vihaan, as if blaming the young man for his own demise.

Koliya *was* glaring at Kosala, daring her to say something, though at least he showed enough decorum not to further disrupt the funeral.

Ruhi spotted several of the other rajas as well. There was the older woman, Jasleen Lal, with three younger women grouped around her, their features so like hers that these were clearly her daughters. All of them looked fierce and capable, watching the crowd as they hovered protectively, but Jasleen's face showed only sorrow, the grief of someone old enough to have outlived many friends and loved ones.

Not far from that quartet was the sharp-featured woman, Falguni. Another one Ruhi recognized but didn't remember hearing speak was beside her. Then there was the other female raja, whose name she didn't know either. Was that everyone? She did a quick mental count. Yes, that was seven, and Vihaan and Udayin had made nine. They were all here. She also recognized several people who had attended the Council meeting the way she and Sundra had, as observers or perhaps petitioners.

The doctor was there as well, and his face was troubled. *Hadn't he started to say something about Udayin's death before being interrupted?*

And of course the governor, who looked anxious and kept checking on Kosala as if worried she might somehow escape Pillai's care and attack someone else.

There were no other outbursts, and the service was brief, the priest saying all the correct prayers with a clear voice and a confident manner. When he finished, Chetan and Koliya strode up beside him, each accepting a lit torch from men waiting to the sides. They set the torches to the boat, the fires transferring to the oil-soaked wood and quickly rising to a full blaze, the heat crackling across Ruhi's face and making her skin feel taut, though at least the smoke was blowing out to sea. Once the boat was entirely afire, men with long poles pushed it away from the dock, and it drifted out to sea, the young raja already engulfed in his own private inferno, the flames burning away his body so that his soul might rise and move on to its afterlife unhindered.

CHAPTER TWENTY-FIVE

SUNDRA

Sundra was ready to climb the walls by the time the door creaked and Ruhi slipped into the room followed by the tavern's wizened old proprietor. "Well?" he asked before they'd even had time to shut the door behind them. "What happened? Are you all right? Did anyone see you?"

"I'm fine, we're safe, and there's a lot to tell," she assured him, moving to her bed and gathering a few items from her bag. "But first let me change back to Rawal. I'll return shortly." She was gone again before he'd even registered that she was leaving, the older woman accompanying her with a smirk, and the door clicked shut, leaving him alone once more.

The wait was far shorter this time, and when the door opened, it was the now-familiar bearded visage of his brother Rawal that greeted him.

"Shall we?" Ruhi suggested, her voice pitched lower and rougher again. "I'm starving."

So was he, now that she mentioned it, and he followed her downstairs, where the older woman had already set out food at one of the tables tucked in back beneath the balcony. She'd also put out three plates and claimed a chair at the table herself, tearing into fresh roti and a simmering, spicy-smelling fish stew without ceremony. "I know who you are now. I wasn't sure until the funeral, but you're the two everyone is looking for."

Sundra eyed her warily, wondering how much they should admit to and how much danger they were in, but Ruhi nodded.

"Yes," she admitted readily, pouring tea for them all and then sipping at hers before filling her plate with rice and stew and bread. "And we didn't hurt anyone, but you knew that, or you'd have turned us in already, probably back at the docks. Neither did Kosala—she instructed us to prove that and find who did."

The old woman nodded. "Thought as much. You don't strike me as killers, and if you were, why go to all that trouble to see who's there and hear what they're saying?"

"Thank you." Ruhi smiled at her, then turned to Sundra. "Padmini's already been a tremendous help. Not just with my appearance before but with getting into the funeral unnoticed."

He turned to their hostess and performed a seated bow. "We're in your debt," he told her, and she smiled, reaching out to pat his cheek.

"You have fine manners, young man, but be careful saying things like that around here. Some people might take you up on it." She grinned at them both. "Besides, things have been a little too quiet here for my taste. Something like this is just what I need to get the blood pumping."

They ate in silence for a moment or two. Then Ruhi filled him in on what she'd seen and heard at the funeral.

"So, no one was shouting 'I did it!'" Sundra concluded when she was done. "That's unfortunate." He sighed, dipping a piece of roti in the stew. The fare was as excellent as it'd been yesterday, though clearly either Padmini had help in the kitchen or she'd made the stew the night before.

"At least we know where to go next," Ruhi replied. "The doctor."

He pondered that and what she'd said about seeing the man

there. "Yes," he agreed at last. "He knew something back at the Council meeting but didn't get to say. We should go find out what that is."

"Prasenajit Dara," Padmini supplied. "A good man, and a reliable vaidya. He's the one the Council calls upon whenever they have medical needs. I can tell you how to find him."

Sundra was considering and turned to Ruhi. "Might it be better for you to… change appearance once more? Pillai and her guards are looking for two young men, not a man and a woman."

She at least took the time to think before shaking her head. "I'd rather not. Right now the only people here who know my true nature are the two of you, but the more people see me out and about that way, the more they're likely to put the pieces together. Especially if they find you and me and recognize you." She smiled. "Better to keep that in reserve for when we truly need it."

Plus you're enjoying the freedom of being a young man and not having to deal with the expectations you've always faced, Sundra guessed but didn't say. If she was happier playing at being Rawal Chera for now, what harm could that do?

"I may be able to help with the guards," Padmini offered, a smile splitting her lined face. "Come with me."

Leaving the remains of their lunch behind but taking the small lantern that had graced the table, they rose and followed her to a door past the staircase. That led into what must be the working part of the tavern, including the kitchen, judging by the rich cooking smells filling the air. She turned to another door that led into a small windowless room packed with overflowing shelves on all sides.

"People leave things behind all the time," the proprietor explained, holding the lantern high. "Some come back for them, but most never do. Every so often I'll sell off some of it, enough to make space again." She gestured toward one side. "Clothing is mostly over there."

"What would changing our clothes do?" Ruhi asked. "We'd still be two young men."

But Sundra had grasped Padmini's intent. "They're not looking for two men," he explained, digging through the garments neatly folded and stacked. "They're looking for two young men who are indentured servants. Aha!"

He pulled out a sadri, but unlike the plain vests they already wore, this one was leather with stitched patterns and silver buttons. "Much better!" He tugged off his own vest and, after a second's thought, his shirt as well, replacing them with the new, finer sadri. The clothes seemed to be organized by type, and looking on a higher shelf, he found a handsome headcloth that shaded from darkest to lightest blue, which he swiftly wove into a small, dense pagri atop his curls. "How do I look?" he asked, striking a pose.

"Less like a servant and more like a pirate," Padmini agreed, moving past him to another shelf and searching around until she located something she then handed to him. "Try these." They were sturdy leather cuffs with crisscrossed straps and brass buckles, and the one on his left completely covered the metal bracelet there.

"Perfect."

Ruhi had joined them, though now she shook her head ruefully. "I don't think my going barechested would help any," she pointed out, and they all chuckled at that.

"You just need to wear something that says 'pirate' instead of 'servant.' Here." Sundra pulled out a kurta that had been dyed a bright scarlet, pairing it with a black leather vest and a headcloth of wavy red and orange, patterned to look like flames.

He turned his back while she switched shirts then helped her wind the cloth into a turban. Padmini had found another set of bracers, black leather ones that were long enough to cover her entire forearms, and Sundra had to admit that, thus garbed, Ruhi looked a good deal different, enough so that most would never think to compare her to the missing servants. There were also earrings, still copper or brass but braided hoops instead of studs, and a few chains that glittered well enough when they caught the light, plus a few heavy rings with cheap stones that still looked impressive to the untutored.

"Just one thing missing," Padmini told them and went to a cabinet in the corner. This she opened to reveal an array of weapons crammed within. "No proper pirate would walk about unarmed."

Sundra stepped over to examine the hoard and selected a simple talwar that, though it lacked the fine detail of his own stolen sword, was still clean and well-balanced. He slid it through his sash opposite Sanga's dagger and felt nearly whole again, having that comforting weight at his side once more.

Selecting one for Ruhi was more challenging, as she'd probably only hurt herself if she ever tried using it.

"Here," he said, finally handing her one. She took it, and gasped at the weight, nearly dropping the sheathed blade. "I know," he apologized. "But if you can't actually fight, the next best thing is to convince people they don't want to risk it." He tapped the sword with his forefinger. "A tegha like this is just the thing."

She unsheathed the weapon, studying the broad, double-edged blade and the way it curved and widened toward its tip. "I'd run if someone came at me waving one of these," she agreed.

"Exactly. You just brandish it, look fierce, and scream. I'll take care of the rest." He turned to Padmini, who was watching approvingly. "All right," he said. "Tell us how to find this doctor."

❧ ❧ ❧

Unsurprisingly, Prasenajit Dara lived and worked not far from the Parishad Hall—it made sense that the Council would've provided him with a home somewhere he could be reached easily. As a result, Sundra and Ruhi only needed to head north through a wide open gateway in an impressive stone wall—there weren't even gates, just a pair of thick stone pillars to either side—then among narrow streets to a bright red door. A wooden shingle hung from the porch awning stating "Prasenajit Dara, Vaidya."

Approaching the door, Sundra knocked twice, clear and sharp, the sound reverberating within. "Coming!" someone called from inside, and a moment later the door opened to reveal the average-looking man they'd seen at the Council meeting. "Yes?" he asked, frowning at them and pushing his glasses back up his nose.

Sundra spoke first. "Vaidya Dara, we have a medical question for you. We can pay."

Beside him, Ruhi patted her pouch, which jingled obligingly.

"Come in." The doctor stepped back to let them enter, revealing a small but tidy room with low chairs on both sides. "Sit and tell me what the trouble is," he instructed, gesturing to two seats and taking a nearby one for himself. Fortunately, there was no one else there at present.

"Well—" Sundra waited until the man was sitting down before continuing, "the truth is, it isn't about me. Or either of us. It's about the dead rajas."

Dara bolted to his feet—or tried to, except that Sundra had a hand on his shoulder and kept him from rising. The man's eyes widened as he stared at them both. "You're the two servants. The ones they say killed them!"

"We're the two servants, yes," Ruhi agreed, moving up beside Sundra. "But we didn't kill anyone. We're trying to find out who did."

"Why should I believe you?" the doctor demanded, glaring at Sundra. "You're holding me against my will!"

Sundra removed his hand and stepped back a pace. "Sorry. But we truly are just looking for answers." He grinned. "If we were the killers, we wouldn't exactly need them, would we?"

Dara considered that, taking off his glasses and polishing them on the corner of his shirt. "No, I suppose not," he admitted warily. "All right, what do you want to know?"

Now that it appeared the man would cooperate, Sundra sat in the chair he'd initially suggested, Ruhi following suit to his right. "What killed Udayin and Vihaan? At the Parishad meeting, you tried to say that it hadn't been the fall itself that did Udayin in or that at least there was more to it than that."

"Yes, there was." The doctor slid his glasses back on, forgetting his earlier concerns as he warmed to the subject. "Judging by the color of his face, the bulging of his eyes, and certain other features, I am convinced he was poisoned."

Sundra nodded, remembering the bullying raja's last moments. "He and I were shouting at each other. Then he suddenly started thrashing about. His face turned purple, and he was gasping for air. That's when he doubled over and toppled down the stairs."

"Exactly." Dara looked oddly pleased for someone discussing such a gruesome death. "Technically, what killed him was the fall—he broke his neck. But if he'd survived that, I'm certain he would've been dead moments later anyway." Now he was the one leaning in. "And Raja Vihaan? You were the last to see him alive as well?"

That made him grimace. "I was. Lucky me. But it was the same thing, only without the fall—he was shouting, though not at me this time, and then suddenly started contorting and clutching his chest and throat. Then he fell to the ground, gasped, and died."

"Yes, definitely poison," the doctor affirmed. "With nothing to obscure it this time. I was allowed to examine Vihaan's body, if briefly, and I can tell you that whatever did this was also highly caustic. Much of his hands and face looked nearly scalded." He frowned. "Also, there was a faint floral smell about."

"So you're thinking it was a poisonous plant of some sort," Ruhi put in. "But what kind of plant could do that?"

The doctor smiled at her, though that look of delight quickly faded. "There are several, in fact. The problem is, without more detail, I can't narrow it down. This would have been something extremely potent, in which case it only required brief contact. The safest, quickest way to administer a poison would be through their food or drink, especially since regular herbs and spices could mask any scent. But coating a needle and then scratching them could also introduce it into their systems in a hurry. Powders could be blown in their faces. There are endless possibilities." He shook his head. "I wish I had more to work with, so I could give you a clearer answer."

"It's a start," Sundra promised him. "If we find out more

details ourselves, we'll let you know. Then maybe you can tell us exactly what it was and how it was used on them."

Dara nodded, standing up as they did the same. "If your master truly didn't do this, I'm only too happy to help prove that. But be careful. Whoever did this is clever. And they've already killed two men—and rajas at that. Trying to catch them could put you in danger as well, and there's no way yet to know what to watch out for."

"We'll be careful," Ruhi assured the man as they moved toward the door. "Thank you for your help."

The doctor mustered another smile. "I'm just glad someone wants to know the truth. Perhaps you can figure things out before anyone else has to die."

CHAPTER TWENTY-SIX

RUHI

They walked away from the doctor's home and office, and Ruhi was impressed it took Sundra several minutes before he asked, "So, what now?"

"We need more information, right?" Beside her, her companion nodded. "The best people to get that from would be those who know Kosala. They're the most likely to know who might be out to get her."

"Out to get her?" Sundra protested. "But she's not the one who's dead."

"No," Ruhi agreed. "But she's the one being blamed for it. You're right, though—we need someone who knows all the rajas. We just don't know enough about rivalries, alliances, things like that, to be able to tell who might benefit from this the most."

Sundra frowned, tapping a finger to his lips as he thought, doubtless unaware of just how attractive that pensive expression made him. "So we should go to one of the other rajas? They'd know what's going on, surely."

"They would," she replied, for that had been her first thought as well. "But would they tell us? Those are the very people most likely to be involved, after all. Why would they want to help Kosala prove her innocence if they stand to gain from her conviction?"

"Surely they don't all hate her," Sundra protested as they rounded a corner, lowering his voice as the foot traffic thickened on this larger street. "She must have friends among them."

Ruhi thought back to what Sanga had told them. "I'm not so sure," she answered slowly. "She doesn't exactly have the most winning personality, does she? And even if she did have a friend there, that person is still a fellow raja, which means he—or she—would have their own agenda. They could easily send us in the wrong direction, either deliberately or just because it suits their own needs. One of them might have a grudge against another, for example, and assume that person is the most likely to have done all this."

"Ah. Yes. Right." Sundra scowled and scuffed his boot tip across the hard dirt of the road, sending up a small puff of dust. "Who can we ask, then?"

She smiled. "Who's the one person present at each meeting who's not a raja and specifically not beholden to any of them?"

"Oh, of course!" He clapped his hands together, a sunny smile spreading across his face and chasing the gloom away. "Surpakat's esteemed governor. He knows them all, but he's not one of them—he's supposed to be completely neutral." He grabbed her hands and spun them both around in a circle, causing a surprised squawk from a woman they nearly bowled over. "Yes!"

Ruhi laughed, caught up for a second in his exuberance. "There's just one problem," she admitted after a moment, when they'd stopped spinning and had pulled apart to catch their breath. "I don't know how we're to get in to see him."

But Sundra's restored good mood wasn't so easily shaken. "Leave that to me," he stated confidently. Before she could respond or ask, he was turning toward that same woman to apologize and, after flirting outrageously, to ask directions to the governor's offices.

The Governor's Hall proved to be farther south in a section of Surpakat they'd not seen before, and Ruhi was apprehensive as they found themselves in unfamiliar territory. The entire tenor of the town seemed different here than around Udayin's or the doctor's or even Kosala's, the streets broader and the homes and buildings farther apart and more elegant, with fewer evidences of wood or brick and more of stone.

There were just as many people about, but not as many wore the garb of seafaring folk, and more and more she felt nervous. Their own borrowed attire was more colorful than many of the others she saw walking and it drew the occasional glance.

"Relax," Sundra advised, walking beside her as if he had not a care in the world. "If you look like you did something wrong, people are more likely to wonder if you did." He smiled, nodding at a couple passing by, and they nodded back.

"I just don't think we belong here," she whispered once the pair had passed. "Or rather, I don't think the people we look like do."

"Of course they do. He's the governor of the whole town, isn't he? And we're residents of that town. I'll tell you what I think. The area we were in before, especially around the Parishad Hall, that's the original port. The streets weren't planned, nor the houses; they just grew up as more and more people came to live here. This part?" He waved a hand about them. "This came later when it went from being just a pirate hideout to a real town. They still had to follow the land, which is why the streets curve, but they planned them out a bit better and made them wider too. And the houses were all added to meet demand, particularly from merchants and craftsmen and the like—the people who deal with pirates, rather than pirates themselves."

It made sense—the upper portions of Surpakat did have a denser, rougher feel. She was also surprised Sundra would've reasoned all this out.

As if guessing her thoughts, he shrugged. "The benefits of

a classical education," he explained. "Lots and lots of history, including how and why towns and cities form and what works or doesn't work in various examples."

That hadn't been part of Ruhi's curriculum, of course, since Auntie Rudra had only taught her the traditional feminine skills, and what she'd learned from her father and Ganath and the other workers was entirely practical for their business.

They finally reached the Governor's Hall. It was impossible to miss since there was a cleared area all around it with nothing but decorative gardens whose carefully sculpted hedges lined broad circular walkways between lush grass. A profusion of vibrant flowers filled the air with a heady, sweet scent which might've been cloying if not for the leavening effect of the cool salt air from the sea.

The building itself was fairly large and more round or faceted than squared, with handsome red walls set off by white arches over the windows. It had squared white columns inset at each corner, and white edging around the façade. A dome perched over all, coated in perfect, eye-searing gold as it shone almost like a torch in the noon sun. One side of the building had columns running all the way up with a deep-set door behind them, the door's arch matching that of the windows in shape. A pair of guards stood to either side of the door, spears in hand.

"Just follow me and act like you know where you're going," Sundra warned and headed straight for the guards. The guards each took a step forward, spears starting to angle down to cross and bar the path, but Sundra waved them aside. "No time for that. We've got urgent news for the governor regarding the recent rajas' deaths!"

That got the men's attention. They paused, glancing at each other, and the older one shook his head and shifted his spear to his other hand—so that he could tug open his side of the door instead. "Go right on through, shri," he said, and Sundra nodded thanks as he sailed on past, Ruhi doing her best to keep up with him.

They didn't stop once they were inside, the smell of the flowers outside now faded and masked by an aroma of furniture polish and strong tea, and she had a fleeting impression of a high, vaulted ceiling inlaid with a bright blue mosaic as they rushed forward across an equally intricate gold and green floor. Up ahead, Ruhi saw a wall of handsomely carved wood, and two more guards beside the doors there.

"Urgent news for the governor!" Sundra announced again, and the men obligingly stood aside and let them through, no doubt reasoning that their counterparts outside would not have done so without good reason.

The room they entered had whitewashed outer walls above polished wood paneling, and a rich red carpet covered the floor. A fireplace occupied one side, though it was unlit at the moment, and a wooden desk was placed just to the side of a pair of tall, paneled wooden doors. A young man sat there, and he started to his feet as she and Sundra approached.

"We need to speak to the governor at once," Sundra demanded. "It's regarding the rajas' deaths. We have important information for him."

The man—slim and boyish with a clean, heart-shaped face and large, light eyes—started to protest, but Sundra had already angled past him and stepped to the doors.

"You can't disturb him!" the secretary protested, but Sundra was already pounding on the door with one hand even as he opened it with the other.

"Governor Laghari?" he called, stepping through the portal and gesturing for Ruhi to join him. "We need to speak with you."

"What?"

The room here was much like the secretary's only far larger and with a much richer rug. Tapestries hung on the walls between the windows, and a low couch sat to one side, flanked by a pair of matching chairs, each with pillows decorated in a pattern of marching elephants.

The governor rose from behind his desk, which was much larger and grander than his secretary's, and looked surprised both at their interruption and at the way Sundra firmly shut the door behind them. "Who are you?" Laghari demanded, crossing the room to confront them. "What do you want?"

"We want to talk," Ruhi replied, and for the first time the governor turned to her—and his eyes widened as he took in her features rather than her clothes.

"You!" he gasped, falling back against his desk. "Kosala's assassins! Are you here to kill me too?" He opened his mouth, no doubt to scream for help, but Ruhi acted first, stepping up to him and placing a hand on his arm and used her Gift to ease his fear.

She felt him relax as it took effect. "We aren't here to hurt you," she promised. "And we didn't kill anyone. Kosala has charged us with finding out who did."

"Then why come to me?" he protested, though at least he wasn't shouting. "I didn't do it."

"No, but you know everyone involved," Sundra pointed out, walking over to the couch and sinking down onto it. "We thought you might be able to tell us who has a grudge against Udayin, or Vihaan—or Kosala. Who would want to see the first two dead and the last one blamed for it?"

"Ah." The governor straightened, but he seemed calm enough now that he knew he wasn't in immediate danger.

Ruhi backed away as he joined Sundra, claiming one of the two chairs. She took the other end of the couch, and it seemed almost civilized, just three people chatting. Albeit about murder.

"Yes, I understand." He steepled his fingers, the pudgy digits resting lightly against his equally plump lips, his eyes narrowed as he visibly collected his thoughts.

At last he sighed. "To be plain, no one liked Udayin. He was an entitled young fool who never did a day's work in his life. He was also a bully and mean—my belief is that he was insecure about his own position, since his father designated him as heir from birth, and that was why he felt the need to throw his weight around constantly to try impressing upon people that he did have power and authority."

That also fit with what they'd seen of their first master, yet Ruhi found she couldn't muster any sympathy for the dead raja.

Truly he would not be missed.

"Now, Vihaan was a different matter," Governor Laghari continued, glancing up at them both. "Though he, like Udayin, had inherited his wealth and ships and his place in the Parishad, he was far more amiable, far more at ease with himself and others. There were arguments, of course. He and Kosala often didn't see eye to eye—nor did he and Chetan or even Jasleen—but it was more in the nature of them despairing at his youth and inexperience and the overconfidence that came with both." He shook his head. "In all honesty, I can't picture any of them truly wishing him dead. With time, he could have matured, gained wisdom and caution, and become a great man and a great raja."

Ruhi found herself moved by the description. She, too, had liked what she'd seen of Vihaan, and she knew that Sundra had as well. "What of Kosala? Would anyone among the remaining raja want to see her... removed?"

"Oh, yes." Laghari chuckled. "I am sorry to say your master is not well liked either. She tends to rub people the wrong way. She and Chetan are constantly at each other's throats, and she and Koliya frequently wind up shouting at each other. She and Udayin couldn't stand each other, and she despaired of Vihaan's wild schemes." He frowned. "I believe she and Jasleen have always gotten along though. I don't know of any issues between her and Ehsaan, or her and Falguni either. I don't think she holds Tarabai in high regard though, and I suspect the feeling is mutual."

"So Chetan seems the most likely," Sundra mused aloud. "I remember Shivaji asking if I worked for him, so it sounds like he didn't like Udayin much either."

Remembering the argument Kosala had with Koliya during the funeral, Ruhi privately added the big raja to their list of potential suspects as well.

"Well, I wish you the best of luck in your search," the governor told them, rising to his feet and prompting them to both do so as well. "If you're right, and Kosala is innocent, I hope you can prove it in time."

"Thank you," Sundra replied. "And thank you for seeing us." He flashed a quick, boyish grin. "Sorry for barging in the way we did."

"That's all right," he insisted, waving off the apology. "You were right to come here. I only wish I could offer more help. If you do find anything though, please let me know at once."

"We will," Ruhi promised, bowing as Sundra did the same.

"Chetan next then?" Sundra asked as they strolled away from the governor's office through the gardens and toward the street beyond.

"I think so," Ruhi agreed. "We'll have to ask where he lives, I suppose." A flash of light caught her eye, and she looked in that direction—and winced to see a familiar figure striding toward them, spear tip catching the sunlight, burnished mail coat making her almost shimmer in anger and single-minded focus. "First, however, we may need to find a way to get away from *her.*"

Sundra followed her glance and sighed at the sight of Captain Pillai hurrying toward the governor's office. "Yes, I suppose we'd better."

Chapter Twenty-seven

SUNDRA

Studying the guard captain's face as she drew near enough for them to make out her features, Sundra sighed. She looked determined, and moderately angry, which meant there was little chance of talking their way free of her. He wondered if one of the guards they'd bulled their way past had sent for the commander or if it was just bad luck that she was showing up now and spotted them. Regardless, the damage was done, and with talking off the table, that only left running.

The problem being, they were out here in the open, in the middle of these gardens. The hedges were nearly up to his head, and thicker than his middle, so hopping over them was out—even if they did, it wasn't like Pillai wouldn't be able to follow.

So what were they going to do?

He said as much to Ruhi, who scowled. "I hate to do this," she muttered, drawing the heavy sword he'd given her, and for a moment he thought she planned to fight their way free. While he applauded her spirit, he was sure the guard captain was a competent swordswoman and knew for a fact that Ruhi wasn't. Even two against one, he wasn't sure he liked those odds.

But once she had the hefty tegha unsheathed, she raised the broad blade—and began to hack at the shrubbery immediately to their left. The weapon made short work of the foliage, being far better equipped for such trimming than his own, slimmer talwar, and within moments, Ruhi had carved a deep divot into the top of that hedge.

"Let's go!" she announced and proceeded to jump over the mauled greenery with surprising grace. Sundra followed, a bit more clumsily, but he still managed to mostly clear the hedge and only stumbled a step on the landing.

The area they were in was mostly grass, with stands of flowers rising up in circles and spirals in the center. They skirted that section, darting across the neatly trimmed lawn instead and soon reached its far side where another hedge blocked their path. Ruhi attacked this one as well, carving a crude exit, and then they were back on the gravel path, but a good distance from where they'd been.

Pillai stood staring—now from the far side of this expanse of garden. Not surprisingly, such a bastion of law and order wasn't willing to deface one of the town's public arrangements, and even if she used the path they'd created, she'd still be too far behind them to catch up.

"Well done!" Sundra congratulated as he and Ruhi hurried away, with her sheathing her blade once more. She flushed with pleasure and grinned at him, though she did glance back guiltily at the damaged hedges.

"They'll grow back," he assured her. "Which we wouldn't, if we were locked away." It hadn't even occurred to him to cut into the plants, after being trained by his mother to respect her own gardens, but he was glad his companion had had no such scruples.

"Right, let's find out where Chetan lives and go see him," she replied, brushing off the compliment in a way that suggested she wasn't used to receiving them. Which was a shame.

They walked for several blocks with no particular destination.

He was still considering what different lives they'd led before they'd met when they rounded a corner—and nearly ran full into a large man in an open black leather vest and a deep red turban.

A man they unfortunately knew all too well.

"You!" Shivaji growled, grabbing Sundra by the arm and giving him a shake that rattled his teeth. A slow, nasty smile spread across the pirate's face. "I've been hoping to find you two again."

"Leave him alone!" Ruhi shouted, trying to yank Sundra's arm free, but Shivaji backhanded her hard enough to send her careening off the nearest building and sprawling to the ground, narrowly missing a collection of urns and jugs someone had set out to catch rainwater.

"I'll deal with you after," the pirate warned, his eyes never leaving Sundra's face. "But first, this one and I have a score to settle."

"Fine by me," Sundra replied. He kicked Shivaji between the legs as hard as he could, and although his foot skewed to the side and struck the thigh instead, the big man still doubled over, gasping in pain and releasing Sundra's arm as his own hands both went protectively to his injured leg. When he straightened again his face was nearly crimson with both pain and rage—but Sundra had stepped back, putting enough distance between them that the pirate couldn't simply grapple him again.

"You want to settle this?" he offered now, his hand going to the talwar at his side. "Let's." He drew the blade, which made a faint hiss as it slid from its scabbard and glinted in the light as he held it before him, low and at the ready. "Draw your sword and face me like a real man. If you dare."

He wouldn't have thought it possible for Shivaji's face to turn even darker, but it did. "You sniveling little worm!" the pirate bellowed, yanking his own sword free—a tegha like Ruhi's. But the big man held it easily, and his stance indicated long familiarity with the weapon. "I'll split you in two!" And, eyes wide and mouth open in a soundless shout, he charged.

Sundra stepped out of the way of that mad rush. His sword flicked out as he dodged, the tip slicing his opponent's cheek and leaving a thin red line oozing there. That made Shivaji scream with pain and rage, and he rounded again, but was still too worked up to do anything but charge a second time with the same result.

"Is that the best you can do?" Sundra asked with a deliberate sneer. He shook his head. "All those times you hit me, if I'd only known you were so pathetic with a blade I'd have challenged you then and been done with it."

"You're dead, little lordling," Shivaji replied, gathering his wits enough to at last stand his ground, his heavy sword out before him. "You just don't know it yet."

"I very much doubt that." Finally, a chance for him to show what he could do with a sword. Sundra raised his talwar, preparing to cut and thrust, aware that his foe's larger blade could snap his if they met head-on but also aware that his weapon was far faster, already calculating attacks and defenses and working out the best strategy—

—when a heavy water urn crashed into the back of the pirate's head, shattering with an explosive noise and raining pottery shards down on them both. Shivaji straightened, his eyes wide and confused, his mouth going slack with surprise. Then his sword fell from his fingers, hitting the ground with a dull clatter, and he followed it, toppling like a tree that had just been chopped down.

Ruhi, standing behind him, looked down at the unconscious pirate, then at her own hands, which were now dusty with bits of pottery. She withdrew a fals and set it in the damp ring where that pot had been resting before she'd snatched it up. "Let's go." There was a darkening bruise blooming on her cheek where Shivaji had struck her.

"Why did you do that?" Sundra demanded, his sword still in hand as he looked from her to the man at her feet. "I had him!" And, belatedly, "Are you all right?"

"Did you?" she asked, focusing on the first portion of his response, and he hated the question in her voice. "And what about them?"

She jerked her hand behind her, and Sundra looked past her—

to where several men were approaching with shouts and drawn swords. Men who all looked vaguely familiar. It was the rest of Shivaji's group of thugs, evidently just now catching up with their leader. There were at least six of them, which was far more than Sundra could handle on his own.

"Ah. No. Perhaps not," he admitted, sheathing his sword. "So—time to run then?"

"Yes!" Her words were almost drowned out by the screams now and the sound of pounding feet as the men picked up their pace. Sundra didn't wait for them to arrive. Instead he turned on his heel and took off the way they'd come, back around the corner. From there, he picked a direction at random, cutting between a pair of houses and then another set to emerge on a different, narrower road. Ruhi was right beside him, neither of them speaking as they conserved their energy for fleeing the men now racing after them.

The streets changed appearance slightly, indicating that they were back in the upper, older portion of the town. Fortunately, that also meant the houses were packed in more tightly, providing narrow alleys to duck into instead of the wider lanes below. Sundra ducked down a side street and then came to an abrupt stop before drawing his sword, scabbard and all, and holding it down at his side as he sidled between two buildings, motioning for Ruhi to follow him. She did, and they both froze once they were far enough back for the shadows to conceal them.

A moment later, Shivaji's men went charging past, shouting and waving their swords and daggers.

Once the sound of their pursuers had faded, Sundra managed to twist his head to look down the narrow crawlspace he'd crammed them into. There was light there, so he slid and scraped toward it, finally emerging into a patch of dirt and grass between the backs of two rows of homes. From there they were able to reach the street at the far end, though they paused before emerging long enough to check and make sure the band of thugs wasn't lying in wait just beyond. The road was empty, however, and they stepped out, restoring their swords to their sashes and adjusting their clothing before walking away as if nothing untoward had happened.

"Nothing like a little light exercise to work up an appetite," Sundra declared as they headed north once more, keeping his eyes open in case of another attack but effecting nonchalance. "So, look for Chetan's home now or head back to the Quiet Fire for lunch first? I'm famished!"

Chapter Twenty-eight

RUHI

A helpful woman directed them to Chetan's home with the simple, clear instruction, "Upper right corner."

"That's it?" Sundra asked after they were out of earshot. "Upper right corner? Of what? I don't think this town is exactly a square, do you? Shouldn't we go back to the inn first? I'm sure Padmini can give us better directions than that—over some food."

Ruhi rolled her eyes at him. "Let's check the northeast corner and see if that's what she meant. Then we'll go back." She elbowed him in the side. "Unless a big, strong guy like you is too tired to make the walk there?"

"No, of course not!" he insisted, puffing out his chest. "I can handle it, obviously. I was just thinking of you!"

She was chuckling to herself as they continued up toward the town's northern edge.

The farther they went, now that they were back in the older district, the rougher things became. And not just the buildings and the paving stones in the road either.

"I'm amazed the guard doesn't break this up," she commented

as they edged around a pair of pirates brawling in the street. The two men were punching and kicking each other, growling curses as they each struggled to grab the other and throw him to the ground.

"Doesn't look like they care much," Sundra replied, gesturing with his chin.

Ruhi looked where he'd indicated and was surprised to see a guard leaning against a building across the street, watching the fight occur. He did straighten, however, when one of the men succeeded in laying out his opponent with a solid punch to the jaw—and then drew a dagger as his rival sprawled there in the dirt.

"That's enough of that," the guard declared, striding over and placing himself between the two men. "You know the rules. You started with fists, you end that way. You want to duel, you do it proper."

The pirate glared at him, but the guard didn't move. Finally he spat, "Fine!" and shoved the dagger back into its sheath. "But next time," he told the man still groggily struggling to sit up, "it's blades from the start, and I'll run you through!"

"Strange place, this," Sundra commented as they continued on through the crowd of onlookers who were now dispersing since the entertainment was over. "Good to know you can beat someone bloody without getting in trouble, or stab them, but you can't try for both at once."

"She did say duels were allowed," Ruhi reminded him, careful not to say Kosala's name. "But I guess they consider switching from punches to blades to be dishonorable."

"It would be," he agreed.

She wondered if the pirates' code was all that different from the sirdars', with their emphasis on "we'll treat our own with respect but everyone else is fair game."

They continued, crossing a road she thought would have lead back to the tavern—with Sundra casting a longing glance in that direction but not arguing as she kept their pace brisk and their course forward—and then past the Parishad Hall as well. The streets were even narrower here, the houses smaller and cruder, and ahead, past them, she could see a scattered row of trees with what looked like a tall stone wall behind them. "I'd say we've hit the top of the town," she said as they slowed beside that last row of houses. "Which means, if we go this way, we should find the upper right corner."

"It's well-planned, actually," he stated as they followed the street to the right, keeping that wall on their left side. "Looks to me like there's no natural barrier to the north, so they added one of their own. I'm betting where there're cliffs or such they didn't bother, since in those spots they wouldn't need a wall for protection. And of course the waterline is entirely docks, with plenty of eyes on the ocean at all times. Probably sentries at the outermost edges, to provide warning if any ships try sneaking in unnoticed."

That did make sense, but again she was impressed he'd thought it through so well. *Evidently lords did learn something more than dancing and drinking and dueling.*

The road ended, the ground becoming rockier and more uneven, but ahead, Ruhi could see a small cluster of buildings. The outer wall slanted down behind them, and she could make out a matching barrier on the farthest building's other side. "I think we've found our corner," she pointed out, picking her way over the rocks and gravel and sand.

"Yes, and they don't like visitors much," Sundra agreed. "Still, tough to sneak up on someone out here." Which was true—they were sending up showers of pebbles and dirt with each step, and the crunching was nearly constant. The people in those houses would hear them the entire way along.

Sure enough, as they approached, she saw four pirates emerge from the second building and head toward them.

"What do you want?" one of them called out. All four were bigger than her or Sundra and built burly, and all four had hands on the swords at their belts. Their leather vests were all undyed, she noticed, as were their turbans, which gave them all a subdued but weathered appearance much in keeping with how she remembered their captain.

"We want to talk with Raja Chetan." she called back, coming to a halt perhaps a body length from the men.

The one who'd spoken glanced behind him at the last building in the row, which was by far the biggest and grandest, with two stories, an upper balcony, and a limestone façade. Though it was a handsome building—with a stair-stepped ridge over each of its two rounded corners and a parapet between them—there was a certain rough-hewn quality about it, a boldness and strength that would not have been present with finer carving or more delicate windows.

"He's not seeing visitors today," the pirate replied, which made his friends laugh and him along with them. "Come back tomorrow; maybe he'll be in a better mood then."

"It's important," Ruhi insisted. "It's about the other rajas' deaths."

That killed the laughter, but the man scowled at her instead. "He's definitely not at home for talk about that. Now go back where you came from before we decide to teach you a lesson about going where you aren't wanted."

She might've stayed and tried to argue further, but Sundra tugged at her sleeve. "We should go," he suggested, his voice low and taut, which surprised her. There were only four of them—hadn't he been ready to take on that many before? But then she saw where he was looking, as motion caught her eye too. It was the same house these four had come from, and four more pirates were stepping outside and heading over to join them. Yes, eight was considerably more than they could handle if things got ugly.

"Fine, we'll go," she said. "But we'll be back."

That got scoffs and jeers as she turned and let Sundra lead her back across the rough terrain to the start of the street once more.

"We'll ask Padmini," Sundra suggested. "Maybe she'll have an idea on what to do next."

Maybe, Ruhi agreed. But she wondered just how much more time they had.

● ● ●

"Ha, good luck with that one," the innkeeper told them as they ate, after telling her about their abortive encounter. "Chetan keeps to himself out there. Doesn't like visitors."

"So we noticed," Sundra agreed, helping himself to another piece of roti he used to scoop up more rice, lentils, and stewed meat and vegetables before shoving the whole mass into his mouth. Funny how his manners disappeared when he was hungry! "But we need to talk with him. He's our best suspect."

The older woman snorted at that. "He'd never poison someone. He'd take them on openly, no question."

That did match what Ruhi had seen of him so far, making him much like Kosala herself in that way. Plain-spoken to a fault.

"Even so, we do have to speak with him. What about the other rajas?" she asked their host. "What can you tell us about them?"

"Not as much as you'd think," she owned, sitting and pouring herself some tea. "It's just that I was indentured to both at one point."

The dining room was quiet enough, with only a few other patrons, that she didn't need to jump up and serve anyone at the moment. "The lords and their sailors don't exactly frequent my establishment—they prefer to stay above the Line, which is fine by me."

"The Line?" Ruhi repeated.

"Oh, yes, the Pirate Line, it's called," the older woman explained. "You passed through it on your way to reach Vaidya Dara—the wall with the wide, arched opening?"

Sundra snapped his fingers. "It's the same wall we saw behind Chetan's house, isn't it?" he asked. "And it's back behind Kosala's as well, only the crops hide it there, but I bet it runs all the way around the original town."

"That's right." Padmini beamed at him like she was a tutor and he her star pupil. "Where it cuts across the city there, we call it 'the Pirate Line' because it's the divider between the two halves, old and new. Up above the line, that's mostly pirates still, and they like it there, with the narrower streets and tighter quarters, and all the older docks that're narrower and closer together for more access to the water."

She smiled. "Most of my customers are merchants, craftsmen, the occasional plantation owner—people coming to town for business who don't want to stay on the docks or risk going above the Line but can't afford one of the larger, fancier inns farther down. I'm close enough to everything to be convenient, cleaner and quieter than any pirate tavern, but cheaper than those high-end places, while still being just below the Line, so I'm respectable."

"You've managed it for years," Ruhi reminded her, "plus you pay attention. So I'm guessing you know something. More than we do, at any rate."

"Ha, well, that's not hard, is it?" the older woman retorted, but she seemed amused rather than annoyed, and after a second and a sip of tea, she spoke again. "Let's see, you have Kosala and Chetan and Vihaan and Udayin, them you know. There's Jasleen Lal, she's a fierce one even now, though these days her daughters run the fleet on her behalf. Koliya's a big blowhard, but he also has more ships than anybody else, so he can afford to be mouthy. Tarabai Banerjee's an odd one. She's only got a few ships, but her husband's the governor of their stronghold, Riyassat, which gives her a pretty decent power base. Ehsaan is quiet, I couldn't tell you anything else about him. And Falguni, she has a stronghold up north somewhere, almost never comes to town."

Ruhi thought back to the Parishad meeting which seemed so long ago. "What about a man named Khatri? Something about plantations?"

"Oh, aye, he's the master of Bahut Saare. Big plantation the next island over. He's always on about representation and rights, I've heard some of my guests going on about it."

Sundra frowned, puzzled, and the older woman noticed.

"Plantations don't have a seat on the Council," she pointed out. "So they don't get a say in how things are run. Yet some of them are rich as any raja—and some have exclusive arrangements with a particular stronghold or even a particular pirate lord."

Thinking back, Ruhi nodded. "None of the rajas were all that interested in hearing him out. They laughed in his face, in fact."

"Well, yes, the rajas don't want to share power with anyone, much less a bunch of glorified farmers. To them, ships and strength of arms are all that matter, with money a distant second, mainly just a way to keep score. These plantation owners though, they clearly think things should be a bit more equal." Sundra laughed. "Good luck with that—those in power are never interested in sharing it."

Ruhi nibbled at some dried mango, just to occupy herself somehow. She sighed. "We're no closer to figuring anything out, and we don't have anything to go on, anywhere to look." Because Padmini was right, Chetan simply didn't make sense.

"There's someone you could speak with," the proprietor said. "Someone who'd know better than anyone who might have it in for those two rajas—or for your own employer."

"Who?" Sundra asked, but Ruhi had already realized what she meant.

"Yes, you're right, she would be the one to ask," she agreed, shredding the piece of mango she held, though her eyes stayed locked on Padmini. "There's just one problem with the idea—how exactly are we supposed to get in to see a woman being held for two murders without winding up behind bars ourselves?"

Their host grinned, a dangerous expression on her lined face as she eyed Sundra in particular. "Oh, I'm sure we can think of something."

CHAPTER TWENTY-NINE

SUNDRA

Sundra sighed. "This is ridiculous," he complained. "I feel like an idiot—and probably look like one too."

"You look fine," Ruhi assured him. "Now hush, they're coming." He could tell, even without seeing her, that she was grinning. "Play dead."

"Not dead, knocked out," he muttered, but did as he was told nonetheless, keeping his eyes shut and laying completely still there on the floor. He heard footsteps nearby but growing softer, which had to be her retreating so as not to be caught up in all this. Not that he could blame her—he wished he could get up and run away too.

There was the sound of a door opening. That would be the tavern's front door, no doubt, with Padmini there to greet the new arrivals she'd summoned. A part of him couldn't help wondering if this was all just some way for the old woman to mess with him, but he hadn't offended her as far as he knew. And this was the only plan they had for getting what they wanted.

Assuming it worked.

"He's over here," he heard the proprietor explain and then

more footsteps, growing closer. Several sets of them, both her thumps and sharper, crisper sounds that had to be hard-soled boots. They stopped right beside him, and then what must be a toe nudged him in the side. He groaned obligingly and shifted like he was just coming to.

"You say he stole from you?" a man asked. Deep voice, serious tone. No nonsense.

"What'd you hit him with?" another asked. Higher pitch, mildly amused.

"This." Sundra knew she was brandishing a heavy iron skillet. "And yes. Money's missing, and he's the only one who could've taken it."

"So you only *think* he stole from you," the first voice corrected. "What do you want us to do about it? Without any proof and no one who witnessed it, we can't bring him before the judge. There wouldn't be any point."

"I need you to cart him on out of here before he scares off the rest of my customers," Padmini answered in an aggrieved "do I have to explain everything" tone. "I'm going to be looking, either here in the inn or with them gamblers he bets with, and then I'll have proof."

The pause after this felt monstrous to Sundra, still stretched out on the tiles of the dining hall. But it was probably only a few seconds before the guard said, "All right, fine, but if you haven't found anything by tomorrow, we'll have to let him go."

Then a hand was grasping him under his right arm and another under his left, and Sundra was hauled to his feet.

"Wha—?" he made a show of waking and groggily peering about him. "What happened? My head hurts."

The two guards holding him up didn't look terribly sympathetic, and neither did the third one facing him. "Come along without any trouble or we'll truss you up and drag you," he warned, his tone matter-of-fact enough to show he took no pleasure from the idea—but that he would absolutely follow through with the threat if necessary.

Sundra nodded meekly, not having to pretend anxiety as he let the three guards lead him away. Off to the side, he saw Ruhi peeking out from behind a door but otherwise staying out of sight. That was good. They'd agreed that having two young men get in trouble would just encourage people to connect them to Kosala. One pirate on his own though, that was probably something the guards dealt with every day.

The trick, of course, had been coming up with something significant enough for them to arrest him and cart him off to jail but not so severe that they'd kill him or sentence him. There were, after all, only a few offenses the guards would even interfere on, and the most potent of those—murder and sabotage—weren't ones they wanted to risk. That had left theft.

"Will they really care?" he'd asked when Padmini had laid it all out for them the evening before. "I mean, no offense but isn't the code 'no stealing from our own'? And you're not exactly a pirate."

"No, but I live here too," she'd explained with surprising patience. "Above or below the Line, I'm entitled to the same protections. If it wasn't for that, the pirates would just steal from everyone all the time, and there wouldn't be restaurants and taverns and inns or tailors and blacksmiths and brewers either!"

"And you're sure I'll actually be able to talk to Kosala in there?"

Padmini had smirked at him. "Believe it or not, I've been in there a time or two myself. If they don't think you're a threat, they just dump you in the general holding room. And she's a raja, so they'd let her stay there too—more space, more light. So you shouldn't have any trouble."

"Just make sure not to leave me in there too long," he'd warned more than once, including right before she'd paid a boy to run to the guard and tell them she'd caught a thief. "I don't want them to get any ideas about meting out some justice of their own."

"We won't," Ruhi had promised each and every time. "Just an hour, no more. Long enough to talk to her."

So he'd found himself agreeing to this insane idea, and now he was being led out of the Quiet Fire and onto the street, where people paused to watch as he was hauled along by the guards. They weren't mean in their treatment, but they weren't gentle either, and when he stumbled once, they yanked him to his feet hard enough that it rattled him right through.

It was with mingled relief and dread that they eventually slowed before a massive building, easily the largest he'd seen here in Surpakat. Two wide towers rose on either side of a wide, flat front, broken by a tall arch over a shorter one filled with a set of iron doors—the towers had to be at least sixty feet tall, he estimated, and even the doors were a good twenty feet high or more. Narrow slits provided light to upper floors, with arched windows lower down covered in metal grates.

The building was constructed of large, rough-cut sandstone blocks. The space before the entrance was paved with the same, and as they marched through the doors—which were opened on their approach by a pair of guards stationed inside—he saw that the same flooring continued into and through the building. It was a veritable fortress, and his heart sank a bit as those iron portals clanged shut behind him, sealing him within.

"Let's go," the one in charge ordered, still staying in front as he guided them through the inner doors, across an open courtyard, and into a squat inner building beyond. There was a brief respite as they stopped before a wrought iron door to explain their presence to the guard behind it.

Sundra was asked his name, and he replied with "Nalan Dhar," stealing pieces from two of the men he'd met at Udayin's. They unlocked the heavy door in that wall and pushed him through it into the basement below.

He sighed with relief when the door at the base of the stairs was unlocked and shoved open to reveal a single, vast chamber, just as Padmini had said. The walls were the same stone as the rest, but the floor was uneven and unbroken, making it clear the room's base had simply been chiseled out and then walls raised around it. Barred slits just below the vaulted ceiling provided adequate light to see a few heavy, crudely made benches bolted in place along the sides, one of which was covered by a sprawled figure—and one of which was occupied by a lone woman sitting upright and watching them closely.

He did his best not to show any sign of recognition as the guard shoved him forward through the door and then bolted it behind him.

"Grub at dawn, noon, and dusk," the man explained through the small grate at head level. "Water over there." Glancing where he pointed, Sundra saw a small basin carved into the floor in one corner. "Waste there." That was a similar but deeper crevice in the opposite corner. "Don't get 'em mixed up." With that, and a laugh at his own joke, the guard turned away, lumbering back up the stairs.

Then, finally, he was able to turn and approach the woman.

"I didn't expect to see you in here," Kosala stated when he reached her. She eyed him up and down. "What happened? Pillai finally catch up with you?" She pitched her voice low enough that the room's other occupant wouldn't hear her.

"No, nothing like that." He took a seat on the other end of the bench. "This was the only way to get in to see you. We're not having much luck. I'm sorry. We're trying though." He explained what they'd done so far, and what little they'd found or been told.

His employer listened carefully, not interrupting. She didn't look any the worse for wear, other than being slightly dusty and perhaps tired—the air here did seem a bit musty and thick, and Sundra's nose tickled as he spoke.

"Those all sound like reasonable approaches, though I don't believe Chetan would do something like this. He'd have gone for their throats outright if he'd wanted them gone—or mine." A faint smile touched her lips. "He and I are much alike in that way."

"That was the impression we had too," Sundra acknowledged. "Which is why we thought we needed to speak with you. We're not sure where else to look."

She gave that some thought, tapping a finger to her lip as she did. "I'd—" she started but stopped as the door above clicked and creaked open. "Odd," she noted. "Two new arrivals in one day? It's much too early for the noon meal, and you missed the morning's, I'm afraid. Not that it holds a candle to Madhav and Laila's work."

They both waited, listening to the sound of footsteps coming down the stairs. Heavy ones, and more than one or even two of them. Realizing that it might not be best to be seen consorting with the suspected murderer, Sundra rose and strolled quickly over to the far wall, leaning against it as casually as he could. The rough stone pressed into his shoulder and hip, but he ignored that, watching as the door to the stairs was unlocked and swung open, yielding a quartet of guards.

Oddly, they had no prisoner between them, nor did they carry any food. "Here to let me out?" Sundra called, but all four ignored him, entering the room and making straight for Kosala where she sat. "Hey!" he tried again, taking a step, and one of the guards turned and gave him a glare.

"Quiet, you," the man warned, "or you're next."

Next? That didn't sound good. Nor did the fact that, Sundra suddenly realized, these guards were both unfamiliar to him and all armed. The one who'd brought him downstairs, he now recalled, hadn't had a weapon on him, presumably so that, if any prisoners did get the drop on him, they still wouldn't have anything they could use in a fight. Why, then, had these four entered with heavy clubs? And why clubs at all, when most of the guards he'd seen carried swords? Things were definitely not right here.

Kosala clearly felt the same way. Not that it cowed her any. "Here to shut me up?" she demanded, rising to her feet to face the men more squarely. "Better make sure you do the job right, then."

"Oh, we will," one of the men retorted, raising his club. "We won't leave a bit of you unbroken."

"A reasonable plan," she agreed, even as Sundra crept away from the wall and sidled closer, moving carefully so his boots would not make any noise on the rough floor. "There's just one problem. How will you kill me if you can't even see me?"

Her right hand snapped forward, and something small, sleek,

and silvery shot from it—and the man she'd been trading jibes with screamed, dropping his club to clutch at his face as blood spurted from his left eye.

Sundra charged, crouching at the last second and then straightening like an arrow shot from a bow to slam his shoulder full into one man's legs and rear. The guard went flying forward, crashing into one of his fellows and sending them both toppling to the ground, which they hit with heavy thuds. That left one upright and unharmed, and he hesitated, clearly surprised by this unexpected show of resistance and unsure which of his two foes he should confront.

Sundra solved that problem by stooping and scooping up one of the fallen clubs. It was nothing more than a stout stick, perhaps an inch in diameter and three or four feet long, that tapered from a wider head down to a narrower handle before flaring out again slightly at its base. Still, it had a good, solid weight when he swung it, and though it wasn't a sword, it would do in a pinch.

Seeing him armed, the man turned to face him fully, raising his own weapon in a way that indicated he was more used to a sword himself. "Right, you first then," he blustered, advancing quickly and swinging with all his might at Sundra's head.

The blow was clumsy and easily avoided, and Sundra ducked beneath it, jabbing instead so that the blunt but solid head of his own weapon struck the man full in the throat. That sent the guard stumbling back, choking, and grasping at his neck, his face purpling, and Sundra suddenly recalled the two dead rajas with a sick jolt.

Then a club came down on the man's head and he slumped to the floor, unconscious.

"Nicely done," Kosala complimented, the appropriated club still at her side after that swing. She studied the other men, banging the two who'd tripped each in the head to quiet them before kneeling next to the wounded one. Sundra didn't see exactly what she did there, but the man twitched. She wiped something on his coat sleeve, something small and metallic, then stood, making it vanish once more. "It seems I owe you my life."

Sundra just stared. How could she be so calm? These men had just tried to kill her! And not in a duel either. This had been outright murder! "How did they even get in here?" he wondered aloud, his thoughts racing as fast as his pulse, which was hammering in his ears. "Or are they real guards?"

She gave a thin smile at that. "No, I think not. The uniforms are right but they didn't wear them well. Borrowed, stolen, or bought, I'd think."

"So all I had to do to get in here was steal a uniform?" Sundra shook his head. "That would've been so much easier."

"No," she corrected with a frown. "Even in that, you'd never have gotten past the front gate. And certainly not into this building. Definitely not through that door and down those stairs. No, these men were allowed in."

"Which means the guards are in on it?" He was horrified at the thought and only slightly mollified when she shook her head.

"Not necessarily. Someone is though. Someone high up enough to order a guard or three to look the other way." She glanced at him. "How were you planning to escape?"

The sudden change in topic made him laugh, though he knew that was more from nerves than any actual humor. "I wasn't. Not exactly. I—" Again they were interrupted by the noise of the upstairs door opening. *Reinforcements, come to finish the job?*

"Quick, drop that and move away," Kosala warned. "They can't know you were involved." She smiled at him for real this time. "Go back to the beginning. Look for connections. They must be there—otherwise no one would be trying to keep me from living long enough for you to find them."

He smiled back and bowed. "We're on it."

Then the door to the stairs opened. "Right," the guard who'd brought him down before said even as he entered. "Looks like you can go, it was all—what in the deep blue sea?" He stopped and stared at the four bodies clumped on the floor, and Kosala standing over them, club in hand. "What happened here?" the guard demanded, backing up until he was on the far side of the door once more.

"These men snuck in somehow and attacked me," the raja replied. "I dealt with them. You might want to get someone down here to clean this up." She tossed the club onto the nearest body with a meaty thunk before resuming her previous seat.

"Yes," the guard agreed slowly. "Come on, you," he told Sundra, beckoning him over. "Charges were dropped—found the money, sounds like." He half-shrugged, still watching Kosala warily. "Let's get you out of here."

Sundra was only too happy to follow him up and out.

CHAPTER THIRTY

RUHI

R uhi looked at him yet again, once more restraining herself from putting a hand on his arm or shoulder.

"I'm fine," Sundra insisted, ducking his head to avoid her gaze. He glanced up though, and his smile helped put her heart at ease, at least a little. "I promise you, I am fine."

"But you almost weren't," she protested, knowing that she was repeating herself but unable to help it. "You could've been killed! Both of you!"

"Bah, he's fine," Padmini stated, setting a tray down on the table. It held a teapot—its brightly enameled spout releasing a steady spurt of steam—three mugs, and a plate of dates, nuts, and dried fruits, perfect for a refreshing snack in mid-morning—or something to wash away the taste and feel of being thrown in jail and attacked by thugs.

"See?" Sundra said, sitting up and accepting a mug of tea with a nod of thanks. "I told you. Everything's all right." He sipped at the tea before amending, "Well, there's someone who's trying to kill Kosala even though she's already in prison and likely to get convicted of two murders she didn't commit, and we still don't have anything that can help her prove her innocence. But otherwise…"

"Right." With a sigh, Ruhi tried to focus her thoughts on that new wrinkle. "It doesn't make any sense. Why wouldn't whoever it is just let the Council condemn her and be done with it? Unless they really do worry that we'll find out who's behind all this and prove it somehow."

Padmini sat and pushed the second mug into Ruhi's hands before claiming the final cup for herself. "Aye, and whoever it is has a lot of pull," she pointed out, snatching a date with her forefinger and thumb and popping the delicacy into her mouth. "To get men in past the guards like that."

"Well, good luck getting them back out again or explaining what happened in the first place," Sundra said, looking pleased with himself.

Admittedly, if what he'd said was true, he and Kosala had fended off four armed men with nothing more than their wits, their own bodies, and some kind of tiny knife or needle. Still, the sudden, significant increase in danger had Ruhi worried, even if he wasn't.

"Let's return to what she said," she suggested. "She told you—told us—to go back to the beginning and look for connections."

Across from her, Sundra nodded, his mouth full of nuts and fruits, making him look like a young boy gobbling up forbidden sweets before someone could tell him to stop.

"Back to Udayin's, then?"

"We could," he agreed, fortunately after swallowing, else he'd have sprayed food everywhere with each word. "But I don't know. We were there already, and if Shivaji catches us there, he'll have even more men with him this time." He shook his head. "I think we should try Vihaan's instead."

She considered that. "The guards're probably done there by now. So you're right, this might be a good time to look around there, see if we can find out anything. All right." She rose to her feet. "Let's go."

"What, right now?" he protested, looking at the food before

him. "I'm still eating! I need to restore my strength after that ordeal." Then, seeing her look, he took two quick gulps of tea and grabbed a handful of nuts and fruits before finally pushing away from the table and standing up. "Fine."

She rolled her eyes at him, but secretly Ruhi was happy to see him behaving so—in other words, the way he usually did. If she'd been the one dragged off to jail and then brutally attacked, she wasn't sure she'd be so nonchalant, or able to act so silly.

❦ ❦ ❦

The doors were shut and there was no sign of any guards around, but even so Ruhi slowed to a stop across the street and a few doors down from the place. "How do you think we should approach?" she asked, glancing about. She hadn't realized it before, but Vihaan's home was up at the top of Surpakat, not far from Chetan's, and there was far less foot traffic here, which meant that the two of them loitering nearby would stand out more to anyone watching.

Sundra stroked his chin, no doubt hoping to look wise. "We could just walk up and knock on the door."

She slapped him on the shoulder. "And say what? 'Hello, we work for another raja, one your dead master didn't like much and who didn't like him either and who's currently in jail on suspicion of killing him—can we ask you some questions?' How well do you think that's going to work?"

He rubbed his shoulder. "Ah. Yes. You're right, that might not work. What's your idea, then?"

She hated to admit it. "I don't have one. Not yet, anyway."

She was still thinking about it when Sundra returned the previous blow. "I've got it!" he declared and pointed. Startled, annoyed, and mildly bruised, Ruhi massaged her wound but did follow his gesture toward the side of Vihaan's house where a pair of women were emerging, both garbed much as she and Sundra had been back at Kosala's, in plain, simple, sturdy clothing.

The garb of a servant or worker. Though finer than what Kosala's staff wore and with a bit more decoration around the cuffs and hems and collars.

"Oh. Of course." He had a point. Going to the front door wouldn't work—they'd either be recognized, in which case no one would want to tell them anything, or they wouldn't, in which no one would bother to tell them anything. But if they went around the side as servants, they might be able to slip in and go unnoticed long enough to poke around. It was worth a try, anyway.

"We'll need different clothes," she warned, catching Sundra as he was already striding across the street.

"No problem," he assured her, not pausing in the slightest. "If there aren't any hanging out back to dry, we'll find some in one of the rooms or hanging by the back door. Come on, don't dawdle, that'll just look suspicious."

Cursing him under her breath, Ruhi followed as they ducked down the alley on the house's near side, taking the same path they'd just seen those servants emerge from a moment ago. As they went, she unbuckled and pulled off her leather cuffs, stuffing them into her belt pouch. Seeing that, Sundra nodded and did the same with his own wristlets, so that both of their indenture bracelets now showed again. Next they tugged off their turbans, clutching those in their hands. They'd have to find some place to stow those and their swords while they were inside.

She was still doing a mental inventory of what they could and couldn't carry or wear as servants when they reached the back of the house. A small patio stood there, covered by a small wooden pergola, the benches and stools around its edges indicating that it was often used, but the simplicity of those items suggesting the area was frequented by servants rather than the master himself. Beyond it was a modest doorway, and the smells of baking bread and roasting meat that reached her from there and the adjoining window suggested it led straight into the kitchen.

Fortunately, there was no one out on the patio at the moment, and they were able to duck through and into the house without notice. A pair of cooks were hard at work inside, but they were too busy with pots and pans and plates to notice as Sundra and Ruhi sneaked past.

A hallway just beyond the kitchen led to the laundry, and sure enough, Sundra was able to snag a pair of big, loose kurta off a line there. "Put this on," he instructed, tugging the other shirt on over his vest. Ruhi did the same, leaving her bright red shirt on beneath this white one, and hoped it didn't show through too much. Because the borrowed clothing was so large, she was able to shove her turban into her belt and have it hidden from view. And the hilt of her sword shouldn't be too noticeable as long as she was careful not to let it jut forward too much.

Thus disguised, they strolled out into the main courtyard, doing their best to move at a normal pace and with an air of belonging. Other servants were walking about, some carrying things this way or that, some cleaning, a few just lingering to talk, so Ruhi grabbed the first thing she saw, a handsome nilavilakku set inside a small alcove along the wall, and motioned for Sundra to do the same. This way, hopefully anyone who did spot them would think they were taking the brass lamps out back to polish and clean and refill for use that night.

She was still looking around, trying to get her bearings and figure out where to start their search, when she rounded one of the columns at the courtyard's far end—and nearly ran into a solidly built man in clothing that was far from a servant's, stolen or otherwise.

"Watch where you're going," the man snapped, then his eyes fell on her properly and widened. "You!" They darted past to Sundra, who'd frozen half a step behind her. "And you! Kosala's little pets!"

For her part, Ruhi gulped.

Up close, Raja Chetan was a good deal more intimidating. He was her height, for one thing, and significantly broader, not as large as Koliya but still a big man. His clothing smelled of salt air and sweat and was more plain leather than silk or cotton or even brocade. Wide shoulder guards and a heavy baldric sat above a hand-stitched tunic. A worn headcloth looped almost lazily around the top of his head with the undyed ends dangling scarf-like down the front of his chest. He had sturdy leather bracers covering his entire forearms and tall boots reaching up to his knees.

His dark hair, flecked with gray, was pulled back in a simple but effective knot, and his beard was short and bushy but well-maintained beneath a strong nose and fierce, dark eyes that now stabbed right through her from a weathered face covered in deep, fine lines at eye and nose and forehead.

"What are you doing here?" he demanded, latching onto her shoulder with one big, meaty hand and Sundra's with the other. Both of them squirmed but were too terrified to seriously try breaking free. At least, she was.

"We could ask you the same question," Sundra managed to squeak out, right before the big pirate lord shook him. "This isn't your house, you know."

"No, we both know whose it was," Chetan shot back. "And that's why you're here, isn't it? Looking to get rid of whatever would prove your master put you up to this? To killing him?"

"We didn't kill anybody!" Ruhi protested, but all she got was a grunt in reply. "That's why we're here, to prove we didn't do it and that Kosala didn't either!"

Instead the pirate lord snorted. "Good luck with that. Your master's a hard one, and she'd have no problem killing Vihaan if he got in her way or crossed her somehow."

"True," Sundra agreed, "but not like that, she wouldn't. She'd have challenged him to a duel. You know that. She said the two of you were alike in that way."

"We're nothing alike!" the weathered raja insisted, eyes narrowing. He shook them again, and Ruhi's teeth rattled in her head, her vision swimming from the aggressive motion. But she kept her calm, and once he'd stopped, she was able to catch her breath and chime in.

"You know that's not true." She held up her hands placatingly when he started to retort. "You may quarrel, but you know she'd never do something this dishonorable. Disagree with her, sure, but when have you ever seen her stoop to anything like this?"

He scowled at them both, but at least he didn't argue—or shake. Instead, after glaring a moment more, he let go, wiping his hands on his sturdy cotton trousers as if to rid himself of their stain.

"So why are you here, then?" he asked at last. "What're you hoping to find?"

"Anything," Sundra answered, shifting to resettle his shirt where the raja's manhandling had tugged it up around his neck. "Something. No idea. What were *you* hoping to find? Because you didn't just wander over on your lunchtime walk."

For an instant, that shut Chetan up. Then he growled, "I don't answer to you!" before gesturing back the way they'd come. "Go on, get out. There's nothing here for you."

Sundra started to argue—of course—which was when six men burst into the courtyard from that direction. These men didn't look nearly clean enough to work for Vihaan. They weren't dressed like servants either, in their leather and their hoops and chains.

And their drawn swords.

She hoped they didn't work for Chetan, because if they did, she and Sundra were now trapped between the man and his thugs, and that didn't bode well for the two of them, not at all.

CHAPTER THIRTY-ONE

SUNDRA

Ah, lovely," Sundra muttered as the men surged toward them. He could already guess who they were, at least in vague terms—despite the lack of guard uniforms. He hadn't been here in the Islands nearly long enough—or had the opportunity to flirt enough—to have people sending thugs and killers after him for any other reason yet!

"Here now," he heard the surly pirate lord behind him call out. "Who in the nine hells are you lot? You don't belong here."

So, not working for Chetan, then.

Not that this was much better. "They're here to kill us," he muttered over his shoulder to the raja. "Some of their friends tried with Kosala earlier today in the jail. They didn't succeed." He grinned at the men, which at least made one or two of them pause for a second. "Neither will these."

"Brave words, pup," one of the ones who hadn't halted shot back, hefting his sword. "But there's six of us and two of you, and you aren't even armed."

For a second, that last part puzzled Sundra. Then he understood and smirked. His borrowed kurta was covering his blade, so these men hadn't spotted the sword. Excellent! That gave him an element of surprise, as he tugged up the shirt's hem to draw his blade—and discovered he couldn't.

A string of curses he'd learned from the servants back home spilled from his lips as his own spirits sank back down. The shirt was too snug, particularly with his turban shoved into his belt, for him to budge it easily. He'd have to wriggle out of the garment completely in order to reach his weapon, and somehow he didn't think these men were going to stand around waiting while he did.

"Problem?" Ruhi mumbled beside him, and he sighed. Of course she hadn't tried drawing her own sword, not that she'd have any better luck than he had.

"I can't reach my sword," he explained quietly. "Which means we're defenseless."

"Speak for yourself." And she hefted the heavy lamp she was still clutching to her chest. "I figure these could do some damage."

She was right. The nilavilakku was good and solid, a handsome piece some two to three feet tall with a stylized bird fashioned at the top so the wick there could emerge from its open beak. The length of the lamp swelled and subsided in a series of smooth curves, providing an excellent grip, and it wasn't all that much shorter than the club he'd handled earlier today, and even easier to hold.

Sundra readied himself, shifting his feet apart a bit for better balance, bending his knees for more flexibility and adjusting his grip on the lamp for more control—when someone pushed past him and Ruhi both, shifting to place weathered leather and bright steel between them and harm.

"Whoever you are, walk away now," Chetan warned the approaching men, his own sword now in hand. "Otherwise, this won't end well for you."

That did make all six stop a second, staring at the raja in their path. Clearly none of them had expected serious resistance, much less from a pirate lord known to actively dislike the one whose servants they'd been sent to eliminate.

But after a moment the one who'd spoken before shot back,

"Stand aside, raja. We've no desire to hurt you, but we have our orders. Those two are done for, and if you insist on helping them, we won't hold back."

"Neither will I," Chetan promised, raising his blade. "I hope you two can fight," he muttered to Sundra and Ruhi. "Because otherwise this might not go well for any of us."

Then the thugs charged, and there was no time left for talking.

Sundra ducked the first blow and lashed out with his nilavilakku, smashing the heavy top into his foe's knee. The man howled in pain, slashing downward reflexively.

Sundra barely yanked his arm back in time to avoid losing it at the wrist. He backpedaled, and his opponent followed, but limping now, his balance completely thrown off by the injury.

The clang of metal on metal distracted him a second, and he glanced over, past where Chetan was battling two men at once, to see Ruhi desperately batting at a sword with her own lamp. The man she faced was clearly toying with her, a sly smile on his face as he stayed well out of her range and jabbed with his sword.

Sundra knew his friend wasn't going to last long without a lot of help. But he was a bit busy himself, so what could he do to even the odds?

It was the difference in length as much as skill that was putting her at risk, he knew. But the first, at least, could be turned around. "Back among the columns!" he shouted to her, and she started then nodded. One big swing that swung her around completely made her foe retreat out of sheer prudence, enough that she was able to dash back among the columns lining the courtyard.

"Smart," Chetan agreed, not taking his eyes off his two foes, one of whom now sported a slash across his upper arm. "Any more tricks you want to share?"

Sundra risked a quick look around, but the servants had all wisely retreated from the conflict, and there wasn't so much as a stool here in the courtyard for him to use. Which left him only his wits, the nilavilakku, and whatever else he had on him. He twisted to avoid a blow, the tightness of the clothes binding his waist hindering him a little, and grinned as an idea struck. "Maybe one," he admitted, reaching under the outer shirt to tug his turban free.

He hurled the wad of cloth as hard as he could at one of the other men, who'd been quietly circling around behind them. The man batted the soft missile aside but took a step back as he did so, which bumped him up against the nearest column.

Before the man could extricate himself fully, Sundra spun and charged, knocking the man's sword aside with his lamp and using his shoulder to slam the man fully into the sturdy support. The thug's head banged back, and his eyes rolled up as he slumped to the ground, unconscious. Sundra leaned down and grabbed for his turban—he'd rather have taken the man's sword, but it was still firmly in his grip, and there wasn't time to pry it loose.

"Clever." That from the raja, who'd dispatched one foe and was now beating another back while the one with the wounded knee tried to find an angle to aid his friend. "You might want to help your brother a bit more though."

Sundra looked over and saw that Ruhi was frantically weaving in and out of columns, trying to evade the swords of not one but two of the thugs.

"Coming!" he shouted and charged across the open space. The man he'd fought before tried to strike him down as he passed, but that leg made him clumsy, and his swing went wide. Sundra saw the opening and took it, swerving into the other man and hammering him in the face with the heavy lamp before stumbling over and away as the man dropped.

A second later he was among the columns himself. He threw the turban at one man, distracting him for a second, and then clubbed the other's sword arm hard enough to make him drop the blade with a yelp.

Ruhi followed that up by bashing the man over the head, and Sundra was able to deal with her other opponent immediately after, the shorter nilavilakku able to swing freely in the narrow corridor here while the longer swords kept getting caught up on the columns or the courtyard's outer wall.

"Thanks," she managed, gasping, after both men were down.

"Don't mention it. Come on." He slipped back out into the center where Chetan was still fighting off the last man, the one who'd taunted them before. About to be ringed on three sides, the thug made the mistake of looking back to where Sundra was, and the pirate lord's sword batted his blade aside and took the man full in the chest. He stiffened, then slid off the bloody weapon with a gurgle to fall limp at their feet.

"Not bad," Chetan declared, stooping to wipe his sword clean on the dead man's vest before sheathing it. "With a real weapon, you might almost be dangerous."

"I *am* dangerous," Sundra promised, his heart still racing from battle. His mind was too, and so he added, "But I'm not a killer. Not the kind that would poison a man, anyway."

The weather-stained raja scowled, but after a second he nodded. "No, perhaps not," he admitted, though it was clear he wasn't happy about having to acknowledge that. Even less so when he grimaced and added, "And I suppose Kosala isn't either. Nor would she be stupid enough or crazy enough or twisted enough to send men after herself or her own employees." He studied them both. "Men really tried to kill her in the jail?"

Sundra nodded. "They did. I was there. They were dressed as guards—but they weren't guards. We don't know who they were, or who they work for, but whoever it is, they're powerful enough to get men inside there."

"Which isn't good," the pirate lord stated, tugging at his whiskers. He shook his head. "Most of us, we'd never stoop to this. Shouting at each other, yes, of course. Challenging each other, maybe, but not even that often. But poisons? Fake guards?"

He frowned, the lines cutting deep into his brow. "The only one I'd have thought capable of such deception, such trickery—such cowardice—was Udayin himself. He was a slippery little monster, and I could easily see him resorting to such tactics, anything to avoid a fight himself. For the rest though?"

He held up his hand and began ticking off rajas one by one.

"Jasleen would never, and she'd kill anyone who even suggested it. She's a true pirate, faces you head-on or not at all. Same with Koliya, though with him that's mainly because he's too big and too dumb to think he can ever lose. Tarabai stays out of fights, concentrates on her own territory, but she's too weak to risk anything that could bring the rest of us down upon her. Falguni, she's sharp but most of the time she just lets the rest of us skirmish and goes her own way. Could she do something like this? Maybe, but I can't see why. And Ehsaan?" He smirked a second. "He might be capable of it, but if he'd planned this, we'd all be dead now. He's too careful to miss."

Ruhi frowned as well, crossing her arms over her chest, the nilavilakku still dangling loosely from one hand. Her forehead was slick with sweat, and her beard and hair matted. Sundra made a mental note to remind her to wash it later, otherwise he worried that the false facial hair might stop looking realistic.

"What about someone who isn't a raja?" she asked. "There must be a few with a grudge and enough money or power to bribe or bully some guards."

Chetan nodded slowly. "Perhaps. I'm not sure who though. I'll think about it." He shot them a sharp, knowing glance. "Where can I reach you, if I find anything out?"

That actually drew a tired laugh from her. "Nice try. We'll find you instead, how's that?"

He chuckled, evidently not offended by her lack of trust. "Fair enough." Then he sobered. "Good luck. I may not like Kosala much, but I like someone framing a fellow raja even less. Find who did this, and fast, before they throw even more men at you, and you don't have someone around to help."

Then, without waiting for a reply, he turned and walked away, heading across the courtyard and through the wide doorway at its front. Because of course he could walk openly out the front gate, and no one would dare stop him.

CHAPTER THIRTY-TWO

RUHI

The next morning, Ruhi was surprised to be woken by someone pounding on their door. As Sundra groaned from his bed, she rose from hers and stumbled toward the door, rubbing sleep from her eyes. It was bright outside their window, and she guessed it to be mid-morning already. They'd both been exhausted after yesterday.

Reaching the door, she thought to lean against it and call out, "Yes?" rather than just tugging it open. After all, this wasn't back home where it could only be her father or aunt.

"It's me," Padmini said quickly, and Ruhi did open it because the older woman's voice sounded strained. "You need to come down. Both of you." Then she was gone again.

Ruhi glanced over at Sundra, who was still blinking, his hair a tangled mess half obscuring his handsome features. "Huh?" he asked, sitting up and scrubbing at his face. "Whuzzat?"

"Get dressed," Ruhi told him, glad that she still slept in her kurta—and both the beard and her amulet—and thus only needed to pull on her trousers before she was at least fit enough for a quiet table at the back of the dining room. "Meet me downstairs." She slipped out, shutting the door behind her, and headed off to find their host.

By the time Sundra reached them, some ten minutes later, she'd already had a cup of hot tea and a fresh pastry filled with mango preserves and was feeling far more awake. Also frustrated, since Padmini had refused to say anything about the early summons until they were both here.

"Something has happened," the older woman explained without further prompting, passing Sundra a mug of steaming, strong tea as well. "I got up early to buy for the day—always best to get fruit and fish and meat when things open at dawn, beat the rush and have your pick of things—and the market was already abuzz. No one seemed to know more than that it has to do with the two dead rajas—and your master."

※ ※ ※

"Still not seeing visitors. Better luck tomorrow." It was the same pirate who'd stopped them the last time they'd approached Chetan's home, so clearly his role was to serve as some sort of lookout and sentry. At least one of the others with him looked familiar as well, though the rest had perhaps changed. Ruhi couldn't be certain, as they all wore such similar attire, and she'd only seen them from this distance.

This time, however, she would not be so easily dissuaded. "He'll want to see us," she promised, continuing forward. That made the men abandon their perches along the porch of their building and hop down to quickly cross the sand and stone and plant themselves in her and Sundra's path.

"I don't think so," the first one started, but Ruhi cut him off.

"Tell him," she instructed, glaring at the man and refusing to give way even an inch. "Tell him Rawal and Sundra Chera are here. He'll see us."

The pirate scoffed, but when she didn't budge, he grunted and turned to one of his companions. "Go on then," he agreed, and the other man, after a single disbelieving look and a shake of his head, hurried off toward the main house. "But when he says no, be ready," the first one warned her with a stern look. "'Cause we tried being all polite. Now it's gonna get rough."

"No," she replied confidently. "It won't."

Sure enough, the second man returned—followed by Chetan himself. "Thought I'd be seeing you two," the pirate lord called while closing the distance. "You heard, then?" A wave of his hand sent his men away, the first one deflating a bit. Ruhi tried not to laugh at him.

"Some, yes, but no details," Sundra replied for them both. "Just that something happened. We figured you'd know more about it."

"Aye, I know all right." The raja reached them and glowered, though not at them. "Nayak Laghari's called for a meeting of the full Parishad, first thing tomorrow. Says he's got evidence, just unearthed, that proves Kosala's behind Udayin and Vihaan's deaths."

"That's impossible," Sundra argued. "She didn't do it, and you know it! Someone's setting her up!"

To her pleasant surprise, the sturdy raja nodded. "Looks like. Tried to shut her up once already. Then came after you to keep you quiet. Neither worked, so now they're out to bury her, keep anyone from figuring it out for real." He scowled. "But something like this, it'd have to be good, almost perfect, otherwise they've shown their hand for nothing."

Ruhi was watching him closely. "We need to know what it is, otherwise we've no idea what we're up against or how to disprove it."

"Aye," Chetan replied. "I'm not of a mind to walk in tomorrow and get blindsided either. Problem is, there's only one person likely to know, isn't there? Besides whoever's behind it."

"Laghari," she said, at the same time as him and Sundra. They all nodded, but then Sundra gave a rueful laugh.

"He might be too busy to speak with us right now."

That didn't faze the pirate lord, however. "He'll see me. One of the advantages to being on the ruling Council, I can go pretty much wherever I want." He strode past them, heading toward the road away from his little corner of the town, then paused and glanced back. "Coming?"

This time Ruhi laughed along with her brother as they hurried to catch up.

"Doesn't mean I like you all of a sudden," Chetan warned as the three of them walked. "Or that I'm looking to be in bed with your master. Just can't abide lies and cheats, is all."

"Of course," Ruhi agreed. But, behind the pirate lord's back, Sundra winked at her.

This time, no guard attempted to block their path as they marched right up to Governor's Hall. The two on duty outside its front door took one look at them, blanched as they recognized the raja, and hurriedly pulled the doors open, saluting as they passed. Laghari's secretary opened his mouth to protest as Chetan swept by but sank back into his chair without uttering a word, just watching mutely as the raja knocked once, a firm rap, before pushing the door open and stepping through.

"Raja Chetan!" Laghari rose from behind his desk, coming around to bow deeply. "This is an unexpected honor." His gaze moved past the raja, and his eyes widened upon recognizing Ruhi and Sundra. "I am… surprised to find you in such company," the governor managed diplomatically, sagging slightly at the sight of this evident alliance.

"We're united in common cause," Chetan replied bluntly. "That being to make sure Udayin and Vihaan's true killer is the one punished for their deaths. You have new evidence against Kosala?"

"I do, yes," Laghari agreed, wringing his hands as he moved to sit, placing the bulk of his desk between them like some sort of protective barrier. "We just received it this morning, but it is compelling enough that I felt it needed to be brought to the Parishad's attention at once. I believe you will find the matter quite clear, once you see it."

"Oh?" Chetan crossed his thick arms over his broad chest. "Let's hear it, then."

"I—" The stocky little governor hesitated, clearly not wishing to reveal anything ahead of time, but quailed beneath his guest's stern gaze. "Yes, of course." He sighed then straightened and stated, "We have found the poison used to kill them."

"Go on," the raja urged, making it clear he would not be satisfied until he'd heard all.

"It is called aconitum," Laghari continued, wiping his brow with a hand cloth. "I understand it is exceedingly deadly."

"Where did you find it?" Chetan demanded, towering over desk and owner both, and the governor flinched back but nodded quickly to show he was willing to comply.

"In Kosala's study," he answered. "Sitting upon her very own writing desk. There can be nothing clearer." His voice bore a note of entreaty, as if begging for agreement. "I've already spoken to Vaidya Dara, and he confirms that it would cause all the symptoms he observed and all that you yourself described," he added, glancing past Chetan to Sundra, though that seemed an odd point to make, given that he was essentially accusing the younger man of this crime.

"Who found it?" Ruhi asked. "And when?"

The governor glanced her way, and for an instant there was something in his eyes that wasn't fear, something harsher as if he resented her asking him anything. But his gaze flicked to the raja still glowering at him, and he relented.

"One of my guards did," he replied. "I stationed men there to watch. This morning, he noticed the study door ajar and glanced in to make sure nothing was amiss. That's when he noticed the vial on the desk—he said the sun was striking it just right, or else he might not have seen it. Something about it disturbed him, and so he brought it straight to me."

"Where is this deadly poison, then?" Chetan asked, studying the governor's own desk which had several papers and parchments and ledgers scattered across it and a cup of tea cooling to the side but nothing else.

Laghari straightened. "It is in the custody of my guards, of course. I couldn't risk anything befalling it before you and the other rajas had a chance to see it for yourself at the Council meeting I've called." The look he shot Ruhi seemed oddly triumphant.

Chetan said nothing for a moment, eyeing the governor, who did not back down. "Fine." The raja spun about. "Let's go."

Ruhi followed him, Sundra trailing behind, and left the governor of Surpakat sputtering impotently at their abrupt departure.

She waited until they were back outside, and past the outer guards, before saying anything. "This is absurd," she stated clearly. "Someone obviously planted that vial there. I was in Kosala's office, the day Vihaan died. I was standing right beside her at her desk. There was no such thing there."

The burly raja chuckled. "Of course you'd say that. If she's convicted of this crime, the two of you will be implicated as well— even though you were just doing her bidding, it's still murder, and of two raja at that." He held up a weathered hand, forestalling the protests already forming on Sundra's lips. "I know you didn't do it. Or at least, I'm coming around to that. It's all too neat." He tugged at his beard. "I don't like it when things are that neat. Always feels like they're not natural."

"What can we do about it though?" Ruhi asked. "It's our word against theirs, and we're the ones they think did it!"

Sundra was pacing, his face twisted in thought. "Maybe. Maybe not. I need to get my hands on that vial. Today. I have a Gift. I can see where things have been, but only as far back as dawn." He shrugged. "It might not help any, but Laghari said they found the vial there this morning. Maybe I can see who put it there or something else that'll help us."

Chetan was frowning at him. "Prove it," he demanded, pulling a ribbon from his pocket and handing the thin scarlet cloth to Sundra. "Tell me where it was this morning."

Sundra took the item, and his eyes seemed to unfocus for a second. "It was… in a woman's hair," he replied. "Older, gray hair. A cook? I saw a kitchen."

The raja nodded, accepting the ribbon back. "My cook," he confirmed. "The end frayed. It's her favorite color, so I took it so I could find a match. All right, I believe you," he declared with his customary bluntness. He sighed, rubbing at the bridge of his nose. "And again, you didn't make up those men who attacked us, and you don't seem dumb enough to have left your poison just lying about back there. Why wouldn't you have at least taken it with you when you ran off to evade the guards? So, all right, let's go."

"Will they really just let us in to see it?" Ruhi asked as they began walking again, heading back up toward the guard headquarters. She noticed Sundra shuddering slightly, no doubt reliving his previous visit there. "Even if you're the one asking?"

"Maybe not," the raja said, not slowing his pace any. "But if not, we'll figure something else out."

CHAPTER THIRTY-THREE

SUNDRA

They'd only just left the gardens behind when a boy came hurrying over to them. "Raja Chetan!" the child shouted, racing up to them, his little chest heaving from the effort, his face shiny with sweat, eyes wide. "Raja Chetan! Come at once!"

"Wha—Erish?" It was clear from the way he stopped mid-stride that the raja knew the boy. "What are you doing here? What's happened?" he demanded, though gently as he crouched down beside the child.

The child was still gasping for breath, hands on his legs, but he lifted his head and managed to utter one word, which sent a thrill of fear through Sundra as well.

"Fire!"

"What?" Now Chetan was upright, lifting the boy without apparent effort to cradle him against his own broad chest. "Fire? Back at the house?"

The boy nodded.

"We need to get back there at once!" Chetan started walking again, at a far quicker pace, but that soon escalated to a jog, and then a full-out run. Sundra, after a quick glance with Ruhi, charged after, but there was no way he could maintain that furious pace and especially not all the way up to the top of the town and the raja's far corner of it.

Glancing around, he saw something that could help.

"Chetan! Chetan!" Lunging forward, he managed to get a hand on the raja's shoulder. "Stop!"

The look he got from the burly pirate lord was furious and a bit wild. "I need to get back there!" he insisted, ready to bolt again, but Ruhi had sprinted to get on his other side, boxing the man in for the moment. They were taking their lives into their own hands—it was clear the raja would cut them down if that's what it took to get back to his men, so Sundra spoke quickly.

"I know, and we'll help. But even if you could run the whole way, you'd be useless when you got there." He pointed past them at the cluster of horses tied to a post there. "Can you ride?"

The pirate lord frowned, but at least the question brought him up short. "No," he admitted after an instant. "Never saw the need." His expression brightened. "But that I can do." And then he was striding forward again, brushing past Ruhi and headed, not for the group of horses Sundra had seen... but for the wagon that had just rounded the corner farther down.

"You there!" the raja shouted, and the man driving the wagon tugged on the reins, pulling his pair of horses to a whinnying halt. "I need your wagon!"

The man took one look at Chetan, either recognizing him or at least realizing that here was a man of some importance who would not be denied, and nodded. "Yes, raja, of course," he stated, and hopped down, offering the reins. "Might I come retrieve them after?"

"Of course." Chetan deposited Erish on the long bench up front before clambering up beside the child. "Get in."

Sundra and Ruhi barely managed to jump aboard before the wagon was in motion, the raja spurring the horses into a mad gallop down the block and then left to head due north, toward his home.

The man had been delivering goods, and the wagon was half full of sacks and barrels and crates. Sundra managed to punch and shove a pair of sacks into passable seats, and he and Ruhi sprawled upon them, clutching the wagon's sides as the pirate lord drove recklessly through town, shouting at people to clear a path.

That at least gave the rest of them time to think, and to catch their breath.

"What happened?" Ruhi asked the boy, who twisted about to regard them. He glanced up at Chetan, waiting for his master's nod before he replied.

"Don't know," he began. "I was in the kitchens helping with breakfast when we heard the shouts. Rushed outside and saw the barracks in flames. Da told me to find you, quick as can be, and said you was down at Governor's Hall. So I ran."

"You did well, boy," Chetan assured him gruffly, and the boy's chest swelled with pride. "Was anyone hurt, do you know?"

The boy shook his head. "They was all milling about outside it when I left, and Bhuvan had everyone getting buckets from the well."

"Good."

They rode in silence after that, other than the raja's shouts at people blocking their path, and the town flew past beneath the horses' hooves. Soon they'd passed through the Pirate Line back into the older part of town, the streets growing narrower and more twisted, but Chetan didn't slow in the slightest, forcing people to dive out of the way to avoid getting crushed by the horses or the wagon bouncing along behind. Up they went, veering right just as the wall came into view and then along that narrow street that ended in the short bridge to Chetan's.

When the buildings there came into view, Sundra couldn't help but gasp at the sight.

Flames were writhing about the first building—the barracks, the same one the men had emerged from twice to warn them off. They rose high into the air like some enraged plant or angered beast, their intensity almost too bright to look upon even in full daylight, the heat intense enough to make him break out into an immediate sweat, the air thick with an acrid smoke.

The next building over had also caught fire, and men struggled to splash water on both, trying to keep the flames from consuming the two structures and also to keep them from reaching the next building beyond. Chetan's own house stood in the corner, but so far, it and the row of smaller buildings beside it against the back wall appeared untouched.

"Where is Bhuvan?" Chetan demanded even as he reined to a halt and vaulted down from the wagon, striding toward the men. "Bhuvan! Don't bother with those two, they're gone—concentrate on the second bunkhouse!"

Sundra hopped down as well, coughing from the smoke, and was helping Ruhi over the wagon's lip when her startled yelp made him turn. There was Chetan, shouting orders at the men, one of whom was approaching him to confer. Other servants and sailors were milling about, some splashing water onto the fire with no visible effect and others struggling to carry items out of the next building, lest it too take blaze. The fire and smoke were casting strange silhouettes everywhere, throwing the farther buildings into shadow—

And rising up against those buildings he saw the figure of a man with a drawn bow in hand, arrow aimed straight at the unsuspecting pirate lord.

"CHETAN!"

There was no time, so Sundra turned and hurled himself at the raja, colliding with him and sending him stumbling back. There was a twang, barely audible over the crackle of the flames and the shouting of the men, and an arrow suddenly sprouted from Chetan's left shoulder. Then the two of them crashed to the ground.

"Bowman!" Ruhi was shouting beside the wagon, pointing toward the figure, who was already reaching for a second arrow. "There!"

Chetan's men turned as one, pausing their firefighting to stare at the man who'd just attacked their master. With a roar, half of them charged him, dropping buckets to draw swords instead.

The man, whose features were impossible to make out in

the distance, darkness, and flickering light, took one look at the enraged crowd surging toward him and ran, dropping his bow in his haste. He darted toward the bridge, dashing across it and down the street before anyone could close the distance, and disappeared among the buildings there a second later.

Some of the men pursued, but most of them pulled up short, realizing the futility of the chase and reminded by the crackle and hiss all around that they had other matters to attend.

Ruhi hurried over to Sundra's side and knelt beside him and the wounded pirate lord. "How bad?" she asked, reaching tentatively for the arrow jutting there.

That wrung a harsh laugh from the raja. "Hurts like all the hells," he replied, but levered himself to a sitting position, twisting to study the arrow himself. "Still, a foot to the right and I'd not be here speaking to you now." His gaze caught Sundra's. "Thank you. Saved my life."

Sundra shrugged, though he could feel his face flushing with pleasure. "You're welcome." He stood, wincing at the bruises and aches their collision had produced then offered a hand to help Chetan rise as well. "I'm guessing we have our mysterious killer to thank for that?"

The raja nodded, groaning as the gesture aggravated his wound. "No doubt. Clever too—set my place on fire to draw me back here, station a man to shoot me down once I show."

"How did they know where we were, though?" Ruhi asked, studying the scene.

The men had now switched their attention from the two still burning buildings to the one beside them, at Chetan's orders, and were wetting down that whole structure instead.

Ruhi was still speaking, and Sundra forced himself to concentrate. "Plus, a day ago you were convinced it was us behind all this, but clearly someone knows you had a change of heart, otherwise they'd not have bothered to target you today."

"Right," Chetan agreed, brow furrowed in thought and presumably some pain. "And they knew I wasn't here either, else they'd not have needed to set these fires. Which means someone's been talking. If it's one of mine, I'll see 'em strung up!"

"I'm betting it was a guard," Sundra put in, drawing the attentions of both Ruhi and the raja. "It makes sense," he added defensively beneath their gazes. "We were just at the governor's, right? So clearly you've sided with us, at least for now, and we know a guard or someone the guards would answer to was involved in the attempt on Kosala, otherwise they never could have gotten those men into the jail. So a guard who saw us enter the hall sent word to someone, and they realized you weren't fooled anymore and had to be taken out. That's when they sent that man up here to start the fires and wait for your return."

The look he got from them both was admiring, grudgingly so on the raja's part.

"It does make sense," Ruhi agreed. "And it's stopped us from our original plan, which was to get a look at that poison."

"You need to keep on after that," Chetan urged, waving away the men approaching him for a moment. "I'm out of this for the moment—" he indicated his shoulder "—but you have to get there and get to it before day's end." His lips quirked into a smile. "Tell me what you find." It was a command, not a question, but the smile softened the edges from demanding to conspiratorial, and Sundra nodded at once.

"We will," he promised, already backing away. "Soon as we find anything out, we'll come tell you."

Ruhi was kind enough to wait until they were well out of view and out of hearing before turning to him. "So," she began. "We need to get into the guardhouse, find this poison, and get your hands on it. All before sunset. And without the aid of a raja or anyone else while the guards are actively searching to arrest us. How exactly where you planning to do that?"

Sundra glanced over, regarded her, and gave her his best, most winning smile. "I have absolutely no idea."

Chapter Thirty-Four

SUNDRA

Are you sure," Ruhi asked again as they walked down toward the guardhouse, "that this can't wait until morning? Chetan might be recovered enough to go with us by then."

Sundra shook his head. "It needs to be today, or at least tonight. I can only see as far back as the most recent dawn. Not sure why, maybe because I'm a child of the dawn myself, born at first light." When he'd first discovered his Gift a few years back as he'd transitioned from boy to man, he'd tested that, tried pushing it, but always it was the same—he could only see to dawn of that day, even if it was mere moments after the sun came up. "Besides, the Parishad is meeting tomorrow, remember? We can't afford to wait."

"I know, I know," she groused, fingers beating a frantic pattern against her leg. "I just don't know how we're going to pull this off. You said the place is like a fortress!"

"Oh, it is and filled with guards, obviously. And we don't even know where they'd keep something like this."

To that, at least, his companion had a ready answer. "The

captain's office." She shrugged at his surprise, then elaborated. "If it's that important, Pillai will want to keep it safe herself."

"So we just need to get in and get to her office." Sundra smiled. "Simple."

They reached the guard headquarters, and he noticed how Ruhi stiffened at the sight of the place.

"I told you," he reminded her softly, but he understood. The massive stone building was impressive and forbidding. So of course he marched right up to the front and banged on the closed double doors there.

A panel in the front slid open and a helmeted face peered out at him. "State your business," the man declared sternly.

"We're… here to become guards!" Sundra blurted out, latching onto the first thing that came to mind. "We want to join up."

The guard regarded him suspiciously. "Why?"

"Sick of being on the water," he replied, leaning in as if confiding this dark secret. "Tired of hauling rope and even more tired of uncertain pay. We want something steady, on dry land."

"Sorry." The man didn't sound particularly apologetic. "We're full up." He started to shut the little panel again, and Sundra knew if that happened they'd be sunk.

"Captain Pillai told us we could," he all but shouted. That stopped the closure, but now the guard looked even more doubtful. "We met her when she was looking into those recent deaths, and she said we were helpful. Thought we'd make good guard material. Told us to come on by if we were interested. So here we are."

He waited, and beside him he could practically feel Ruhi holding her breath. *Please work,* he thought desperately, sending that prayer up to the heavens. *Please!*

After a second, the guard told him, "The captain isn't here at the moment. She's reporting in to the governor right now. I suppose you could wait for her though."

"Perfect!" Sundra told him happily. "Yes, that would be great, thank you. Once she sees us, she'll remember." Oh, she'd remember them, all right, but his luck was holding—if she'd been here they'd have had to explain themselves quickly indeed to keep from just getting thrown into jail right alongside their master. This way, they at least had some time before they had to figure out that next step.

"Hm." The guard still didn't seem entirely convinced, but something about Sundra's genuinely hopeful expression must have swayed him because he slammed the panel shut, but then there came a heavy click and a loud creak as the door itself began to open. It didn't swing back fully, just enough for the two of them to slip through, and when it shut behind them it did so with an ominous thud, but at least they were inside.

"This way," the same guard told them, turning away from his partner and the door.

Sundra was relieved to see that they weren't heading toward the jail itself but instead turned to the side, entering a much smaller but still solid wooden door in the outer wall and following a narrow, stone stair that wound up and around. They continued up three flights, none of them speaking, and finally reached the top floor where a tight corridor led the length of that corner, pierced by doors on both sides. The guard continued on to the far end and stopped at the door in the back corner, which looked much the same as all the others, wood with heavy iron fittings in a deep-set frame.

"This is the captain's office. Wait here." And then he turned on his heel and retraced his steps, his boots clattering on the stone floor.

"Not bad," Ruhi told him once the man had gone, leaving them alone—they'd seen a few other guards walking across the courtyard when they'd entered, but no one since they'd taken the stairs, and this floor seemed almost eerily quiet, lit only by lamps hanging from iron brackets spaced high along the walls.

"Thanks. It was a spur of the moment thing." He frowned at the heavy door barring their path. "Now we just need to figure out how to get in there before the captain herself returns."

This time it was his companion who grinned, gently pushing him out of the way as she stepped up to the solid portal. "Allow me."

Digging in her pouch, she came up with a small paring knife and a small comb meant for beards, with a narrow metal handle. Reversing the tool, she crouched and inserted both its handle tip and the knife blade into the door's keyhole, then began fiddling with them, shifting them this way and that.

Sundra watched, dumbfounded, as she worked. He was even more astounded when, after a minute, the lock clicked and she straightened, smiling as she turned the handle and pushed the door open. *Where had a nice, quiet girl learned to do something like that!*

"We had an employee once," she explained, answering his unspoken question. "Bit of a colorful past and inclined to be a bit light-fingered. Manpreet taught me how to pick locks. We fired him, of course. Turned out he'd been using those same skills to help himself to the cashbox. Useful skill to know though. Shall we?"

She stepped inside, leaving Sundra shaking his head. Just when he thought he had her figured out.

They entered Captain Pillai's office, quickly shutting the door behind them, and looked around. It was a good-sized room with a curved outer wall broken up by two of the narrow windows they'd seen outside, though most of the light came from the wrought iron chandelier suspended from the high ceiling. The inner walls had been plastered and painted white to offset the bare stone of the outer, and a thick but plain rug in a simple banded pattern covered much of the floor. Shelves took up one side wall and a massive wooden cabinet the other, with a plain wooden desk occupying the center, a lower cabinet positioned against the wall behind it.

"Tidy," he commented, and it was. Pillai was clearly someone who thrived on order. Nothing was out of place, her quill and ink neatly in their stand, her papers all aligned, the shelves crowded with row upon row of neat folders. No doubt each was carefully and properly labeled and in either chronological or alphabetical order. The notion of such slavish attention to detail made him cringe.

Ruhi, on the other hand, was nodding. "A woman after my own heart." She went straight to the desk. "If I were her, I'd have put the poison either in here or in the cabinet behind me—there's no specific place for such things, so she'd have to just find someplace secure with enough room to hold it safely."

Sundra followed her over and saw that the desk had a narrow drawer right in front and then a set of taller drawers down each side. There was a lock on the front one and at the base of each drawer on the right, and she readied her tools to start working on the first when he stopped her.

"Maybe that would help," he suggested, pointing at the inkstand—and the small key nestled within it. "Probably keeps it there in case she needs it in a hurry."

"Ah. Right." Ruhi nodded and snatched up the key, trying it on the first drawer. It fit perfectly. She slid it open, the wood gliding along with an ease and silence that suggested it was kept well oiled, and they both peered at the contents thus revealed. More papers, a folder, a small dagger, and a surprisingly fine necklace of gold and amber, but nothing that screamed "poison."

Closing that drawer, Ruhi went to the next, the top drawer on the right. She unlocked it, but it contained only more folders, carefully packed into that space. "Don't," she warned, slapping his hand away when Sundra tried extracting one. "She'd notice."

"I was only curious," he protested but let it go, watching instead as she opened the lower drawer. This one was, curiously, completely empty save for a small pouch he suspected contained money—and an even smaller vial of some dark glass.

"Your turn," Ruhi told him.

He stepped in closer, stooping to reach into the drawer more easily. His fingers closed around the vial—

—and the world around him melted away as his Gift showed him a different place altogether.

It was dawn, the light streaming in from large windows. The vial sat upon a desk, massive and polished to a mirror sheen. The room around it was large and airy, wood paneling extending up to the windows but white plaster above that, and a rich red rug covered the floor. Tapestries hung on the walls, and a long, low couch sat to one side, elephants marching across the pillows that decorated it. The air smelled of polish and tea leaves, and Sundra didn't need to see the stocky man seated at the desk to recognize the place. He'd been there just an hour or two ago, after all, and speaking to that very same man.

"Governor Laghari." he said softly, then looked up to meet Ruhi's puzzled gaze. "This was sitting on his desk this morning, not Kosala's!"

"He did say a guard had brought it to him," she argued, but Sundra was already shaking his head.

"Brought it to him after finding it this morning, but what I saw was dawn, and it was already on his desk. There's no way a guard found it and delivered it that fast—remember, he said the guard only noticed it because the light was striking it."

She nodded slowly. "So Laghari lied to us. The bottle didn't come from Kosala's, he had it and pretended it did so as to make her look guilty."

"And he'd have the authority to let those thugs into the jail," Sundra added, closing the drawer and standing again. "Plus, it was right after we saw him that someone tried to kill Chetan. We thought it might be a guard who warned the real killer, but what if it was the governor himself?"

He stared at her, and she returned his gaze, her face showing the same concern he was feeling. They'd known someone must be in on this, but the governor of the whole town? How were they supposed to compete with someone like that?

Chapter Thirty-Five

RUHI

A s luck would have it, the same guards who'd been stationed at the outer doors before were still there now, and Ruhi called out to them, "Chetan ordered us back— the governor asked for updates as soon as we had any." The men, clearly recognizing them both, just nodded and opened the doors, allowing them into Governor's Hall without hesitation.

The governor's secretary didn't even bother calling out to them, just glared as they passed him and went straight to the inner office's door. But Ruhi was surprised enough to freeze in place when she'd pushed that one open and stepped through—only to find that Laghari wasn't alone.

With him were a tall, distinguished-looking older man and a slim woman in a long mail coat. The former was unfamiliar to her but the latter was all too familiar. The woman's look of surprise changed to one of contentment, even pleasure, as she stalked forward to greet her and Sundra—and incidentally, to slide between them and the door, effectively trapping them here.

Sundra wasn't slow to realize what was going on nor to try twisting it to their advantage.

"Ah, Captain Pillai," he said as smoothly as if he'd been expecting her here. "Good to see you. This saves us having to send for you. Excellent." He strolled into the room like he owned the place.

Ruhi could have laughed at his bald effrontery if she hadn't been so terrified, but she was still impressed.

Pillai, for her part, was taken aback by this unexpected response, but she recovered quickly. "Good to see you both as well," the guard captain stated, not bothering to hide her relief. "I have some questions for you, and they're becoming more urgent by the moment."

"I'm sure they are," Ruhi told her, "but we have some questions of our own. Or rather some information. Things you will be very interested to hear." And she skirted the other woman to follow Sundra over to the governor's desk.

Laghari, for his part, looked glum and deflated. "What do you two want?" he demanded, though his voice emerged without any real force or anger. "Captain, can't you just escort them out? Girish and I still need to finish deciding whether we're raising the import tariffs."

But Sundra was clearly not about to be shunted aside or carted off so easily. "That can wait," he declared firmly, walking right up to the governor and putting both hands on the desk so he could lean in and confront the shorter man from mere inches away. "We have information. We know where that poison is really from."

Ruhi didn't fail to notice the way the governor blanched at that statement. "What do you mean?" he managed to squeak out. "It was found on Kosala's own desk!"

"No, it wasn't. It wasn't anywhere near Kosala's house this morning—it was right here instead!" And he banged his fist down on the desk, making the governor jump.

"That—that's ridiculous," Laghari muttered after a moment, though he was still pale as flour. "What are you saying?"

"How do you know?" asked Pillai.

Sundra explained his Gift. "Can you give me something on

you, something I can tell you where it was this morning that I couldn't know any other way?"

In response, she pulled a coin from her belt. "Fine, here."

Taking it, Sundra's face took on that same slack expression Ruhi had seen back at the jail. "You got this off a fruit vendor," he said after a moment. "A man, middle-aged, stout, short tufted beard, blue turban."

"That's… right," the guard captain agreed. "Fehrun. I bought a mango."

"That's how I know," Sundra told her. "I did the same with the vial. And it was here. Were you informed about the attempt on Kosala's life?" he continued, his tone sharp and his gaze unwavering. "The one at your own jail?"

"Yes, I heard," she admitted. "And I'm looking into how that could have happened. The men who did it, none of them were in any condition to talk, but they were dressed as guards—yet none of them are in my employ."

"I know. I was there when it happened. I helped Kosala fend them off. But someone had to let them in. Which means either one of your guards is working for someone else—or someone with enough authority ordered them to stand aside."

He let that sink in a second before continuing, "Did you know that more men tried to kill the two of us at Vihaan's house? They were wearing common sailor's garb, but I'd bet they were sent by the same person. And just now, after speaking with the governor in this very room, someone set fire to Chetan's home to draw him back and then tried to kill him when he showed."

"What?" That came from all three of their audience members, and Ruhi thought the governor looked no less surprised than Pillai or the other man, Girish. "Is he—?"

"Alive, yes," Ruhi answered. "He took an arrow to the shoulder. But someone sent that assassin there, and they did so after we were here." She stared at the governor, who glanced away. "Someone here is working with whoever actually killed Udayin and Vihaan. And that same someone produced that poison this morning to seal the case against Kosala before the real culprit could be exposed."

Now even Pillai was studying the governor, who was squirming beneath their collective gaze. "You told me one of the guards found it in Raja Kosala's study this morning," she reminded him. "And brought it straight to you when they should've alerted me first and not moved it. Which guard did you say it was?"

"I—I don't recall," Laghari claimed, sweat already beading his brow. "What does it matter? They brought it here instead, and that's that."

"Except that it isn't," Sundra corrected. "Because you said they only noticed it from the sunlight hitting the bottle, but it was already on your desk at dawn."

Now the man glared at him, some color returning to his face and some strength to his voice. "You can't prove that. I say it was brought to me by a guard. And I am the governor. You're just a poor indentured servant, and you work for Kosala, so of course you would be trying everything to distract us from the evidence of her—and your—guilt."

Ruhi saw her friend hesitate and could guess what was going through his mind. He could explain about his Gift to the governor, but in doing so they would have to admit they'd broken into Pillai's office, into her desk itself. That wouldn't do much to help convince anyone. And Sundra couldn't share the vision itself, so it really was his word against Laghari's.

Turning away so no one would see the despair she was sure was etching itself onto her face, Ruhi's eyes swept the room, taking in the details she'd seen before—the fireplace, the table, the chairs, the couches, their handsomely patterned pillows. Something about that last item made her pause, and she crossed the room to pick one up, studying it. *Where have I seen this pattern before, with its entwined elephants all in a neat row?* Then it came to her, and she gasped.

Swiveling back around, she stared at Laghari, narrowing her eyes. Yes, she could see it now—the round face, the wide features, the stocky build. They were so much alike, once you knew to look.

And from what she remembered, and the clear age difference, there could only be one explanation. "You're Meera's father!" she blurted out.

The effect was startling and immediate. Governor Laghari sat bolt upright, shifting to stare at her, his eyes gone saucer-wide and his face flushing wine dark. "Don't hurt her!" he cried out, half rising before slumping back in his chair and burying his face in his hands. "Please, don't hurt her!"

"Hurt her?" Ruhi and Sundra both said at once.

Pillai asked, "Who's Meera?"

The taller man stayed silent and out of the way but was clearly listening to everything.

Laghari sighed and glanced up at them, his face now streaked with tears. "My daughter," he admitted. "She came to Surpakat only recently—in Kosala's employ. Damn that woman! Using my own child against me!"

Now he had the guard captain's full attention. "Explain," she insisted, her tone quiet but forceful, and the governor complied, all resistance clearly gone.

"She's my only child," he started, gazing off into the distant past. "Her mother was from one of the plantations; we met when I was still just an inspector and had visited there. I didn't even know about Meera until after she was born. Her mother flatly refused to marry me or leave her home. I only saw them whenever I visited on my rounds, once or twice a year."

He sighed. "Her mother passed away when she was ten. I tried to convince her to move here with me then, but she chose to stay with her grandparents and aunts and uncles and cousins instead. Until this past year, when she decided to go out on her own and find employment elsewhere."

"And Kosala hired her on as a housekeeper," Sundra offered.

Laghari nodded. "At first I was thrilled. She was here in Surpakat! We got together for lunch and dinner several times. She made me those." He gestured toward the pillow Ruhi was surprised to discover she was still clutching to her chest. "But then—" his fist clenched "—Then I found out that it was all a ploy."

"By Meera?" Sundra asked, blatantly disbelieving, but the governor shook his head.

"No, by Kosala! She'd found out about our relationship and had hired Meera just to gain power over me, keeping my only child hostage against my good behavior." He pounded his hand on the desk. "I couldn't let her take control of Surpakat. I just couldn't!"

The man was clearly incensed, but Pillai held up a hand. "Back up," she commanded, her tone cutting through his outrage. "Did Kosala make demands of you?"

Which would be a problem, Ruhi realized—Surpakat hosted the Parishad specifically because it was the one stronghold none of the rajas controlled. If Kosala had found a way to influence Laghari, that would've given her an unfair advantage over the other pirate lords.

She was relieved when he shook his head. "No," he admitted. "But she was about to. Bhadra warned me just in time."

"Bhadra? Bhadra Khatri?" That sounded familiar, and after a second Ruhi recalled the name and its owner. He had been the oily man who'd greeted Kosala at the Council meeting, the one she'd clearly not liked much. He wasn't a raja though—he'd been seated in the gallery, same as her and Sundra. But he'd also been the one to speak up, requesting that the Council consider representation for the plantations—an idea Vihaan had quickly shot down.

"Yes," Laghari was saying. "That's where Meera grew up, at Bahut Saare, his plantation. He's the one who found out about Kosala's plans and told me. I had to stop her, don't you see?" That last was a clear entreaty to Pillai and even the rest of them. "Not just for Meera's sake but for the town's."

But Pillai's whole stance showed she was unsympathetic. "So you framed her for murder," she clarified. "Did you have Udayin and Vihaan killed, as well?"

The governor looked truly shocked at that accusation. "What? No! I had nothing to do with that. I was as surprised as anyone at their deaths. But Bhadra said it was the perfect opportunity. All I had to do was let the Parishad find her guilty, and Meera would be safe."

"But that wasn't enough for him," Sundra guessed. "Not once you told him we were poking around. So he sent men to kill her instead."

Laghari shuddered. "I didn't know he would do that!" he insisted, wringing his hands together. "He just told me he needed the guards to let a few of his men into the jail to rough her up so she wouldn't be able to argue her own defense. When I found out after, I forbade him from going near her again."

Ruhi nodded. "At which point he decided the case against her had to be so ironclad it wouldn't matter what she said."

"Yes. He brought me the vial late last night, told me all I had to do was say it had come from her house, and the matter would be settled. Meera would be safe." He had drooped in his chair again, and though his color had returned to normal, his eyes were still awash in tears, and his hands trembling as he rubbed at his cheeks. "I was a fool, wasn't I?" he said after a moment, his voice small.

"You were blinded by a father's love," Ruhi corrected, cutting in before Pillai could say something more cutting. "I think anyone can understand how Bhadra Khatri manipulated you using such a bond."

She confronted the guard captain. "Kosala clearly didn't like Khatri much, and Vihaan cut him off when he spoke to the Council. What about Udayin? I'm guessing he couldn't have liked the idea of diluting his own power by giving any to the plantations."

"No," Pillai agreed slowly, rubbing her jaw. "The three of them were the most vocal opponents every time the topic was raised."

"And now two of them are dead and the third accused of their murder," Sundra chimed in. "I'd say we've found the one behind this." His eyes widened. "Oh! And I think I know how too."

He turned to Ruhi. "Remember the day Udayin died? He was wearing a new pair of gloves—awful, garish things, clashed with everything. And Vihaan, his looked new too."

"You're right," she agreed, thinking back. "And when we were at the Parishad, Khatri said something to Kosala about a package. You think the gloves were poisoned?" She went back through the last day at Udayin's in her head. "Your cheek! Where Udayin struck you, you had a welt for days!"

"I did," he recalled, unconsciously rubbing that same spot. "Far more than I should've, given his slap. But he did it with his glove on—then pulled the thing off to suck at his knuckle like a child. If the poison was in there, he shoved it into his mouth all on his own!"

"And Vihaan had his off as well when he died," Ruhi remembered. "His hands were all red too."

"The horse!" Sundra burst out and looked oddly pleased. "I didn't take Vihaan for a man who'd beat his steed, and he didn't. The poison on his gloves left those welts instead."

The others had been watching this back-and-forth with some confusion, but now Pillai stepped in. "You're saying that Shri Khatri sent each of the three of them a pair of poisoned gloves," she restated clearly. "Udayin wore his at once and compounded the issue by transferring the poison to his mouth. Vihaan wore his, but not right away. And Kosala never wore hers, which is why she wasn't affected."

"Correct," Ruhi agreed. She was reliving her last exchange with her master before Vihaan's death. "When we were in her office, there was a gift box there. Like one for a scarf—or a pair of gloves. I asked her about it, and she said it was a bribe from someone she hated, so she wouldn't touch it. Which meant there was no chance for the poison to affect her. When the blame for the others fell on her instead, Khatri must have been thrilled."

The guard captain didn't so much as bristle at the accusation. "It made sense at the time. Now, however—yes, I can see it. We'd need proof, however. There are no clear marks on the vial to indicate where it came from, and Khatri may not be a raja, but he is rich and powerful in his own right."

"If Kosala still has those gloves in her office, that would help,"

Sundra pointed out, already moving toward the door. "We'll go look for them."

"I'll come with you," Pillai stated, and it was obviously not a request. "That way, if we find them, there can be no question of tampering." Ruhi nodded, as did Sundra. It was a fair point, and they could use all the help they could get.

CHAPTER THIRTY-SIX

SUNDRA

Will you release her, now that you know the truth?" Sundra asked as they exited Governor's Hall and started the walk back up toward Kosala's house.

"Once I know for certain, absolutely. Until then, I think it's safest for everyone if she stays exactly where she is." Pillai frowned as if guessing his next thought. "No one except my actual guards—and only the ones I completely trust—will have access to the jail until then."

That was something, at least. As was the fact that they were with the guard captain themselves right now and not under arrest. Sundra didn't know how long this strange new alliance would last, but he certainly preferred it to having to run and hide constantly.

Having Pillai with them served another purpose, which was to clear a path. Whenever there were people on the street, they took one look at the guard commander's serious, set expression and melted out of her way. Thus the trek up through the Pirate Line and then left on the first street past it went a good deal more quickly than he'd have expected, and within minutes they were approaching the broad, low-slung building with its shingled roof and wide porch that already felt like a second home.

What was unfamiliar was the fact that no one came out to greet them as they approached, not Sanga or Meera or anyone. In fact, the front of the building seemed almost eerily quiet.

"Where is everyone?" Ruhi asked aloud as they stepped up onto the porch. "Hello?"

Pillai was scowling, and Sundra noticed as he drew his sword that hers was already unsheathed. "Stay behind me," she warned and pushed open the heavy front doors, which weren't barred. With those out of the way, sounds did now reach their ears, but not the normal noises of people moving about, talking, and doing chores. Instead, Sundra heard shouts, curses, screams—and the telltale clang of metal on metal.

"They're after the gloves!" Pillai shouted, turning toward the fight. "Go get them."

Sundra ran toward Kosala's office, Ruhi right on his heels. Fortunately, the door to the study wasn't blocked, and when he opened it, he was relieved to find the room unoccupied.

"Let me," Ruhi told him, circling around him and heading not for the desk itself but for one of the chairs beside it. A pile of papers covered the seat, and from the top she plucked a long, flat box. "Got it!" She started to open it but then clearly thought better of the idea, instead clamping down to keep it sealed between her fingers.

They turned to go, emerging into the hall—and a pair of unfamiliar men crashed into them, sending all four of them sprawling on the stone tiles. Sundra managed to keep hold of his sword and shoved the men off him with his free hand, then twisted about and got his feet under him so he could spring upright, blade at the ready. "Back off!" he warned.

"Not likely," one of the men retorted, also standing, though a bit more clumsily. He was big and beefy, and his sword was twice as heavy as Sundra's. In his free hand he held the flat box Ruhi had found seconds earlier but lost in the scuffle. "*You* back off or die."

"Never. Stand and fight!" Sundra raised his blade.

The big man smirked at him—then shoved the box up under his arm to grab a heavy urn from a small table there beside him. "Fight this!" And he hurled the big pottery piece at them.

There was no time to think, only to react—Sundra spun around, crouching down and covering his head with both arms. The urn shattered against his back and shoulders, showering him with shards and dust, and he staggered but managed to keep his feet. By the time he was able to face them, however, the men had gone, barreling down the hall toward the sounds of battle.

"They've got the box!" he shouted to Ruhi, who'd been staying safely behind him. "Come on!"

He raced after, but upon entering the inner courtyard found himself in a small battle. He saw Sanga and Pillai fighting off several thugs at once. A few of Kosala's men also fought, but most of the people here were housekeepers and groundskeepers and cooks and so on, with no fighting experience or skill. These cowered along the room's outer edges or ran from the thugs chasing after them, attacking them, and generally causing havoc and chaos in every direction.

"Let's go!" he heard a man yell, and then all the attackers spun about, fleeing toward the back of the house and out the door into the yard. Sundra gave chase, but several of them threw more pottery or just tugged it down onto the floor behind them, and dodging over and around those slowed him considerably. The last man disappeared through the door while he was still a good ten paces behind, and they were already halfway across the yard when he emerged out back.

He would've kept up the chase except that Ruhi caught up to him and laid a hand on his arm. "Don't. You won't catch them now. And even if you did, you'd be badly outnumbered. You getting yourself killed won't help anything." She managed a small smile. "And I'd hate to have to find a new brother."

"Yes, well—" Through the haze of battle and the thrill of the chase he saw the wisdom in her words and stopped, sheathing his sword and watching the last of the attackers disappear. "Damn."

Returning to the house with her, they found Sanga speaking to Pillai, with Meera close by. "They came out of nowhere," Kosala's second was explaining, nodding to them as they approached. "Pushed their way in at the front, must have snuck around to the back; one minute it was quiet, and the next we'd half a dozen strangers shouting and punching and breaking things. They didn't draw steel, at least until a few of us pulled ours, so I don't think anybody got hurt too badly. No idea who they were or what they wanted though." He had a small slash on one upper arm but otherwise looked none the worse for the unexpected bout.

"I know what they wanted," Ruhi told him with a touch of bitterness. "And I had it in my hands too!" She held up the hand in question, then brought it closer to her nose, and made a face. "I can smell it too. Faugh!"

"Can you?" Sundra frowned as she waved her hand in the air and he caught a whiff of something as well. Something oddly familiar. "Let me see." Grabbing her wrist but remembering to be careful so as not to hurt her, he brought her hand right up to his face and took a big, long sniff. The scent that hit him was definitely floral, but not even remotely sweet—in fact, there was a hint of bitterness beneath its woodsy odor.

It was a smell he definitely recognized. After all, he'd been skirting it for years.

"Vatsanabha!" he declared, releasing her arm with a grimace. "I'd know it anywhere!"

"What's that?" Pillai demanded. "You know the poison?"

"Yes," he told her. "It grows near my... near home. They use it around estates there to keep animals away. The flowers are small, and a bright, rich purple in tall clusters. Just touching it can give you a rash. Rubbing up against it causes welts and worse after a while. Eating it... well, that would kill you, no question, and in an ugly, ugly fashion."

Meera was frowning. "I know a plant like that. I haven't seen it here at all, but back in Bahut Saare, where I grew up, they plant it around the outer edges. Animals won't go near it, and they were always careful to keep us children clear of it too. What would that be doing here?"

Sundra wasn't sure how much it was safe to tell her, but fortunately that wasn't up to him.

"We think someone sent Kosala gloves laced with it," the guard captain explained. "And the same to Udayin and Vihaan. We came to retrieve them, and it looks like we weren't the only ones with that idea."

Sanga, oddly enough, beamed at this news. "Then you know the raja didn't do this. Not if someone was trying to kill her too." He towered over Pillai. "You need to release her at once!"

Their height difference didn't cow her in the least. "I will—when it's safe." She didn't explain who she was trying to make it safe for, but her firm tone and steady gaze quelled any other protests he might've made.

Unfortunately, that didn't improve their current situation any. "That was our only chance to prove who was behind all this and how," Ruhi pointed out to him and Pillai, the three of them edging away from the others to continue their conversation in private. "With those gloves gone, what can we do? If we just accuse Khatri without proof, he'll laugh it off and say we're inventing stories just to free Kosala."

Pillai nodded. "I believe you. I was leaning that way already, after what Laghari said, but this proves it—someone didn't want us to get those gloves, and all the pieces fit. But you're right, if it's just your word against his, the Parishad won't convict him, even if they do agree to release Kosala." She scowled. "I hate it when people get away with things in my town. Especially something as serious as murder. It makes me look bad."

"What if we don't need proof after all?" Sundra suggested to them both, thinking fast. "What if we can get Khatri to admit what he did in front of everyone?"

"Why would he do that?" Ruhi demanded. "All he has to do is stay quiet and call us crazy and he's home free. He'd be stupid to do otherwise."

Sundra brightened as an idea began to form. "So we get him to lose his temper and do something stupid instead." He grinned. "Fortunately, I'm good at pissing people off so much they can't think straight."

CHAPTER THIRTY-SEVEN

RUHI

Pillai frowned, which seemed to Ruhi like the woman's default expression. "I don't like the notion of us separating," she told them bluntly. They were out on Kosala's front porch, giving Sanga and Meera and the others space to clean up after the recent incursion there. "What if someone comes after you again?"

"We'll be fine," Sundra promised with his usual confidence, patting the handle of his sword. "We can handle ourselves."

Ruhi was far less sanguine about the prospects, but she nodded nonetheless. "It has to be this way. You need to get back to the guardhouse, explain everything to Kosala, and get her ready, then return to the governor and brief him on his role."

A role which he would be given no choice in, and she'd have felt bad about that, if not for the part he'd already played in endangering their lives.

"We need to go to Chetan and ensure his participation." Which she hoped would be as straightforward as she made it sound once they'd explained everything to the injured raja. He did strike her as an eminently practical man, so hopefully he would see the sense to this plan—and that it was their only real option. "There isn't time for all of us to go together to all three places," she concluded, glancing up at the sky, where the sun was already well past the midpoint and beginning its inevitable descent toward dusk and then night.

"I know, you're right, but I still don't like it. As resourceful as you two have proven, I shouldn't worry. But I do." Pillai scowled as if hating to admit this concern, then nodded sharply, almost fiercely. "Fine. But go straight there, don't dawdle and no side trips. Then get yourself someplace safe until morning."

She'd carefully not asked where they'd been staying, just if they had someplace they felt safe, which Ruhi appreciated. She hadn't wanted to have to lie to the woman, but definitely preferred to keep the Quiet Fire a secret. The fewer who knew she and Sundra were hiding out there, the better.

"We'll be fine," Sundra repeated, clapping Pillai on the shoulder the way he might a good friend. "See you tomorrow." Then he'd turned and started away, leaving Ruhi little choice but to follow after a short nod and wave of her own. "We'd have stood around another hour while she dithered," he muttered once Ruhi had caught up to him. "Better to just head off and leave her to her own tasks."

Glancing back, Ruhi saw that the guard commander had indeed started off in the opposite direction, south toward the guard tower and Governor's Hall while she and Sundra traipsed once more all the way to the top right of the city to Chetan's little realm in that corner. Several times along the way, she jumped when people emerged suddenly from buildings or around corners, and Sundra laughed at her each and every time.

"Relax," he said after one such incident. "No one knows where we are or what we're doing. Laghari is no longer sharing our whereabouts and plans with Khatri, so we're safe."

Speaking of the governor brought another topic to mind. "Did you tell Meera anything?" she asked him.

He glanced down and away, studying his boots as they kicked up small clouds of dust with each step. "No, not really," he admitted with less enthusiasm than before. "I wasn't sure what to say—'sorry, it turns out your father is the one who was betraying us, working with the man who owns the place where you grew up?' What good would it have done to tell her all that now?"

"She deserves to know," she argued. Then felt like a fraud. After all, she hadn't exactly raced to tell the young housekeeper either. "We can send word," she decided. "After speaking to Chetan. At the very least she should hear that her father was involved and Khatri." It was a cowardly decision though, and she amended it quickly, "We'll go back ourselves and tell her. The two of us together."

Her companion sighed, but finally nodded. "All right. Together." The thought of not having to brace Meera alone buoyed them both, and they picked up their pace, pacing the turns for Indentures Hall and then Udayin's house with nary a tremor.

Ruhi was just starting to relax and enjoy the exercise and the pleasant breeze that ruffled her hair and fluttered her beard as they turned onto the street that would lead them out to Chetan's—and found a man standing there waiting, arms crossed over a black leather vest, crimson turban seeming to almost glow blood-red in the afternoon light.

Shivaji.

"At last," Udayin's former second growled, a slow, nasty grin spreading across his face. "I knew if I waited here long enough you'd come running back to your new master. Or is he your old one? Was this Chetan's plan all along, to do away with his rivals by whatever means necessary? If so, you've certainly done your work well—Udayin, Vihaan, and now Kosala too. Shame you won't live to reap whatever rewards he promised you."

He drew his tegha with deliberate slowness, drawing it out to give them time to feel properly terrified.

At least, that had no doubt been his intent. But they were both tired from the walk, everything that had already happened today, and the past few days in general.

"Oh, put it away, Shivaji!" Ruhi snapped, startling the big pirate with her tone. "We don't have time for you! Come back later."

"My brother's right," Sundra agreed, his talwar already unsheathed. He spun the blade so that it caught the light, sending sharp little glares into the pirate's face and causing him to wince and blink each time. "You're not part of this, and we're terribly busy. Why don't you make an appointment with us for some time next week, and we can settle this then?"

Ruhi wanted to curse at him. She'd had Shivaji confused, uncertain, and from there she could have talked him down, convinced him to leave them alone at least long enough to wrap things up and reveal the true culprit. But Sundra's taunts had the opposite effect. The big pirate straightened, and was all but snarling as he glared down at them both.

"I demand satisfaction!" he bellowed, raising his sword high over his head where it gleamed like a sliver of sunlight. "You killed Udayin, and now I'll kill you!"

This had gone on long enough. "We didn't kill anyone," Ruhi informed him sharply. "It was a man named Bhadra Khatri. He owns the plantation called Bahut Saare."

Shivaji sneered at her. "I know who he is. Is that the best you can do? He's a rabbit, a moth, a flea. Insignificant." At least he'd lowered the sword, though that might have just been from the strain of holding it aloft like that.

"That's exactly the problem," Ruhi agreed, talking quickly to keep him from attacking. "He isn't taken seriously. And who were the three raja who treated him the worst?"

That made the big man pause and think, anyway. "Udayin, Vihaan, and Kosala," he conceded after a moment. "But so what? That means nothing!" The sword tip rose once more, and he took a heavy step toward them.

Ruhi stood her ground, even though she wanted to turn and run. But if she did, she knew he'd just chase them down. Better to try settling this now, while they still could. "He meant to poison all three of them. Think! Udayin had new gloves the day he died. Where did he get them?"

The pirate stopped again, face scrunched up in concentration. "They were delivered by messenger," he recalled at last. "An admirer, was all Udayin said. He was thrilled. He put them on immediately." He scowled at Sundra. "Then you killed him."

"Not me," Sundra countered, finally realizing words might serve better than blades here. "It was the gloves themselves. Poisoned, like Rawal said. On the inside. It's a plant called vatsanabha, just touching it will give you welts—close contact like that, it seeps into the skin. Causes pain, cramping, seizures—exactly what happened to him." He shook his head in what might even have been sympathy, and Ruhi reminded herself that Sundra had watched both pirate lords die that way. "It's an awful way to go. And guess what plantation has that plant growing around its borders to keep out pests? Bahut Saare."

For an instant, Shivaji seemed to consider this. Then he shook his head like he was ridding himself of a persistent fly—or an annoying idea. "No!" he bellowed. "You're lying! You did this, and now you're trying to cover it up." But he sounded less certain than before, and that sword tip was wavering slightly.

Which is when an arrow sailed through the air, passing from behind Ruhi and Sundra to strike the pirate. It embedded itself in the top of his turban with a silky hiss.

"Ambush!" Shivaji shouted, that sword rising once more, his face purpling with rage. "You tricked me, kept me talking so you could strike from a distance! Cowards!"

Sundra quickly slashed a second arrow from the air, cutting it in two before it could plant itself in his chest. "Don't be stupid!" he yelled back, turning to face this new threat. "You ambushed us, remember? We had no idea you were even here! The one shooting, he's trying to kill us, not you. He works for Khatri."

"And he's brought reinforcements," Ruhi muttered, twisting about just as screams split the air and three more men charged up the street at them, weapons drawn. "Wonderful."

The one in front, she recognized—it was the same man who'd grabbed the gloves from her at Kosala's less than an hour before.

They must have realized she and Sundra might return to apprise Chetan of recent events and had circled around to come after them. They'd already be at the raja's house now, safe and sound, if Shivaji hadn't gotten in their way!

Then she had no time left to think, as one of the men charged her, his blade already sweeping down toward her head. She barely managed to get her own sword out and up in time to block the blow, and the force of it send a shudder through her hands and arms all the way to her shoulders, the impact almost making her drop the weapon.

The thug grinned at her, sensing her inexperience, and she took advantage of that to kick him, sending him stumbling back. "Help! Sundra!"

"Coming!" he replied, but she could see he was facing two men himself. The last one glanced toward Shivaji but didn't attack.

"This isn't your fight," he said instead. "We're just here for these two. Stay out of our way and we'll let you live."

That had been the wrong thing to say.

"Let me live?" Shivaji shouted, drawing himself up to his full height. "As if you could take me!" And he launched himself at the surprised thug, bashing the man's sword aside before stabbing him through the chest.

"Help Rawal!" Sundra urged, still busy with his own foes. "Or else Khatri wins, and your master goes unavenged!"

That worked, and the big pirate turned toward the man now stumbling back toward Ruhi with murder in his eyes. "For Udayin!" Shivaji howled and barreled into the man, lifting him off his feet and slamming him into the ground almost a yard away. The thug was still trying to get to his feet, head shaking, when the pirate ran him through.

That left Sundra's, and—

"The archer!" Ruhi cried as an arrow narrowly missed her, shattering against the wall just behind instead. She glanced up and saw the man at the street corner. He was already reaching for another arrow.

But Shivaji was quicker. The big man reached behind him and drew a dagger with a long, slim blade. He flipped it over, catching it by its narrow point, and then hurled it with a snap of his wrist, sending the slender weapon spinning end over end—to embed itself in the archer's chest. The man dropped without a cry, only the thud of his body and the clatter of his bow hitting the paving stones.

Sundra had dispatched his foe. He eyed the big pirate warily, sword still out, before asking, "Are we all right?"

Ruhi held her breath, then let it out explosively when the big pirate nodded. "Yes."

He wiped his blade on the last man before sheathing it. "Guess maybe there's something to what you said, after all." He scowled. "But if you lied to me…"

"We know," Ruhi assured him. "And that's fair enough. Come to the Parishad meeting tomorrow morning. See for yourself."

"I will," he promised or perhaps threatened. Then he stalked off, deliberately kicking one of the bodies out of his way as he passed.

"Well, that was exciting," Sundra said, crouching to clean his blade as well. "Did you see me against mine?" He sounded almost boyish, his face aglow with enthusiasm and recent exertion.

"Sorry, I was a little distracted trying to stay alive."

"But I was really good!" he protested.

She rolled her eyes. *Men.*

"Let's just get to Chetan and tell him what's happened and what has to occur tomorrow," she reminded. "Maybe someone else will try to kill us on the way, and you can show me then."

CHAPTER THIRTY-EIGHT

SUNDRA

The next morning dawned gray and cold. Sundra shivered as they headed to the Parishad Hall because he'd opted to return to just the plain, simple, unadorned kurta, sadri, and shalwar Kosala had provided them. He was unarmed, his curls bare, and his sleeves rolled up to prominently display his indenture bracelet as a statement. He braved the weather as they walked, trusting the exercise and his general excitement—and anxiety—about the day to warm him.

Ruhi, on the other hand, had delved into Padmini's stores once more, and was today garbed in a turban of a deep emerald green that matched her shirt and a black cotton vest decorated with patterns in gold and green over a pair of shalwar such a dark green they were nearly black themselves. She'd also reshaped her beard into a shorter, rounder, thicker curve, and her sleeves were down and buttoned to cover her bracelet.

Her new look was why Sundra wasn't surprised when, as they neared the hall and the wide space before it, she peeled off from his side, muttering, "Don't look at me or call out to me once you're inside. I don't want them to recognize me. Not yet."

Not entirely sure what she was up to, Sundra nodded anyway and slowed a bit to let her go on ahead. Once he'd seen her pass through the building's front doors, he followed. The guards at the top of the stairs hesitated as he approached, but fortunately Pillai was right behind them. "Let him through," she instructed.

The room was every bit as grand as Sundra remembered, and there were already several people seated—including Bhadra Khatri. He was right in the front row, exactly as they'd expected, and behind one of the unclaimed table seats so that he would be visible to all. He'd brought three men with him, but—as Pillai had assured they would be, based on previous eagle-eyed observations—they were arrayed in the row right behind him, allowing the seats on either side of the plantation owner to be available for more important people he might wish to chat with. One of those had already been claimed by Ruhi herself, and Sundra noticed Khatri seemed unsure what to make of her, which meant he didn't recognize her.

So far, so good.

Chetan was there as well, his arm in a sling but appearing otherwise unharmed, and he nodded to Sundra before glancing away with a scowl in case anyone noticed. The quiet pirate lord, Ehsaan, was also seated, as was Jasleen, her three daughters standing right behind her.

Sundra wasn't sure where to place himself yet, so he lingered over by the pillars near the window, just watching. Which is why he noticed Kosala's entrance a second before everyone else did.

There was a stir through the room, murmurs mixed with people shifting to look, as the female pirate captain strode toward the table, head held high. There were heavy iron manacles on her wrists, linked by a short, thick chain, yet she looked unbowed as ever, her clothes dusty but her face and hair clean and her expression determined.

She took a seat at the table, and one of Khatra's thugs immediately leaped to his feet. "She doesn't belong there!" the man shouted. "She's a murderer!"

Before he even had time to consider, Sundra had straightened and stepped away from the column. "*You're* a murderer!" he shot back, drawing gasps of surprise that only multiplied as the rest of the onlookers recognized him. He saw the thug pause, unsure how to react to this accusation, and in the row ahead of him the man's employer shifted uneasily, that instinctive retort coming uncomfortably close to the truth.

"No, *you're* the murderer!" The thug next to the standing one accused, coming to his friend's aid. Which is when Ruhi turned and leveled a glare that would have shut down a hundred men twice their size.

"I'd be careful how you throw that word around," she warned, her voice low but still managing to carry through the room. "You never know where it might apply."

The murmurs grew, some no doubt agreeing with the epithet while others were simply confused, but Pillai moved in behind Kosala and cleared her throat. "Any guilt has yet to be proven," she reminded them all in a clear voice carrying over any objections. "And until it is, Kosala is still a raja and still entitled to a seat at the Parishad."

Khatri in particular looked unhappy about this and even more so when Sundra deliberately marched across the room—and claimed the seat on the man's other side. He tried not to smirk as he sat down. If only the oily plantation owner knew what was coming next.

Koliya was also clearly displeased, the big man turning to Chetan as if for support. But Chetan ignored the look, giving Kosala a curt nod no different from their last greeting, which she returned in kind. Without Chetan's backing, Koliya bit down any objections and just sat grumbling under his breath instead, like a great sulking bear.

The other two pirate lords, Banerjee and Falguni, arrived. The former looked nonplussed to see Kosala there but nodded to her nonetheless while the latter gave her a smile that was all the more startling for its brilliance. Interesting.

Shivaji was also there, deliberately sitting right behind one of the empty seats and glaring at Sundra. Hopefully the man would remember his promise to wait until all was resolved, otherwise he might mess everything up.

Last to enter was the governor. Laghari looked terrible, dark circles under his eyes and his face flushed, his hair already damp with sweat. He took the seat directly in front of Khatri, glancing at the man—and at Sundra and Ruhi flanking him—and then quickly looked away, his eyes darting next to Kosala then Pillai standing to one side.

Hold fast, man! Sundra wanted to shout as the stocky man sank into his chair as if already exhausted. *This will all be over soon—one way or another.*

There was silence for a moment, and at last Pillai cleared her throat. Laghari jumped at the reminder, studying his hands guiltily a second before saying, so softly they almost didn't hear him, "As host to the Council, I, Nayak Laghari, hereby call this meeting of the Parishad to order."

"About time," Koliya growled, slamming a heavy fist on the table. "Let's put this murdering sow away and get on with it!"

That raised a wave of excited whispers through the crowd, who were clearly eager for drama and possible bloodshed. Kosala gave no reaction, but Sundra gulped.

Luckily, they had planned for this. Chetan rose to his feet, all eyes going to him as the chatter died out. "Before we get to that," he declared in his loud, gruff voice, "we have something else to deal with. Something long overdue."

"What could be more important than avenging the death of two of our own?" Falguni asked, though without heat—Sundra caught the almost apologetic glance she sent Kosala's way, like she'd have preferred otherwise but had to ask. Which was certainly fair.

Chetan had an answer ready for that. "This could affect the composition of our table and alter any vote we might take after, including the one regarding our fellow rajas' murders." He shifted, widening his stance as he faced not only his peers but the rest of the room. "Because this is a heinous crime, no question, and the person or persons responsible, no matter who they are, must pay in full for such a despicable act."

That wasn't what they'd discussed, and Sundra saw Pillai and Laghari both peering at the burly pirate lord, as if trying to figure out why he had deviated and what that might mean for them.

But one person wasn't studying Chetan. Instead, Ruhi had turned to the man seated beside her. "That's us," she told him, her words carrying. "Do you hear? He means my brother and me!" And then she reached out and grabbed Bhadra Khatri's chin with her hand, dragging his head about so she could look into his eyes. "They're saying we did this, that we killed them!"

This, too, was unplanned, and now Sundra was the one puzzled. *What in all the heavens is she up to with such a strange display?*

"Unhand me, man!" the plantation owner snapped, reaching up to wrench her hand from his face and shove it away. "Show some decorum!"

But, oddly, when she shrank back in her seat Ruhi's expression was anything but upset or even worried. Instead, she looked... satisfied?

Nor was Sundra slow to take advantage of the disruption. "Decorum?" he all but shouted in Khatri's face. "Easy for you to say. You're not the one accused of murder!" He half rose from his chair, leaning into his neighbor as the man tried to pull away. "How would you like it? Murderer! Murderer!"

"That's right," Ruhi agreed, getting into it and adding her voice to his, crowding in around Khatri. "Murderer! Murderer!"

"Get away from me!" he screamed, his eyes wild, hands up to shield his face as if they might switch from words to blows. "Get them off me!"

That last was to his henchmen, who rose and shoved Sundra and Ruhi away from their cowering boss. "Back off," one of them ordered. "Or else!"

"Or else what?" Sundra shot back. "You can't touch us. We work for the Raja Kosala. Your boss is just a plantation owner. He's got no power here!"

"Exactly," his supposed brother chimed in. "We're safe as houses from the likes of him!"

Khatri's eyes were bulging, and he opened his mouth to respond but clamped it shut again at the last second.

Damn! They'd almost had him!

But they weren't done yet. Sundra twisted about as Chetan spoke again, capturing the room's attention once more.

"I'm talking about representation," Chetan stated loudly, setting his unbound hand on the table and leaning in. "For too long we rajas have ruled here without considering those who help govern these Islands yet have no voice in our discussions."

Khatri straightened, a broad smile spreading across his face, and tugged at his expensive jacket, adjusting his cuffs. His fear had vanished, replaced by naked glee. He might be mystified at this strange turn of events, but he was also thrilled. His true goal was suddenly within reach, especially with two of those who'd have objected most strongly now silenced forever and the third in chains.

"I am referring, naturally," Chetan continued, "to none other than the governors of our strongholds. Starting with our own Nayak of Surpakat, Dalpat Laghari."

The governor straightened a bit, trying to preen the same way Khatri just had, while behind him, the plantation owner was startled enough to yelp, "Wait, what?"

Gotcha! Sundra thought. *And just when you thought you'd won.*

Ignoring the interruption, the burly pirate lord went on, "It is thanks to Nayak Laghari that we've received the damning evidence against Raja Kosala. Without his help, we'd still be uncertain who was responsible for these bold if horrible deaths, who'd executed such a brilliant if awful plan, who'd masterminded such an evil yet genius plot to remove Udayin and Vihaan from our number. We owe it all to Laghari, and it is past time he receives the respect and authority that is his due." And Chetan began to thump his fist on the table, over and over.

There was silence for a moment as the rest of the room struggled to absorb this new information. Then someone else started clapping. It was Kosala.

"My hat is off to you, Nayak Laghari," she stated clearly, dipping her head to the man. "Even though it may bring about my own demise, I must respect your brilliance in all this. Well done, sir. You're truly a force to be reckoned with."

"Damn it, it's true," Ruhi lamented, patting the man beside her companionably on the hand. "He's got us for murder, and I still have to admire him. He was just too smart for us."

That did it. Sundra had watched Khatri's face grow redder and redder as praise was inappropriately heaped on the governor seated before him. Now, at hearing even Kosala and her underlings praise the man who'd doomed them, the plantation owner could take it no longer.

"Are you all insane?" he shouted, leaping to his feet. "You want to credit this man for all that? Look at him! He's clearly an idiot!" His men started to stand as well, but two of Pillai's guards had quietly placed themselves beside that row of chairs, and the thugs sank back down in the face of those spears.

"Then how did he hook us?" Sundra demanded, jumping up as well and getting in Khatri's face. "How did he outsmart us? How did he kill them if he's such a buffoon?"

"He has to be smart," Ruhi shouted in the man's face, closing in from the other side again. "He framed us for these murders!"

"He tricked Captain Pillai, and Shivaji, and the entire Parishad," Sundra announced. "That's pure genius!"

"Smarter than all the rest of us put together!" Ruhi offered.

They were inches from Khatri's face, shouting this back and forth, and finally he couldn't take the onslaught. "Shut up!" he screamed, shoving them both aside. "You're all idiots! Laghari worst of all! He's nothing but a pawn, and he didn't even know it!"

"That's ridiculous!" Sundra yelled at him. "If he's not the mastermind, who is?" And then, very deliberately, he stopped and turned, ever so slowly—toward Pillai, as if a thought had just crossed his mind.

"Why are you looking at her," Khatri demanded. "What? No! Are you mad? She's not smart enough!"

"Then who?" Ruhi demanded.

"Yes, who?" Sundra agreed, whipping back around.

The shri looked about at all the scornful faces in the Council, not even noticing Ruhi's hand on his arm.

And, just as Sundra had hoped, seeing the disdain there finally pushed him over the edge.

"Me!" Khatri screeched at last. "It was me, all right! I was controlling him the whole time!"

"Controlling me?" Laghari blurted out, doing a credible job of looking surprised by this outburst. "I thought you were just warning me? You said my daughter was in danger!"

"I lied, you fat fool!" Khatri shrieked, lunging forward to grab Laghari by the shoulders and shake him roughly about. "It was all a lie! And you fell for it, every bit of it! I sent those gloves to them all, I poisoned them, I gave you the vial to prove the case against her—me, all me! I am the genius here, not you!" His hands shifted, moving from the other man's shoulders to his neck, and he began to throttle Laghari then and there. "I won't let you take what should be mine!" he shouted, spittle flying from his lips, his eyes wild.

"What an interesting confession," Kosala's wry voice cut through the man's diatribe. "Commander Pillai, have you heard enough?"

"Absolutely," Pillai agreed. She'd moved stealthily around the table during Khatri's hysterics and now was right beside the man, plucking his hands from the governor's throat and yanking them behind his back. Two of her guards were right behind her and affixed manacles to the man's wrists—the same ones Kosala had been wearing just moments before, Sundra realized as his master rubbed her bare wrists.

"Shri Bhadra Khatri," the guard captain's voice echoed across the room, "you are hereby under arrest for the murders of Raja Udayin Agarwal and Raja Vihaan Dhar." She gestured, and her guards dragged the man away from the table, tugging him across the room and toward the doors. His own men looked on, half out of their seats but evidently unwilling to test their unarmed mettle against the guards, especially as the two from the door stepped forward to meet their fellows.

For his part, Khatri looked dazed. "What?" he managed as he was led away, stumbling over his own feet. "I—no, I didn't do that! Kosala did! The poison proves it!" But his words were weak and without conviction, the rote defense of a man who knows he's caught but still can't admit it, even to himself.

On the far side of the table, another man jumped up, this one big and wearing a dark red turban and a black leather vest. "You're a dead man, Bhadra Khatri!" Shivaji bellowed and would've rushed him then and there if the guards hadn't blocked his path. "I challenge you to a duel! I'll avenge Udayin's death on your bloody corpse!"

"What? No! Stay away from me!" It seemed the plantation owner's fear of Shivaji was greater than his embarrassment at getting caught, because he turned to his captors and pleaded, "Please, get me out of here!" Which they did with obvious satisfaction.

CHAPTER THIRTY-NINE

RUHI

Ruhi collapsed into her seat once Khatri had been escorted out. *It worked!*

She'd known that she'd need to use her Gift on him, to lower his inhibitions and make him more likely to speak the truth. The issue had been, how to manage? Only flesh-to-flesh contact would work. If she'd been garbed as a woman, she might've been able to get away with resting a hand on his or pressing her palm to his cheek in seeming sympathy. As a man, she couldn't get away with such gestures, not to another man. Thus she'd been forced to use a bolder, more unorthodox approach. No doubt that had looked strange to everyone, but it had worked, and with Sundra's outburst immediately after, she doubted anyone had even noticed.

Chetan was speaking again, once more directing his words to both his fellow rajas and the assemblage beyond. "I apologize for the deception. It was necessary to push Shri Khatri to the point where he couldn't help but confess his guilt."

"So you don't actually plan to give Nayak Laghari a vote on the Council?" Falguni stated, her brow arched and a half smile playing on her lips. "I think that's for the best, all things considered."

"It is indeed." That was Kosala, still seated in the same chair, but what a difference a few moments made. She'd been chained before and at least shamming the part of the potentially guilty party, though that had been difficult to convince her of. She hadn't appeared in the least bit penitent, of course, but she hadn't ruined their little play. Now, however, the chains were gone, along with the true culprit. She was once more a full member of the Parishad and a wronged one at that. The way the others all turned to her and offered short bows from their own chairs showed they knew it too.

"Dalpat Laghari," Ruhi's master continued, the faint furrow in her brow the only indication of her displeasure. "I hereby charge you with willfully misleading this Council, with assisting Shri Khatri in the murders of Udayin and Vihaan, with attempting to wrongly convict me of that same crime, and with assisting him in attempting to have me killed while held in the town jail."

That drew gasps, and she paused to acknowledge them. "Yes, Khatri sent his men to kill me," she repeated. "But it was Laghari who allowed them access." Her stern gaze returned to the man in question. "Have you anything to say for yourself?"

Ruhi almost felt sorry for the man as he sat there sniveling, slouched, deflated, and pale. "I can only plead for mercy," he stated, his voice ironically stronger and clearer than it had been earlier when he'd been playing his role of unsuspecting pawn—a role he'd performed all too well in real life. "I acknowledge what I did, and that it was wrong, but I was motivated only by concern for my daughter, and fear for her well-being." He raised his chin in an impressive attempt at salvaged dignity. "I'd do so again if I thought it might save her."

Kosala rose to her feet. "Your daughter is not at risk and never was," but Ruhi noticed that the pirate lord didn't mention Meera by name. "However, I can respect your paternal instinct. I won't ask for your death, therefore, especially since you didn't directly kill anyone—even the attempt on my life didn't come from your hand, you merely provided the avenue of approach. I call for your exile, however. You're no longer fit to govern here." She waited one beat, two, before adding, "But your daughter may accompany you if she so desires. That will have to be her choice, however. Does the rest of the Parishad agree to this sentence?"

"I do," Chetan agreed immediately, and the others' assents were close behind his.

Laghari stood. "Thank you. It is more than I deserve, and I know it." He didn't look as pathetic now nor as lost as he told the gathered Council, "Though I realize my word means little, my lieutenant, Girish Malhotra, knew nothing of this, and was as surprised and betrayed as the rest of you. He is a good man and would do well as Surpakat's new governor."

"I'll second that," Pillai added from the corner pillar she'd reclaimed as her leaning spot. "Girish is an honest man and an able one. You couldn't ask for better."

"We'll take that under advisement," Ehsaan assured her, and indeed Ruhi could see how the Council was already considering the notion.

Girish had been the tall gentleman they'd met yesterday in the governor's office, and she could see that he was not only well-mannered but also careful and considerate. And Pillai's recommendation would no doubt carry a great deal of weight, given both the respect everyone clearly had for her and her own reputation for unstinting honesty.

Which was probably why, now, the guard captain pushed away from the pillar to approach Kosala and bow deeply. "I want to apologize, Raja Kosala," she declared formally. "For suspecting your involvement in these murders and for your treatment thereafter."

That drew a smile from the raja, if only for an instant. "You have nothing to apologize for, Captain. You acted efficiently, as always, and your behavior was above reproach. I wasn't mistreated in any way, and I, for one, am glad to know that you won't let a simple thing like someone's rank and position stand in the way of your quest for justice."

She sat back down and shifted to summon Sundra and Ruhi

to her. "Speaking of honor, honesty, and efficiency," Kosala announced, "I wish to publicly thank my two indentures, Rawal and Sundra Chera. Without their tireless efforts, Shri Khatri's crime would never have come to light, and I might've been convicted of a crime I didn't commit."

Turning to Sanga, she gestured, and without a word, he handed her his pouch, from which she withdrew a pair of heavy gold coins. "I hereby award them each one dinar, in honor of their exemplary service," she stated, pressing one of the gleaming discs into Sundra's palm and the other into Ruhi's. "Thank you," she added more quietly, and Ruhi dipped her head.

Chetan stood. "I'd like to add my thanks as well and that of the entire Parishad," he stated. "You saw what we did not and kept us from doing an injustice to one of our own and from letting two of ours go unavenged."

"Yes, hear, hear," Jasleen Lal agreed, banging the head of her cane against the table. "In fact, I propose the Council reward them with a dinar each as well, to show our appreciation." Her eyes glittered. "And perhaps we'll call upon you two again, if there's ever another puzzle to solve, hmm?"

Ruhi could only bow deeply, Sundra beside her, as the entire Council clapped or pounded the table in agreement, and the audience stood and clapped as well.

Her head was spinning, however, and it was all she could do not to grin beneath her false beard. *Two dinar apiece! That was nearly half their indenture!* Another incident or two like this and they'd be free, and while they were still young enough to appreciate it!

Her mind, however, replayed the last thing the older raja had said, and the look that had accompanied it. Another puzzle? Something about that phrase, and the look, made her wonder if the pirate lord already had something in mind.

GLOSSARY

Achkan: a knee-length open jacket with buttons all the way down

Ayya: an honorific meaning "noble" or "worthy"

Baglah: a large, deep-sea ship, typically with three masts

Chettiar: a landowner or merchant

Choli: a fitted, midriff-baring bodice, worn by women under sari or sadri

Churidar: tight pants

Daniq: a smaller gold coin, six to a dinar

Dhangi: a smaller deep-sea ship, usually with two masts

Dhoti: embroidered silk sarongs tied to resemble loose trousers

Dinar: a heavy gold coin

Dirham: a silver coin, twenty to a dinar, roughly three and change to a daniq

Dupatta: an embroidered shawl that can be draped around both shoulders and over the head, or across the chest, or in several other ways

Durga: a stronghold

Fals (plural Falus): a copper coin, ten to a dirham, two hundred to a dinar

Ghagra: pleated skirts worn under a sari

Gharara: wide-legged silk brocade pants that flare out dramatically at the knees

Kameez: a long, loose shirt or tunic

Khet: an estate or plantation

Kolossoi: the mythic Giants

Kunwar: the son (or Kunwari, daughter) of a Sirdar, essentially a prince

Kurta: a loose cotton shirt

Mekhela: an elaborately beaded or linked belt

Nayak: a governor

Nilavilakku: a traditional oil lamp, typically tall and slim like a candlestick and made of brass or bronze. They are often found at the entrances to homes, and lighting them is considered good luck.

Pagri: a traditional headdress made of a single long cloth wound around the top of the head; also called a turban

Parishad: council or assembly, the Pirate Council that rules the islands

The Pirate Line: a wall running across Surpakat and effectively dividing the older, pirate-run portion of the town ("above the Line") from the newer, more respectable section for business and government ("below the Line")

Pujari: A holy man or priest who performs important rituals

Raja: "king"; a Pirate Lord

Rishi: A holy man or sage who dispenses wisdom and knowledge

Sadhu: An ascetic holy man who engages in meditation

Sadri: a vest, often embroidered

Sari: a long strip of cloth, often beautifully woven, women wear wrapped around them

Sasaka: captain

Shalwar: drawstring trousers, loose at the top and cuffed at the bottom

Sherwani: a longer, heavier jacket, often embroidered or made of brocade

Shri: a polite form of address equivalent to "Mr." or "Ms."

Sirdar: a nobleman of the highest rank, a chieftain

Stanapatta: a band worn over the breasts

Talwar: a long, slim sword with a curved, single-edged blade, a one-piece metal handle and cross guard (and often knuckle bow), and a disc-shaped pommel.

Tegha: a sword with a wide, double-edged blade that curves and widens toward the tip.

Thakur: a minor nobleman

Vaidya: a practitioner of the Ayurvedic healing arts; a doctor

ABOUT THE AUTHOR

AARON ROSENBERG is the author of the best-selling DuckBob SF comedy series, the Relicant Chronicles epic fantasy series, the Dread Remora space-opera series, and, with David Niall Wilson, the O.C.L.T. occult thriller series. His tie-in work contains novels for *Star Trek*, *Warhammer*, *World of WarCraft*, *Stargate: Atlantis*, *Shadowrun*, and *Eureka*. He has written children's books (including the award-winning *Bandslam: The Junior Novel* and the #1 best-selling *42: The Jackie Robinson Story*), educational books, and roleplaying games (including the Origins Award-winning *Gamemastering Secrets*).

He is also an author in the new Eldros Legacy epic fantasy series, with his first novel in that setting, *Deadly Fortune*, out now.

Aaron lives in New York. You can follow him online at gryphonrose.com, at facebook.com/gryphonrose, and on Twitter @gryphonrose.

IF YOU LIKED...

If you enjoyed this novel and the world it's set in, then the creators of the Eldros Legacy would like to encourage you to don thy traveling pack and journey deeper into the mysteries of the world Eldros and all the myriad adventures set therein.

The mortal world of Eldros is coming apart. The Giants, who once ruled its five continents with draconian malice have set their mighty designs on a return to power. Mortals across the globe must be victorious against insurmountable odds or die.

Come join us as the Eldros Legacy unfolds in a growing library of novels and short stories.

You can find all the novels at:
www.EldrosLegacy.com/books

Our website is, of course:
EldrosLegacy.com

The Books by Series
Legacy of Shadows
by Todd Fahnestock
Khyven the Unkillable
Lorelle of the Dark
Rhenn the Traveler

Legacy of Deceit
by Quincy J. Allen
Seeds of Dominion
Demons of Veynkal

Legacy of Dragons
by Mark Stallings
The Forgotten King
Knights of Drakanon (Forthcoming)
Sword of Binding (Forthcoming)
Return of the Lightbringer (Forthcoming)

Legacy of Queens
by Marie Whittaker
Embers & Ash
Cinder & Stone (Forthcoming)

The Dog Soldier's War
by Jamie Ibson
A Murder of Wolves
Valleys of Death (Forthcoming)

The Areyat Isles
by Aaron Rosenberg
Deadly Fortune
Stealing the Storm

Other Eldros Legacy Novels
The Pain Bearer by Kendra Merritt

Short Stories
Here There Be Giants by The Founders (FREE!)
The Darkest Door by Todd Fahnestock
Fistful of Silver by Quincy J. Allen
Electrum by Marie Whittaker
Dawn of the Lightbringer by Mark Stallings
What the Eye Sees by Quincy J. Allen
Trust Not the Trickster by Jamie Ibson
A Rhakha for the Tokonn by Quincy J. Allen

WHEN MAGIC DIES,
ONLY THE DEAD HOLD MAGIC.

Once, the empire of Ritakhou was full of magic. But since the Schism, the realm, renamed Rimbaku, is a pale whisper of its former majesty. Now the only magic is the Relicant Touch, a power allowing talents to be drawn from *aishone*, relic bones that are jealously guarded and widely coveted.

Kagiri and Noniki leave their tiny village with a few aishone and all the hope they can muster, but the world is a larger, more dangerous place than they ever dreamed. Forced into a dark bargain that may cost them not only their lives but their souls, their fates intertwine with an emperor, a warrior, a graverobber, and a killer in ways none of them ever imagined, ways that could reshape the Relicant Empire forever.

This is the first book in The Relicant Chronicles, the Anime-esque epic fantasy series from international bestselling author Aaron Rosenberg.

AARON ROSENBERG

BONES of EMPIRE

BOOK ONE OF
THE RELICANT CHRONICLES

www.ingramcontent.com/pod-product-compliance
Lightning Source LLC
Chambersburg PA
CBHW072123020726
47501CB00003B/955